Also by Cathryn Grant

Cathryn Grant

THE WOMAN
IN THE STORM

An Alexandra Mallory Novel

D2C Perspectives

1

New York City

Rain pounded the pavement outside my apartment. It coated the living room window in sheets of water that turned the trees and the building across the street into a dream-like mirage.

I was half-lying on my love seat, my legs resting on one arm, my shoulder blades on the other. Beside me on the coffee table was a cup of hot chocolate.

Sitting on my belly, highlighted by the white tank top I was wearing to accommodate the steamy temperature of the room, was the old-fashioned key I'd stolen from Jim Kohn after I killed him. It was so beautiful, it hardly seemed like a security device. The intricate loop at the top, the long skeletal look of the body, and the simple shape of the key itself had the look of a sculpture rather than the toothy utilitarian appearance of a modern key. There was something about it that made me feel it was symbolic, not an actual key to open a door or a fancy box.

I hadn't been able to resist the urge to take it. Slipping it off his ring was so easy. I did it almost without thinking. The size and shape of it among a few normal keys and the remote device for his car was startling. The beauty of it didn't fit him at all. He wasn't a fanciful guy as far as I could tell. His house was a classic colonial home made of off-white and coffee-colored brick. It was unlikely it contained a dank, locked basement or a dark, dusty attic filled with relics, whispering buried secrets or hiding tangible wealth. In my survey of the rooms on the first and second floors of his house, I hadn't seen any old-fashioned armoires or cabinets that might be opened with such a key.

There was no rational explanation for why I'd taken it. Curiosity? Yes. Something to remind me that I'd taken and retained the upper hand with him? Maybe.

The last time I'd risked taking something from a man I'd killed it became an albatross. But a key was a thousand times easier to keep hidden than a telescope.

For the most part, I'd taken the key because it was beautiful. It spoke of the past when everything was designed with an eye to beauty over the utilitarian — buildings, the surface of streets, and even keys.

Maybe, it was a lot more than curiosity that made me take a few extra seconds to slide it off his ring. If I could find a way into his house, discover his secrets, I could keep the upper hand with him after death. There was something very satisfying about that.

2

Ten minutes later I was dressed in black jeans and calf-high boots. I wore a pale green turtleneck shirt and a black leather jacket that hugged my shoulders and waist. I went light on the makeup — mostly mascara and a bit of color for my cheeks. I ordered an Uber to take me to Jim's house. The house was about an hour outside of Manhattan in a quiet, luxurious suburb. Because of the rain, Ubers were in high demand, and the app told me it would be ten minutes.

I used the extra time to pull up Jim's house on Zillow and study every room and angle available, refreshing my memory from the unescorted tour I'd taken of the first two floors. There were a decent number of interior photos of the house because he'd purchased the place only four years ago. He clearly wasn't savvy about Zillow — all of the realtor's staging photos were still visible to anyone who was curious. The house wasn't listed for sale yet. Of course, he'd only been dead for a week, and settling ownership of a person's property and possessions takes some time, especially with an estate the size of his.

When the Uber was two minutes away, I grabbed my

umbrella and my camera bag. I left the old-fashioned key in the drawer of my bedside table.

I figured the camera would help me in my attempt to talk my way into the house. If Joe, the man who'd served me perfect martinis at Jim's dinner party, were there, he would remember me as the photographer. Hopefully, he wouldn't get overly suspicious of why I was showing up uninvited. Clearly, there were no more photographs to be taken of his former boss, unless his was the type of family that went in for photographs of their loved ones lying in the coffin, although it was too late for that. Joe was friendly and had seemed warm enough toward me that I was confident he would invite me inside.

Just as I stuck my own key in the deadbolt of my apartment door, I thought of the key safely tucked away. I went back inside and took it out of the drawer. This might be my only chance to get inside of Jim's house. I put the key in the front pocket of my jeans.

Because of the gusting rain and traffic, it took an hour and a half to get to Jim's house.

Locked gates across his driveway provided the first hurdle. The guard booth was empty. I left the backdoor of the Uber standing open as I walked to the intercom on the gate post.

The Uber driver shouted at me. "Hey, I'm not a taxi!" Her voice sounded far away, muted by the pounding rain. "Hey!"

I held up my finger to tell her I'd only be a minute.

She yelled through the open passenger window — "You're on your own."

I heard the window close. I turned and ran back to the car as she was straining over the seat, trying to reach the handle of the door I'd left open. "Can you just wait five minutes?"

"No. I need to get all the way back into the city in this mess. I'm not making money sitting here."

"I'll pay you extra."

"How much?"

"Ten bucks."

She laughed.

"Okay, twenty."

"Five minutes." She picked up her phone and opened the clock. She set the timer. "Close the door, rain is getting inside."

I slammed the door and hurried back to the gate. I pressed the button to speak. There were several minutes of silence during which I pictured the Uber driver's clock counting down the seconds, the minutes disappearing.

"How may I help you?" The voice from the intercom was male. I assumed it was Joe, but I couldn't be sure. I hadn't spoken to him long enough to recall what he sounded like.

I put my mouth close to the intercom. "Hi. Who is this?"

"Who is *this*?"

"My name is Alexandra. I was the photographer at Jim's dinner party in the middle of October. I heard about his death, and I wanted to…"

"Yes, I remember you."

"Great. Is this Joe?"

"Yes it is. How can I help you?"

"I wanted to…I was shocked to hear of his death." I was handling this poorly. The rain was sloshing around me, the driver's clock was shedding numbers.

"We were all shocked."

"I wasn't able to make it to the funeral, and I wanted to pay my respects to his family."

"There is no family here at the moment."

"Oh."

The car horn honked, long and loud. I had no trouble hearing that over the sound of rain hitting the pavement and my umbrella.

"May I come in?"

"Why?"

"He was such a fascinating man." The Uber horn honked again, longer this time. "I felt like I was a part of his life. Taking photographs is such an intimate experience, and I'm feeling a little torn apart…knowing he's gone, and…"

Joe laughed, the sound rich and warm even through the intercom. "Now that you've finished that little performance, would you like a martini?"

"Absolutely."

The gate began to move, both sides drawing inward smoothly and soundlessly. I raced back to the car. The driver lowered the window a few inches. I handed her a twenty and thanked her.

I was soaked from my failure to keep good control of my umbrella while I was leaning toward the intercom and into the car. My jeans clung to my legs. The jacket kept my back and shoulders dry, but the outside was slick with water. My hair was damp and limp.

I adjusted the umbrella to a more effective position, shifted the camera bag so it was better protected, and walked along the curving driveway. I wondered whether the entire staff was still employed and if I might be able to finesse an offer for Jim's limo driver to take me home.

The front door was standing open, no one in sight. I placed my umbrella off to the side on the porch, leaving it open so it had a chance of drying. At least it was well away from spattering rain. I wiped my feet on the mat and stepped inside. Across from the front door was a backless white leather bench with armrests on each end. It stood a few feet from the curving staircase that rose to a landing which framed the entryway. I placed my camera bag on the bench and took off my jacket.

"Vodka and three olives, if I recall."

I turned. Joe stood in the entrance to the living room. I smiled. "Yes, thank you."

He wasn't wearing the tuxedo he'd worn the night of the party. I wondered whether it was because he dressed that way for formal events only, or if his boss's death gave him freedom to wear the blue jeans and white dress shirt he had on now.

"Have a seat. I'll make the drinks, and you can tell me why you're really here."

3

The living room featured an enormous fireplace where several good-sized logs crackled and shot off beautiful orange flames. It was directly across from the entrance that could be closed off with double doors. The front of the room had several tall windows looking out on the trees and shrubs, a rock garden, and the lawn surrounding the driveway. There were two armchairs and a small table in the semi-circular area formed by the windows. A leather couch and more armchairs faced the fireplace, and in the back corner of the room was a large dark blue ceramic pot with a tree growing in it.

I sat in one of the armchairs near the windows and looked out on the pouring rain.

Joe returned carrying two martinis. He stopped near the couch. "You don't want to dry out by the fire?"

"This is fine. I can feel the heat all the way over here."

He came toward me and placed the glasses on the table. He settled in the chair beside me. We toasted Jim, which I didn't really want to do. But I appreciated being invited inside, and the excellent martini I was about to drink, so I figured I could let that little bit of phoniness slide.

We sipped our drinks. The rain sounded far away, insulated by two floors above us and double-paned windows beside us.

He held his glass just above his legs. "Why are you really here?"

"Closure."

He gave me a knowing smile. "I didn't realize you were close to him."

"Like I said, the…"

"Yes. The intimacy of taking another person's photograph."

"It's true."

"I don't doubt that. But it's not the case here," he said. "Your animosity toward him was obvious."

"I don't think…"

"Maybe not to others, obviously not to Jim, but my job is to anticipate, to assess people's unspoken needs."

"You're reading into it. I was being professional."

"Yes, you were absolutely professional, but I'm not reading into it."

I took a sip of my drink. The house was eerily silent, and now I wished for the background noise of the rain hitting glass and wood and stone. "I guess I don't really know why I'm here. Does that make sense?"

He smiled. "No. But I'll accept that you clearly don't want to tell me."

"Then why did you let me in?"

"Curiosity."

I took several sips of my drink, feeling his eyes on me. The room was too warm with the fire and the central heating all working to keep it comfortable. He was a very good-looking guy. I didn't think I'd mind getting to know him, and not just because I needed him to give me access to the house if I was going to settle my curiosity about the key. Although that was first. "Does he have relatives that will be moving in here, or are they selling the house?"

"Nothing's been decided yet."

"And what happens with your job?"

"Jim was good to me in his final wishes."

I smiled. It wasn't an answer to the question. I supposed he was saying there was no need to work, at least for the time being. Possibly for quite some time. Forever?

"I've been asked to stay on, to oversee keeping the house maintained until Jim's brother arrives."

"How long will that be?"

"About a month."

"Do you live here?"

"Yes."

"Where will you go if you decide not to work for him?"

"There are several options."

I waited to hear the options, but he was silent.

"It's an enormous house. It seems strange that he lived here all alone. Except for you."

He took a sip of his drink, then moved the swizzle stick slowly around the side of the glass.

"Were you close?"

"Not really. He appreciated my talents. And I respected his skill with money, even if he was a bit of a prick. But you already know that."

"I just didn't know you agreed."

"As I said, my job is to anticipate."

"*Is* or was?"

He smiled. He raised his glass toward me and took another

sip. When he moved the drink away from his lips, a look of utter satisfaction crossed his face, suggesting he appreciated his own skill in mixing a martini. "I'm surprised you want to be in this house at all," he said. "Dancing on his grave?"

"What do you mean?"

"When you left after his dinner party, you weren't on good terms with him."

I pulled the olives out of my glass and studied them. I thought about eating an olive, but the timing was wrong, I was hyper-alert to what he might say next. I replaced the stick and watched the liquid close over the olives.

"He shoved himself in where he wasn't invited," Joe said.

"Why do you think that?"

"My job, as I mentioned, is to anticipate."

"What does that mean in this case?"

"It was clear what Jim thought was happening, and it was clear to me that you were not at all interested. I was just outside of his study, in case you needed assistance."

He spoke so formally, like a man in his seventies, and yet he was barely past forty, as best I could tell.

It bothered me that he'd seen what happened with Jim. I wasn't sure why. Maybe because I thought it made me look helpless. And yet, he hadn't helped, so he must not have thought that at all.

I tried to remember that night, which I'd worked hard to put out of my mind. I didn't recall being aware of Joe's presence, but earlier in the evening he'd had a knack for seeming to appear out of nowhere, often carrying a martini.

"I don't think you were heartbroken at his death. I think you were quite happy to see him go."

I said nothing. Was he suggesting he thought I'd murdered

his boss? That was paranoia speaking. He couldn't possibly have thoughts in that direction. Could he?

If he was, he didn't seem bothered by the fact. But if he was, I didn't like that at all. I took a long swallow of my drink. I slid two olives off the stick and ate both at once. "You should show me around the house, since no one is here."

"I think you've already seen most of it. On a self-guided tour."

I laughed. "But not the third floor. And not all of the rooms."

"And not the wine cellar."

"Is it actually a cellar?"

He nodded. He pulled an olive out of his drink and ate it.

Watching his mouth move around the small globe was tantalizing. There was something I'd meant to ask, but I couldn't stop watching his mouth. Finally, the thought reappeared. "Is there an attic?"

"Why?"

"If there's a basement, it makes sense there's an attic, that's all."

"No."

The answer was disappointing. An attic seemed the perfect place for an old fashioned key. Maybe the wine cellar...but an attic seemed more fitting. They tended to store old things. I felt the key, unyielding and warm in my front pocket, pressing against my hip bone.

4

Portland, Oregon

Growing up in a large Victorian house was perfect for kids who weren't allowed to watch a lot of TV and as a result, had hungry imaginations. Our fantasy lives were also stoked by Bible stories filled with battles and heroism, cautionary fables, archaic rituals, and illicit sex. There was enough to keep us entertained in the bubble of our restricted home for decades.

With its huge backyard and plenty of square footage inside, we never felt like there were too many people crushed into a constricting space. All the kids were able to relish solitude in their own bedrooms, and there were several small rooms in the living area that allowed us to spread out, putting walls between us. Many territorial fights were mitigated by all those rooms where we could escape a conversation that bored us, a closed window not to our liking, or the unrelenting teasing of a sibling.

Best of all, the house had a full basement and an attic.

I don't know how ownership of this territory evolved because it was established before I was old enough to remember or have any say in the matter, but the basement belonged to the boys and the attic to girls.

The basement had two rooms. One room was used for storage. The main area was given over to my brothers for their activities, especially during the many, many dreary, misty days that Portland offers. The floor was brutally cold concrete covered by a thick area rug, and the walls were brick. Even with the rug, it could get loud down there in a weird, echoing way. It was a solid place, but dank. The storage area had a de-humidifier which helped reduce the dampness that seemed to seep in from the earth even though the entire enclosure was rock-solid.

The artwork on the walls consisted of unframed posters — sports and scenery — since my parents didn't think much of flashy movie posters and certainly didn't allow images of bands or singers like other kids had. Not that we had a lot of friends who didn't belong to our church, but there were a few neighborhood kids and school friends we were allowed to hang out with, as long as we were always alert to the fact that we should be enticing them to believe in god and not allowing them to entice us into anything ungodly.

Two old couches and a few beanbag chairs provided plenty of seating. There was also a cast-off coffee table and a wall unit that had four or five shelves with cabinets below. They had a record player down there, but since our choices in music were limited to religious and classical, it wasn't used much.

My brothers dragged board games down to the basement so when the family went to play a game, half the time it was missing from the designated closet in the main floor hallway. They liked being able to keep games of Monopoly or Risk set up for weeks at a time.

The boys made a big deal of not allowing girls into their area, but the door didn't lock, so of course, I went down there when they weren't around. There was rarely anything interesting to see, but their insistence I didn't belong in their space made me constantly curious. A perverse part of me just liked knowing I was there and they didn't know it. They were unaware that I'd sprawled out in their beanbag chairs and moved a few game pieces on their boards. I never made dramatic moves that would be easily detected, just small things — a little green wooden house returned to the Monopoly box, a dollar taken from someone's cash pile and placed in the bank, or a black cube moved from Germany to Ukraine.

Although they took control of the basement by the default of birth order, I loved the attic and thought it was the better deal. I kept its advantages to myself — from my elevated perch under the eaves, I could see them coming home from school far down the street. I could see every inch of the backyard as well as selected sections in the wooded green belt at the bottom of our sloped yard. Because they never entered the female domain, they weren't aware of how expansive the views were. They obviously had no curiosity about what a small girl might be up to.

Sunlight came into the attic through windows that were wedged close to the peak of the roof in both the front and the back. It was spacious, and it didn't have any of the faint odor of wetness that permeated the space below ground. The attic was not as well-furnished. It only had one couch, but it was soft, allowing me to sink into it, unlike the stiff, cheap couches in the basement.

When a girl my age moved in next door, it was early Spring. The days were filled with near-constant rain. This girl followed me around school for several days not saying anything. She watched me at recess, trailed behind me when I went into the restroom and wiggled into a nearby seat at my lunch table.

Every time I looked at her, she was staring at me, not smiling. I stared back.

After about a week of this, she announced that she lived next door, which I already knew. She further announced that this proximity meant we should be friends. I didn't see any reason to disagree. Her name was Carmen Mitchell.

"You should invite me to play at your house," Carmen said. "Since all it does is rain here, we'll have to play inside."

I complied.

That day after school Carmen walked across the adjoining lawns and rang our doorbell. When my mother answered, Carmen announced she was my best friend and would be spending weekday afternoons at our house. My mother looked as startled as I was, but she didn't argue. She opened the door so Carmen could enter.

"You should show me your room," Carmen said.

I led her upstairs. She began a thorough inspection, touching the headboard of my bed and my nightstand, running her fingers along the length of the drapes, testing my desk chair, and opening the drawers until I told her not to.

She closed the partially opened center desk drawer and moved to my bookcase. "Your books are boring."

I didn't argue. Some of them were. We were nine years old, and all my books had either been chosen by or at least approved by my parents. There were two shelves of easy-reading books about famous characters from the Bible. But there were also two shelves with slender novels I'd bought through the school book club. The bottom shelf was lined with picture books from when I was smaller. I still liked to skim through these — a walk down memory lane, reading stories that I really never read at all because I'd memorized every word when my parents read them aloud.

She turned away and walked to my closet. She turned the knob.

"Don't go into my closet."

"Why? Are there monsters? Bad things?" She giggled.

"No. I just don't like you touching all my stuff."

"Why not?"

"Because I don't."

Despite her aggressive attitude, she accepted this. She sat down in the middle of the carpet. She crossed her legs at the ankles and leaned her elbows on her thighs. "What should we do?"

I sat across from her. Rain was still pounding the earth, so going outside wasn't an option.

I thought about taking her upstairs to the attic, but after watching her open my drawers and give her opinion on my books, I didn't want to let her into that part of my life just yet. Even at nine, I was cautious. I could see that some people will walk through a partially opened door and take over. You have to be constantly on guard.

She sat up straight and crossed her legs in the opposite direction. "Are you glad you have a friend next door?"

I nodded.

"What do you like to do?"

"Lots of things."

She thrust her head forward and peered at me, inspecting my face. "We kind of look like each other, don't you think?"

I nodded. We did. We both had dark hair cut to our shoulders, without bangs. We were both thin and about the same height. At nine years old, that was enough to decree that we looked alike.

"Almost like sisters," she said.

"Not really."

She frowned. "We should become blood sisters."

"What's that?"

She laughed. "You don't know?" She stood and walked to my desk. She pulled the scissors out of the container where I kept pencils and a ruler. She returned and stood over me. "Give me your hand. I'll make a tiny cut on your wrist and…"

"No."

"It won't hurt. I'll make one on my hand, and we rub the blood together. Then our blood is mixed, and we're blood sisters."

"No. Put my scissors back."

She opened them and ran one of the blades gently down the side of her finger. "It doesn't hurt. If you have a pin, that would be better."

"I don't want to do it."

"I thought we were best friends."

"We're friends, but we're not sisters. And I don't like blood."

She laughed. "Are you scared?"

"No. I just don't like blood. And I don't want to give my blood to someone else. It's mine."

She returned to my desk and placed the scissors on the

desk. She sat across from me again and stared at me. "I'm not sure this will work out if you don't want to be my blood sister."

"Do other people have blood sisters, or did you make it up?"

"I didn't make it up."

"Do you have other blood sisters?"

"I have one other one, but we moved away." Her eyes turned glassy. "I thought you wanted to be my friend."

"I'm your friend. But no blood."

She smiled. Her gums seemed awfully red, as if she had too much blood pumping through them.

5

New York

Joe suggested a second round of martinis, and I accepted, willing to sit in that luxurious armchair all afternoon, waiting to see where things might go with us. I wondered when he would offer a tour of the house. He'd ignored my suggestion even though he was the one to tease me with a mention of the wine cellar and the pseudo-attic of the third floor.

We sipped our drinks, and I offered him some carefully curated information from my past — my hit-and-miss approach to college, the basics regarding a few of my jobs, and my impressions of Australia. He talked about his unintended path to becoming chief of a household staff.

He'd started out as a gardener, working with his uncle. After a year or two of this, one of the homeowners asked the gardening staff if any of them were available to serve at a large outdoor party for which they were suddenly short-handed. Joe volunteered and found he liked the people-watching aspect of serving drinks and appetizers. He went to work for a catering company for a while, and it was during a catered dinner at Jim's that the two struck up a conversation. Jim was impressed with Joe's ability to anticipate other's desires before they even recognized their own wishes.

Joe liked being in the background. He wasn't the kind of guy who needed an impressive, enviable career to feel good about himself. He didn't need accolades and power over others. There was something satisfying about serving people, he said. It felt like your life had meaning. It felt like your existence on the earth made an impact. Even though the people you served rarely knew your name or remembered your face, you knew you'd brought something, even if it was just a glass of wine, into another's life.

I had no idea how to respond to this. He sounded like some kind of monk — too good to be true. But there was nothing religious or zealous or even puritanical about him. He was luxuriating in that martini with the same pleasure I have when I sip the icy alcohol.

For all their religious views about not chasing after money, my parents would have labeled him lazy. He didn't have any ambition. And yet, what was all that supposedly necessary ambition for? They wanted us to strive with enthusiasm for top grades, to graduate from college, and find *worthwhile* jobs. For me, they wanted all of that until I found a *worthwhile* man and quit everything I'd planned and worked for in order to take care of children and a home and a husband. But ambition was important. If you didn't have ambition, you were just wasting space in the world. Along with our secular ambition, we needed religious ambition — primarily the desire to convert everyone who came into our lives.

Joe lifted his hand and held his palm toward the window. "I can feel the temperature dropping. Should we sit by the fire?"

"What about that tour?"

"Did I offer a tour?"

"Is there a problem with it? You're in charge now, aren't you?"

He shrugged. He stood and swallowed the remainder of his drink. I did the same.

"We'll start with the wine cellar," he said.

He led the way through the dining room which I was well-acquainted with from the dinner party. Beyond that was an enormous kitchen, large enough to prepare food for a restaurant full of people. There were two center islands, both with sinks, one with a warming drawer and the other with its own small refrigerator. I asked why a fridge was needed when an extremely large refrigerator with glass doors stood ten feet away.

Joe opened the door to the small fridge and showed me two shelves with a few deli containers and a small drawer that was stuffed with produce. "All the ingredients for the meal at hand can be stored here. It helps ensure nothing's forgotten, no missed garnish or forgotten splash of wine. And it saves time. The kitchen is so large, simply moving from the counter to the stove to the refrigerator takes time. When you're juggling meal preparation, every second matters."

He opened a door at the far end to show me a pantry the size of my bedroom. Then we went out into a back hallway and turned a corner. He took keys out of his pocket and opened a door to a steep, narrow staircase. The steps were marble, and the iron railing was attached to the wall. The other side was open to the marble floor below. I glanced at my boots. Surely they were dry by now. Even so, the heels and soles were hard and not conducive to solid footing on a marble floor.

"Why is it locked?"

He gave me a look as if to suggest I was naïve. I said nothing but wondered why anyone would choose to live permanently with people you didn't trust. It seemed money couldn't buy you everything you wanted after all.

We descended slowly, Joe leading the way. It was easier to keep my left palm pressed to the cool plaster wall than to hold the railing which made me feel as if my elbow was jabbing into my ribs as I worked to stay away from the open edge.

The area was bright with recessed light, but even so, there was a sense of the walls being too close, of being trapped in a space where there was no possibility of escape. I could hear my own breath echoing off the thick walls and ceiling, the sound echoed by the movement of air in and out of Joe's lungs.

Taking a claustrophobic staircase into a basement that seemed farther below ground than I would have expected as the stairs continued seemingly without end, with a man I didn't know, might not have been a wise move.

He was friendly. He had a nice smile. He'd treated me well at the dinner party, and he mixed a perfect martini, but the man was a complete unknown. A stranger who had a good six or seven inches on me, not to mention those nicely shaped muscles. He'd watched his boss assault me and stayed back, waiting to see what happened. Not that I wanted to be rescued. I'd taken excellent care of myself, but most men have the societal imperative to rescue, and he had not.

When he'd suggested showing me the wine cellar, the possibility of danger hadn't entered my mind. It was the design of the staircase and the depth of the basement that was causing me to re-think my eager acceptance.

In fact, entering the house at all might have had some risk that eluded me in my desire to find the lock for the artistic key jabbing at my bone each time I moved in the wrong direction.

I continued to keep my palm on the wall and focused my attention on his breathing, trying to see whether I could detect the increased speed and the shallow movement that might suggest he had things on his mind other than a magnificent wine collection.

After what seemed like hours of walking downward, we reached the cellar. It was a palatial room. All four walls except for the space where the staircase ended were lined with narrow shelves fitted with wood racks, angled to hold bottles with the necks forward and down.

In the center of the room was a bar with a cherrywood base and a gray and white granite top. Wine glasses hung from a rack overhead. A refrigerator was fitted into the base, the door the same wood as the rest. The only thing giving away its presence was the inset handle and the thin seams. Jim was obviously big on having plenty of refrigeration close at hand.

As I moved into the room, I saw the shelves had small black labels that indicated what was stored in that section — the vintage, the variety, region, and year. He had wines from France and Italy, and wines bottled in the nineteen-sixties.

"I can't imagine what this is worth." My voice was soft, as if the very closeness and tight seal of the space pressed on my vocal cords to make sure I didn't disturb the atmosphere, unsettle the wines.

"Sixty-four thousand dollars."

I laughed, again, very softly. "I didn't expect an answer."

"It was itemized in his trust, so I had the number at the top of my mind."

I nodded. "It's almost too much."

"You're right. Most of the time when he had a large party, he ordered wine for that particular event. He pulled from his collection when he had smaller gatherings. Special guests."

I shivered, thinking of the glass he'd served me before shoving his hand down the front of my dress.

"Are you cold?"

"No."

"The room is kept at fifty-five degrees. It can feel even colder because the air is dry."

I moved to the bar and placed my fingertips on the icy granite. "What's going to happen to it?"

"His brother inherits most of his estate. A few charities received gifts."

"And you."

"As well as others. But the bulk of it goes to his brother, including the house, and of course, this." He swept his arm in the direction of the shelves surrounding us.

He leaned his hip against the bar and held my gaze. A smile flickered across his lips. They parted slightly, but he didn't speak.

I slid my fingers into my pockets and walked toward the wall at my left. I studied the wines — Cabernets on the first few shelves at eye-level. None of the wineries were familiar to me, but I hadn't studied wines all that much.

I know the names of a few that I like, some that I can afford regularly, others that I always hope someone else will order to share with me.

I was aware of Joe's presence behind me, and I wondered again what might come out of this situation. The key still burned itself into my bone, but there was nothing in this ultra-modern cellar that had a lock, and I'd seen the typical modern key he'd used to unlock the cellar door.

I moved alone to the next section, feeling his eyes on my back. I had no doubt he'd show me the rest of the place. But it didn't seem as urgent as it had when I'd first entered the house. The two martinis floated in my blood, making me feel relaxed and less fixated on finding the lock that drove me all the way out here in the pouring rain. The martinis were possibly the cause of the tremor of caution I'd had descending the stairs. The sensation was gone now, but when I paused to think about the solid, soundproof room where I now stood, I wondered if my caution would prick to the surface again.

It didn't. Instead, I had an overwhelming desire to kiss him — the martinis speaking again. I thought of his lips when he smiled, when they touched the edge of the martini glass, and when he spoke. My body felt warm. It had been a long time since I'd kissed a man. Several months, now. I turned.

As if he knew what I was thinking, he smiled. "Should we try a bottle?"

I took a few steps toward him, and without putting my hands on him, I lifted my mouth to his. I kissed him softly, and after a fraction of a second, he responded.

6

Stephanie poured cream into her coffee and stirred it viciously, knocking the spoon hard against the sides as it circled the ceramic mug. Everything hurt, and the coffee wasn't going to help, but it was her habit to drink a cup after dinner. So here she was, like an automaton, going through the motions of loading grounds, filling the canister with water, inhaling the aroma, and now adding the perfect amount of cream. And it had to be real cream. Always. Coffee with milk tasted like something thin and tired, without distinction. Cream made it rich and soothing and satisfying.

She rinsed the spoon and left it on the counter.

She carried the coffee into the living room and settled into the armchair near the window. The single window in her living room looked out on Sixth Avenue. It was mesmerizing to watch people and traffic move past, aggressive and intent on their destinations. In the rain, they looked as if they existed in another world, covered by a screen of water and wind. It upset her to see so many people passing through her life, people whose destinations were unknown. She would never find out which ones were going to work, which to the hospital for cancer treatment or childbirth, to the gym, or to meet the man they loved.

Tears pricked the backs of her eyelids. She sipped her coffee, recoiling as it singed her tongue. She hadn't had the good fortune of loving a man since Eileen's father walked out on them nearly twenty years ago.

Why did people say that — *walked out*? She supposed because it showed the coldness in the act. Picking up a single suitcase, as if that was all he needed to hang onto after five years together. Walking out the door. There was no passion in the act of walking. No regret, no sadness, no grief, no loss. Nothing. A simple movement from one place to another.

It seemed to suggest that the woman who was walked out upon had absolutely no value. Neither she nor her baby girl. They were casually discarded along with the clothes and meaningless papers and old coffee mugs that were also left behind.

She took another sip of coffee. Starting the evening with morose thoughts like these was not going to pave the way for a good night's rest.

This was the path her thoughts often took. She never wanted to doubt her faith, she didn't doubt it, not for a moment. She believed every single word in the Bible, but wasn't that the trouble? There were so many promises of happiness and good fortune. Why had none of those things appeared in her life?

Yes, she had her daughter. That was a blessing beyond her ability to comprehend. Another life to cherish and provide for during the first eighteen to twenty-five years. She had friends at church where she felt loved and welcomed. But church friends didn't hold you in their arms at night. They didn't smile at you over morning coffee. Only rarely did they offer a listening ear that could help you sort through your problems. It wasn't fair to think that way, but it was true. There was a limit to their desire to hear the details of what you were struggling with. A husband was there for that comfort and companionship every moment of your life.

She'd seen how co-workers and those very same church friends picked up their phones at a moment's notice and shot off a text to their husbands. They sent messages about something funny they'd heard, something aggravating — as minor as having to stand on the subway or the lack of decent bananas at the market.

She swallowed more coffee and put the mug on the table, letting her eyes glaze over, so the traffic and pedestrians became even more of a blur.

Of course, the problem troubling her thoughts and preventing her sleep right now couldn't be discussed with friends. Even a husband, if she had one, might dismiss it. Because the thing she wanted was impossible. The discomfort nagging at her would never go away except by a sheer act of her own will in deciding to move forward, put it behind her. Let it go, as they all said.

When Stephanie first heard of Jim Kohn's death, she'd been elated, disgusting and shameful as that feeling was. Her daughter was finally free of that man's degradation. He'd dragged Eileen into a virtual gutter and turned her away from God. Because of him, Eileen was caught up in chasing a modeling career and all the hedonistic ugliness that went with that kind of life. Jim might be dead, removed from any chance of her daughter crawling back to him, but the damage he'd done was still deeply rooted.

It seemed to Stephanie that Eileen's soul had been sucked out of her. All that girl cared about was making up her face in ever more exotic expressions, the liner on her eyes so thick it took on the appearance of some kind of mask, often painted out into wings that brushed close to her cheekbone. The liner and dark shadow applied beneath her eyes made her look as if she'd been punched. She spent hours in their tiny bathroom conditioning and brushing and ironing and curling her hair, weaving it into ever-more-dramatic styles. When she wasn't in front of the mirror, she was heading out to the gym where she worked her body for two hours and still refused to eat a full meal. She nibbled at crackers and yogurt, fruit and boiled eggs or the scrambled whites. She ate tuna plain because the calories and fat in mayonnaise were *appalling*.

Stephanie touched her mug. The coffee was cooling fast. In another thirteen minutes, she'd be late for Bible study, but she couldn't manage to heave herself out of the chair. She wanted the elation to return. The feeling that Jim was stripped out of her daughter's life for eternity. The thrill had been so short-lived. Long enough to feel pleasure that he was gone, a few minutes longer to tell Alexandra about it, and then, it was gone. The feeling replaced by this deepening gloom.

She felt helpless and alone. So alone. Where was God in all of this? He was supposed to answer her prayers, give her wisdom and guidance. She felt nothing. She felt as if He didn't even exist. Shouldn't there be something? A flutter in her heart? A whisper deep inside of her ear? She was trying to do what He asked, she raised her daughter with prayer and the words of the Bible and church.

Right this minute, she felt that the only soul she could rely upon was her own.

And that was the other thing gnawing at her stomach, making the coffee burn and hiss like spilled acid against her tender internal flesh, despite the thick, soothing sweetness of the cream. She'd prayed for that job. She'd believed she would have that job. She'd trusted it to be delivered into her hands.

Instead, it had been handed to Alexandra.

The unfairness of the situation would not leave her alone. And no matter who she tried to talk to about it, she was smacked down for not trusting God's plan for her life. It might not be the right position for her, they said. Even if she thought it was. God knew best.

Well how come God gave interesting, well-paying jobs to other people and not her?

7

Joe's kiss rocked me to my core.

I had the sense I'd done the same to him. He pulled away from me and settled his hand on my hip. "Does that mean you want to try one of these bottles?"

"How would you ever choose?"

"I know a bit about the collection."

"But the taste of the martinis will spoil it."

"Correct."

"Then?"

"I thought I'd make something to eat. Do you like ravioli?"

"You know how to make ravioli?"

He laughed. "I'm not rolling my own pasta. I picked up a few things from a deli earlier."

"I do love ravioli."

He walked to the rack next to the Cabs and pulled out a bottle. Is Zinfandel okay?"

"Sure."

We walked up the stairs in silence. Once again, I kept my hand on the wall, just a light touch of my fingertips.

While I watched from across one of the islands, Joe tossed

a green salad of arugula and pine nuts and yellow peppers. He heated the ravioli and spooned a serving onto a white plate beside the salad. He did the same for himself. We went into the breakfast room overlooking the back patio. He opened the wine and poured it into our glasses.

The room was surrounded by windows and had three rectangular skylights. Rain pounded the glass on all sides. There was a split in the clouds farther away which cast an eerie light from the disappearing sun on the shadows of trees and grass spread out beyond the breakfast room.

We ate the pasta and sipped the most fantastic Zinfandel I'd ever tasted. We listened to the rain hammer around us and talked about the house and the wine collection. He told me about the staff, all of whom remained for the time being, at the request of Mark Kohn. In addition to the limo driver, there was a gardening crew, a handyman, the chef, and two women who cleaned on a daily basis.

Joe, one of the cleaning women, and the handyman were the only ones who lived on the property. Jim had considered their skills essential — their availability needed around the clock. For this reason, their salaries were slightly higher than you'd expect.

I thought it strange that I hadn't seen a glimpse or heard even the footstep of any of these people during the several hours I'd been in the house. Maybe the rain had something to do with it. Certainly, that would have kept the gardeners away.

When the food was gone, the wine bottle was still half full. Considering the martinis, it was a good thing to be taking it slowly. He poured a small splash into my empty glass then cleared away our plates and flatware.

"Now are you interested in that excellent fire Ed built? I

think it's still got some heat left in it."

I smiled and stood. I followed him to the living room, and we settled beside each other on the couch. He placed the bottle on the table where it caught the flicker of flames in the dark green glass.

Joe took the wineglass out of my hand and placed both glasses on the table. He put his arm around me and pulled me toward him. I felt the long key wedge itself into my hip bone. He kissed me and put his other hand on my waist. He fiddled at the edge of my shirt, waiting for me to give the go-ahead.

I moved away from him. "I need to use your bathroom."

As I stood, he picked up his wineglass and turned his gaze toward the fire.

I went into the entryway and picked up my messenger bag. I found my way to the powder room I'd used during the dinner party. I peed, washed my hands, and ran my fingers through my hair, dry now from my time indoors and slightly warm from the heat of the fire and my own scalp. I put lotion on my hands. I slid the key out of my pocket and tucked it into a zippered pouch inside my bag.

Not knowing where the other staff was located, I wasn't sure it was safe to leave my bag in the entryway. It wasn't that I didn't trust them, or thought them thieves, but I hadn't met them. Not only had I not seen or heard the suggestion of another person in the house, there was an echoing sense of desertion about the place, despite the friendly fire laid by the invisible handyman. I had no idea whether they'd seen me, which was even more concerning. I couldn't risk someone getting curious and finding that key. I could afford to lose cash out of my wallet, makeup, possibly my keys, but I could not afford to have anyone know I possessed that key. Ever.

I brought the bag with me into the living room.

Joe looked at it with a confused expression, as if he wondered why I'd burdened myself with a good-sized bag when the obvious path was toward un-encumbering ourselves of our clothes, but he said nothing. Possibly he wrote me off as a woman who couldn't be separated from her possessions. I was okay with that. In this case, that's exactly who I was.

I snuggled up next to him, and we began kissing in earnest. He slid his hands up my shirt, and soon they were inside my bra. We stroked and writhed around each other for quite a long time. The flames shrank, and I welcomed the cool air drifting over us from the rest of the room and the cavernous entryway beyond.

After a while, he suggested we go up to his suite on the third floor. I took my bag with me.

His space consisted of a sitting area with a large TV mounted to the wall, its tiny speakers tucked into the corners near the ceiling. There was a love seat and two armchairs. Several windows occupied one wall, and the wall opposite the TV held a large abstract painting in blues, some of which transitioned to grays. A shocking thick, red slash of paint ran through the left side.

The bathroom was larger than the powder room downstairs, and his bedroom was spacious enough to contain a king-sized bed with a dark blue fabric-covered headboard and bedding in various complementary shades of blue. There was a chest of drawers and a reclining chair with a table beside it. Bifold doors opened onto a balcony that was lit by a string of small light bulbs.

He removed my clothes slowly, taking his time. When I was naked, he lifted me onto the bed and undressed himself.

I'd never had sex with a man his age before. Not that he was old, but he was certainly over forty, and for some odd reason, his age made me feel more adult-like. I'd been an adult for well over ten years, but there was something about him that made me think of a man rather than a guy. It's hard to describe.

For one thing, he was more interested in me. Not that the guys I'd been with before were selfish, but there was just something more careful and focused about Joe. Giving me pleasure did not appear to be an end-goal toward his own satisfaction. I shouldn't have assumed it was his age, it was just an observation.

I came three times, then fell into a deep sleep that lasted until almost four. When I woke, he was propped up on one elbow watching me sleep. I did not like that at all. I moved away from him and slid out of bed. "I need to get going."

"It's the middle of the night."

"Not really. I have work in a few hours."

He looked surprised. I'm not sure why. He knew I was employed. Maybe he figured a photographer who works at upscale dinner parties keeps her own hours.

He slid out of bed and pulled on his jeans. "I'll get the limo."

"I can order an Uber."

"Not at this hour."

"It's fine. That's what I use all the time."

"It's not necessary. Dirk is used to being called at odd hours. It's expected." He grabbed his cell phone off the nightstand and sent a text message.

The response came before I'd finished hooking my bra.

Standing in the foyer, just over the threshold, Joe gave me a long and spectacular kiss. It made me briefly consider calling in sick. But leaving was better. Once I was out the door, I'd know it was the right choice.

He put his mouth close to my ear. "I'll see you again soon." He kissed my earlobe. He went to a table at the side of the entryway and opened the drawer. He took out a business card and handed it to me. "Call or text."

"I will."

He smiled.

"I didn't get my tour."

He lifted his eyebrows slightly but said nothing.

I retrieved my umbrella from the front porch and closed it. The rain had stopped, and the eaves were no longer dripping. I walked carefully down the wet steps and slid into the back seat of the limo, settling into the creamy leather seat. It was something I could definitely get used to.

8

I climbed the stairs to my apartment, still warm and satisfied from the limo ride and everything that came before. My mind was split between thinking of Joe and knowing I had all the access to the house I desired. I could take my time about finding the lock that matched the old key.

Of course, I'd assumed that lock was somewhere in Jim's house or the surrounding grounds, but really, it was possible it belonged to something in his high-rise office, despite its sleek, ultra-modern look. It might even unlock a cabinet or box at an apartment in the city. It might be the key to a locker at a cigar club or some other type of male hangout for the privileged.

I turned to start the last flight of stairs. The building was silent at five in the morning, the tenants just now creeping from their beds, grinding coffee beans, dressing for the gym. As if to remind me that time was racing forward, I heard the pipes in the walls throb as shower water ran, searching for hot water.

I looked up at the landing.

Victoria from next door was leaning on the railing,

watching me climb. "You're up early." She gave me a cat-like smile, assuring me that she didn't think I was up early at all, but rather up very late.

I continued to the top of the stairs.

As I drew close, she inhaled deeply. "Oh, you had a nice evening. Alcohol. Rain. A warm fire. And sex, absolutely sex."

I shouldn't have let her bait me. "Wrong."

"I smell it."

"No, you don't. Because you're wrong."

"I don't think I am."

She was guessing. That was all. The only risky speculation was the fire, but she'd gambled. There hadn't been a hint of smoke coming from that well-designed fireplace. There was no possible way she could smell it on my clothing. She gambled because she was a gambler. As we'd argued multiple times, day trading is gambling. The stock market is gambling. She might argue that life itself was a gamble, but she never had.

"So there is a guy in your life." The cat-smile remained.

"Shouldn't you be sleeping? Getting your energy to start the race the minute the market opens?"

"I was worried about you."

How had she known I wasn't home? Were the walls thinner than I'd realized? But I'd never heard a sound from their apartment. The only intrusive sounds in the building came from water straining up through old pipes, making sounds like living creatures belching and groaning inside the walls. "No need to worry. And no need to keep a watch on my coming and going."

"It's hard not to with our doors opening right into each other."

"That's only a problem if you're always opening your door."

She laughed.

"Nice chatting." I moved around her and shoved my key into the lock. The door opened, and I stepped inside.

"You're going to have a tough day at work after being out all night," Victoria said.

"I'll manage."

"Did you get any sleep?"

"I said I'll manage."

"You'll definitely miss your morning run." She glanced at her phone, nestled in her left hand. "You should be leaving for your run right about now."

"I'd appreciate it if you'd stop tracking my day."

"I'm not. I just care about my neighbors."

"That's fine, but it's a little creepy."

"Since when is being friendly considered creepy?"

I wasn't going to win the argument. "Talk to you later." I started to close the door.

I should have slammed it because suddenly her foot was between the frame and my door. She'd moved so quickly I felt like I was dealing with a Black Mamba, a reptile that outruns its human prey as she'd done with me.

"Since you have extra time without your run, this might be a good day for us to show you our trading set-up. We can answer your questions and…"

"No thanks. Please move your foot."

Her foot remained. "You said you were interested. We keep putting it off." She laughed as if one of us had said something terribly funny. "It's nothing to be afraid of. The concepts are quite simple."

"I'm not afraid. Move your foot."

"I'll make breakfast. Do you like breakfast burritos? Or are you an old fashioned girl — bacon and eggs?"

"Victoria. You're being a pain in the ass. Move your foot, and we can arrange a time for you to show me your computer set-up, if you think it's that important that I see how it works."

"I'm doing this for you. I'm very good at reading people, and you are beyond curious about our income. You're sort of jealous that you can't work four hours a day and make five times what you're bringing in now."

Again, my argumentative side got the upper hand. Maybe my evening had been too relaxing and satisfying, and I was looking for a debate. I'm not really sure. "You can't assume I'll make five times because you have no idea what I make now."

She smiled.

For a split second, and then longer, that smile made me believe she actually knew what I earned. I tried to shake off the sensation, but it was difficult. The look of superiority, of having figured me out, glimmered in her eyes and wriggled along my spine. "I'm not going to ask you again. Get your foot out of my door."

She removed her foot, and I closed the door.

I began stripping off my clothes as I walked to my bedroom, trying to decide which I wanted more — a shower or coffee. Since my clothes were half off, I opted for the shower. That way I could enjoy the coffee to signal the day ahead rather than drinking it as a pick-me-up while I was still living in the skin from the night before.

While the water ran down the drain and I waited for hot

water to make its way to my apartment, I checked the pouch inside my bag to be sure the key was safe. I'd already checked when I got dressed an hour earlier. I'd checked again while I sat in the silent comfort of the limo, gliding back into New York City with the early commuters.

The constant checking was ridiculous, but I couldn't stop. The elusive nature of the supposed on-site staff made me suspicious of them. Yes, it was an enormous house, easy to disappear in, and they probably didn't have much work on a rainy mid-week afternoon when their boss was deceased, and the new one hadn't arrived, but I still thought I would have at least sensed the presence of the others. The echoing sensation of vacancy suggested they were wary of me, and that suggested my bag hadn't even been safe while I slept in Joe's arms. I'd have to find a more secure way of keeping the key on me during future visits.

How that would happen since I'd obviously be naked on those future visits, I had no idea. But I was confident something would come to me.

9

As if they'd assigned themselves twenty-four-hour
surveillance of my life, Rafe was hanging out on the landing
when I got home from the gym after work. I was carrying a
container of hot and sour soup in one hand, which I was
eager to get inside and into a bowl while it was still hot. I met
his gaze but said nothing.

As I went to my door, he stepped dramatically out of the
way. "What's new?"

I unlocked my door.

He laughed, his tone soft and slightly menacing, although I
might have been reading into it. "Brrr." He shivered with an
overwrought shaking of his shoulders.

I rolled my eyes, but only my apartment door was a
witness. I really could not figure out Rafe and Victoria.
Sometimes I thought they were simply bored with their lives,
anxious to drag me into their world as some sort of
entertainment. Maybe they had a weird sex game going on
between them, and I was the prize in their contest, or a pawn
in whatever moves their game required.

Their desire to unsettle me laughable in its lack of subtlety, and yet, there was a weird kind of mystery, so maybe they were more subtle than I realized. Because I had absolutely no idea what they wanted or what their game was. I could have put an end to the back-and-forth easily enough, but I rarely saw my other neighbors and these two were as entertaining for me as I was for them.

They certainly made the building come to life, bringing excitement if nothing else to the vacant staircase and lobby I usually encountered. Except for a few brief conversations and an evening spent smoking on the roof, I hadn't seen Kent, who occupied the third of four apartments on our floor. The only solitary conversation with him had ended rather quickly and was equally perplexing. He'd suggested the former occupant of my apartment left suddenly and unhappily. When I'd asked Rafe about it, I got his usual dance around the edge of things.

I'd considered knocking on Kent's door, inviting him over for a drink or to the freezing roof garden for a smoke. I had no doubt that if I put my mind to it, I could get him to open up, but I was juggling a lot, so that was further down my list of things to do.

In thinking about my short and twisted interactions with my immediate neighbors, I was suddenly overcome with curiosity about the interior of their apartment. I was holding them off simply to keep the upper hand. But saying *no* doesn't always mean you have the upper hand. Being agreeable often gives you that primary position because it puts others off their guard.

I turned to face him. "Victoria keeps asking if I want to come over to see how day trading works."

"She said you were curious."

"I am." I smiled and tilted my head slightly, playing coy and cute. "But even though you keep talking about it, you never actually invite me over."

"She did."

"But that was when I had to get ready for work. If I arrange it ahead of time, I can go in late."

He shoved his hands into his pockets and cocked his hip to one side. With his white dress shirt, tails out, and blue jeans, he looked like he was trying to imitate James Dean. I wondered if he even knew who that was. For someone who claimed sophistication in the stock market and the culture of New York City, he struck me as slightly ignorant of anything outside his immediate range of experience.

"You can wake up now, the universe has ended," I said.

He didn't respond so I was pretty sure he hadn't recognized the quote from *Rebel Without A Cause*. He lowered his brow. He pulled his hands out of his pockets and pushed his hair off his face.

I nudged my door open and let the strap of my gym bag slide down my shoulder. I eased it to the floor and pushed it inside the door with my foot. "Tomorrow?" I shifted the soup carton to my other hand.

"Excellent. Yes." He grinned as if I'd just accepted his invitation to the prom. "People don't realize the opportunity they're missing — the ability to make money off bits and pieces of other people's money. Cash isn't a real thing anyway. Stocks and company valuation aren't real. Not like a gold bar or diamonds. Even those things, they're only worth what someone is willing to exchange for them."

"True."

"You're a smart girl. I think you'll be intrigued. Most smart people are."

"Is that right?"

"Absolutely. Think about it…"

"I have."

"Maybe not enough. All these geniuses study economics and business models and forecasting and global trends, they're figuring out what's going to be the next wave. They investigate which companies are hiding vulnerabilities, which is all of them, really. You just need to know what they are. The experts figure out where to place their bets and Vic and I follow in the wake. It's natural and it doesn't hurt anyone. Trickle down, right?"

I shrugged. I wondered if Victoria, with all her insistence that this wasn't gambling was aware that he viewed his so-called work as placing bets. "I think I've told you, I'm not a gambler." This was a blatant lie. I might not gamble a lot with money, but I gamble with a lot of other things.

I've taken some serious risks. I just can't help it. The thrill is often irresistible. Maybe I wasn't so different from Victoria and Rafe after all. The old-fashioned key that would tie me to Jim Kohn's murder came to mind. The absurd decision to steal one of my murder victim's telescope. Something that made me question my sanity when I thought back on it — dragging such a large and obvious object from the house and trusting I wouldn't be seen, trying to hide it in my closet in a house where nothing was my own. Never considering how rarely I'd get a chance to use it, and finally deciding it was a large, bulky, obvious threat to my anonymity.

"Life is a gamble, babe," Rafe said.

"I'm not your babe."

"Sorry."

I gave him a hard, tight grimace. Once again, I felt the chill in my spine, wondering at their suggestion they knew what I was thinking. Of course, I was reading into it. It was simply coincidence. It's a common belief, almost a cliché, that life is a gamble. All he'd done was repeat a thought that was not very original.

It still unsettled me. I'm not used to people getting inside my head. Not even close. Mostly I thought my neighbors were simply wannabe players, stumbling through life, happening on things that struck close to the bone. But I wasn't entirely sure.

10

After Carmen went home for dinner that first day she visited my house, I picked up my scissors off my desk. They were a rather large and knife-sharp pair of scissors to entrust to a nine-year-old, but my parents encouraged sewing and other crafts. Good scissors were essential.

I mostly used them only for cutting pictures out of magazines of things I liked or wanted.

I opened the scissors and dragged the blade gently across the underside of my wrist. It didn't hurt, but neither did it break the skin. The side of the blade against my skin felt more like scratching an itch. I'd kept the point far away. I wondered how Carmen had planned to make me bleed. Would she have stabbed that sharp tip into my wrist where a faint purple line revealed the place my blood flowed? Did she want to see my blood rush out of the opening into daylight? What else did she want from me?

These thoughts made the edges of my vision grow dark. I wanted to know what she would have done if I hadn't stopped her. I wanted to know what it would feel and look like. At the same time, I was horrified. What if my blood started to flow out and never stopped? Jake and Tom had both experienced bloody noses a few times, and it had seemed like the blood gushed forever. I'd been so sickened I had to leave the kitchen where my mother was mopping it up as fast as she could, unable to stop the drops from falling on my brothers' legs, dripping on the floor each time she swapped out a wad of paper towels for a fresh handful.

Of course, I'd seen my own blood. I'd had scraped knees and elbows. Those shallow wounds brought out more blood than they should have, but my mother was quick to wipe the scrape clean with warm soapy water, squirt on clear gel that claimed to kill the germs, and hide it from sight with a nice wide bandaid.

Already at a young age, I knew blood should remain hidden from sight. I didn't want my body hurt or damaged in any way. I didn't want the same rips in my skin that covered my brothers' arms and legs. I was careful when I climbed trees, scrambling to keep up with the boys, or rode my bike down a steep hill, also trying to catch them. And possibly that's why I never did keep up or catch them. At least not physically. I was also rather young when I learned there were other ways to win.

Despite my parents' religion and rules, unlike a lot of fundamentalist believers, they did not believe in corporal punishment. They inflicted physically and emotionally brutal experiences — shoving me under the water in an effort to make me repent, punishing me for running away by forcing me to endure a solo campout in the woods behind our house. But they never hit us. Not even a slap on the cheek for bad language or verbal rebellion.

My mother watched over our physical selves like a full-time nurse, making sure our teeth and bodies were zealously cleaned, coddling us when we were sick in bed. She walked up the stairs carrying trays of soup and sandwiches, juice and cough syrup. She patched our wounds and made sure they were looked after diligently until they healed.

The thought of deliberately causing physical injury was shocking to me. I was repulsed and fascinated.

I increased the pressure from the blade of the scissors. A dark pink line emerged, torn bits of skin forming a wake as the blade traveled along the underside of my forearm. That was enough. I returned the scissors to the canister.

I wandered down the upstairs hall and stopped outside of Tom's bedroom. His door was partially opened, as was the household rule. I knocked.

He turned in his chair. He looked surprised to see me and slightly ill. "What do you want?"

"Can I come in?"

He closed the spiral notebook that had been open on the desk. He put the cap on two pens lying beside it — one black and one red. "I guess."

I pushed open the door and stepped inside.

"What do you want?"

"Have you heard of blood sisters?"

He made a face that was half snarl and half smile.

"What is it?"

"It's a stupid girl thing."

"Why?"

"No one ever talks about blood *brothers*."

"I've never heard anyone talk about it at all."

"That's because it's not real. You can't mix your blood with someone else's. Your blood is still your blood. It's not like you mix it and put some of theirs back inside your veins."

"Oh."

"Why do you want to know?"

"Someone told me about it."

"It's a stupid girl thing. It doesn't make you sisters. Anyone who says it does is a moron."

I wondered whether he meant stupid girls did it, or that it was stupid *because* it was a girl thing. "You're not supposed to say that word."

He grinned. "No one heard me but you. And if you rat me out, I'll tell Dad you're thinking of cutting yourself."

"No I'm not."

"Good. Then don't. You can get blood diseases. Like AIDS. Ever heard of that?"

I nodded. I'd heard of it. I had no idea what it was, but I wasn't going to tell him that. Maybe Carmen knew. I would ask her. She'd made it clear she would be coming to my house every day after school. She'd declared us best friends. I didn't think that was true, but she was different from other kids I knew, and she lived right next door. I didn't mind playing with her, for now. I wondered what I would do if I got tired of her.

Tom snapped his fingers at me. "Pay attention! Don't do it, you hear me?"

"I'm not going to."

He started to turn his chair. "Is that all?"

"Yes."

"Then get lost. And close the door as far as you can without latching."

I went out and pulled the door close to the frame. As I turned, it drifted back a few inches.

I returned to my room. I pulled the scissors out of the canister. I went to my closet and took the lid off a shoebox where I kept rocks and feathers. I placed the scissors gently on top of the feathers so they wouldn't split. I replaced the lid, pleased that Carmen wouldn't be able to grab the scissors when I wasn't looking.

I took my math worksheet out of my backpack and put it on my desk. I sat down and began working on problems, but it took longer than usual because I kept seeing red wash across my eyes. I had to rub them to make it go away. I wasn't sure I liked Carmen very much.

11

New York City

The idea was perfect. Absolute perfection.

It had come to her while she was on her knees. She'd been praying with her upper body propped up by her bed. It seemed lazy — supporting her chest and arms on the mattress and wallowing in the warmth and comfort of the bedding. It was not very spiritual, and not what she pictured prayer should be like, but it was hard to remain upright on her knees, especially since she'd turned forty. Her knees grew stiff. Her back and shoulders ached. Itches appeared out of nowhere, demanding to be scratched, interrupting her flow of words.

This was better. Leaning against the bed alleviated some of the pressure on her knees. She wasn't a fifteen-year-old kid who could stress her joints without suffering chronic aches for the rest of the week. She could pray for a longer period of time. Hopefully, God understood that her concentration was more important than an admirable devotional posture.

She was certain the idea had come directly from angelic

whispers in the deepest part of her soul because she hadn't even been thinking about her job. Or Alexandra. She'd been praying for Eileen. Work and the job that had been stolen right out of her hands were far from her mind. The idea rose to the surface like a diver who'd plunged from a twelve-foot board to the bottom of the pool and exploded back to the surface of the water.

It was the perfect way to let Alexandra hang herself in front of everyone. And it didn't involve anything vicious on Stephanie's part, no ungodly or malicious behavior. She would simply provide an environment for Alex's true nature to reveal itself, like a scientist putting bacteria into a petri dish, waiting for the natural activity of cell growth to unfold.

Trystan would appreciate her reaching out to their little team. He would be impressed by her desire to bring them closer together.

She would accomplish all of this by inviting her co-workers to share Thanksgiving dinner at her apartment. If she got Trystan on board first, he would put gentle pressure on Alex and Diana to accept the invitation. All of them were alone in the city. Diana had always gone home to Michigan to spend a long weekend with her family, but she wasn't doing that this year. Instead, she had plans with friends for a Black Friday blowout that included lots of shopping and lunch out, followed by a party on the Saturday after Thanksgiving.

Just before noon, Stephanie left her desk and went into the hallway to check Trystan's office door. It was open. She exhaled slowly and walked toward the welcoming doorway, listening to be sure he wasn't talking on the phone. This needed to be a surprise attack. If he was in the middle of a phone conversation and she had to return after he'd finished the call, he would know already she wanted something. He'd be on his guard. She wouldn't be able to gauge his genuine reaction.

She tucked her blouse more securely into the waistband of her pants. She shifted her slacks on her hips and repositioned her belt buckle directly over the zipper. It was nervous energy. She needed to forge ahead. She strode to the doorway and reached her arm inside to knock on the open door.

He looked up and smiled. "Hi, Stephanie. What can I do for you?"

She went into the office and grabbed the back of the chair that faced his desk, gripping it firmly, as if to support her effort. It was almost like prayer where she needed to support her body. She didn't like noticing the similarity. She removed her hands from the chair.

"I wanted to invite you and Diana and Alexandra to my apartment for Thanksgiving Dinner. All of us are away from our families, and really, our group is like a family. It would be a chance to relax together, talk about things that aren't work-related, build the team, but also celebrate the holiday."

She took a deep breath, realizing she'd spoken too fast, said too many words and depleted the oxygen in her lungs, ending her invitation and the unnecessary explanation on a high-pitched note that sounded anxious and almost tearful. She took another deep breath.

Trystan folded his arms across his ribs. Dark hair covered the backs of wrists. The density of the hair growth was light and masculine, not heavy and animalistic.

She liked that.

He was manly without being aggressively brutal in his appearance. Not that a person could control that aspect of their appearance, but overly husky and hairy men frightened her.

"Thank you. How generous. And thoughtful."

She swallowed. She didn't think of it as generosity. She'd assumed they would all offer to bring side dishes, wine...In fact, she needed Alex to bring her favorite wine or cocktail fixings. Once Alex drank too much, she would show her true colors. Stephanie was sure of it. And she knew Alex liked to drink. "Can you make it?"

"I can. I didn't realize Thanksgiving was coming up so fast." He glanced at his computer screen. "The week after next."

"I know. And then Christmas and another year. Poof." She snapped her fingers.

"Is there anything I can bring?"

"Oh. I...well, wine, of course." She laughed.

"I thought you didn't drink alcohol."

"Sometimes I have a glass of wine. On holidays. Besides... you and Alex enjoy it, don't you?"

He nodded.

"I haven't planned the whole meal. So maybe, bread? And some kind of appetizer?"

"Sure. Anything you need. In fact, why don't I cover the cost of the turkey."

"Oh, I..."

"As long as we agree that you'll cook it." He patted his biceps for emphasis and uncrossed his arms, giving her an eager smile.

"I can get the turkey, but thanks anyway. I'll work up a menu. I might ask you to bring something different. Is that okay?"

"Have you asked Diana and Alex yet?"

"No." She didn't want to tell him that they wouldn't come if he weren't already a guaranteed guest, but she could see on his face that he knew. He knew why she'd asked him first. He knew she was uncertain whether anyone would want to share Thanksgiving with her.

A look of pity took over his lips and brow.

"I just thought of the idea, so…"

He nodded.

"I'll ask them, and then I'll send around a menu."

The pitying expression spread, encompassing every part of him, extending to his hairline, and seeming to drift through the room. He smiled. "Why don't I ask them. I'm not stepping on your toes, am I?"

He didn't spell out that a request from him would carry more weight, would make it seem like an event for all of them, something they couldn't avoid. She wasn't sure she wanted them coming to Thanksgiving dinner under a feeling of obligation, but at the same time, the whole point was to make sure Alex was there, drinking and relaxing and being her true, very nasty self in front of Trystan.

It was an awful feeling, knowing he pitied her, but she had to keep focused on the idea. Heavenly forces were helping her, and she needed to accept that assistance in whatever form it appeared. Trystan was simply enlisted by angels to carry out the plan. What he thought of her didn't matter at all. When she stepped away from the shame of feeling pitied, she was elated. Here was proof that this idea was not her own.

"You're not stepping on my toes." She moved towards the doorway.

"Look for an email from me by the time you get back to your office. I'm sending it right now. And thanks again. It's a great idea. We are a family here, and that needs to be nurtured."

She nodded and retreated before he could change his mind.

It all worked out perfectly, truly orchestrated outside of her control. Trystan sent the email, Diana responded immediately that she would love to join them. Ten minutes later, Alex added her acceptance in a cool, aloof tone, if such a thing can be communicated in an email. Stephanie believed it could.

An hour later Stephanie emailed a menu, assigning pies and side dishes, asking Alex to bring whatever booze she needed to feed her martini addiction, and Diana to bring whatever non-alcoholic beverage she preferred with a nice meal. For some mysterious reason, Diana never touched alcohol. When Stephanie first became aware of this, she'd hoped it meant they were kindred spirits. That Diana had the same beliefs but was quieter about them. It turned out she wasn't religious at all. She'd never explained why she avoided alcohol.

Riding home on the subway, Stephanie closed her eyes for a moment and tried to picture all of them in her apartment. She hadn't mentioned her plan to Eileen. Leaving your daughter out of your Thanksgiving plans was cold, but it couldn't be helped. This was out of her hands. It would really be better if Eileen weren't there. Maybe a little distance would do them both good. Eileen had lots of friends. Surely some of them must have plans that extended beyond their families, plans that could include another friend.

She had a lot of errands to do in order to create a holiday atmosphere. She'd figure out what to do about Eileen later.

12

My visit to Victoria and Rafe's apartment was scheduled for Monday morning. Rafe assured me Victoria would fix a fabulous breakfast, a *real* breakfast. A breakfast like people eat when they live and work on a farm. He said she made the best eggs and bacon and biscuits and gravy of anyone he knew. He said every other breakfast for the rest of my life would be sub-par, once I'd eaten Victoria's food.

His sales pitch made me think of the coffee shop where I'd met Stephanie for breakfast when I'd first started working for Trystan. *The best breakfast in New York City*, she'd insisted. It struck me funny that so many people seemed to think a breakfast could be the *best*. There wasn't a lot of room for skill variation in cooking eggs or bacon. Either they were cooked, or they weren't, in my opinion. Perhaps eggs could have different seasonings, a scramble might have unusual contents, but in the end, eggs were eggs. Bacon was even simpler. In fact, it was the quality of the bacon purchased that made the difference, not the frying or microwaving or baking of the strips.

I knocked on their door at five-fifteen. This time had been

chosen to allow plenty of room for eating the fabulous breakfast, followed by a quick overview of the tools they used for day trading. Once the market opened, I could watch and ask questions, and then leave when I'd seen enough. But Rafe was sure I'd never want to leave. I would fall in love with the beauty of the stock market, and I'd be lured by the realization that if I *delved into it* myself, I would never have to worry about money again. Ever.

The promise was even more flamboyant than the breakfast guarantee.

Victoria opened the door. She wore navy blue yoga pants, pink Ugg boots, and a tight-fitting pink t-shirt. Over that, she wore a pink hoodie. I wasn't sure why she was dressed so warmly, even standing in the doorway, I felt the warmth spilling out of her apartment. It was much hotter than mine. I suppose two bodies warm up a small space more fully.

I didn't smell any bacon. From where I stood, the kitchen lights appeared to be off. She stepped back and invited me inside. "I grabbed some bagels and cream cheese. Do you like dill? Salmon?"

"I thought you were making a big breakfast. Rafe went on and on about it."

"Did he?" She shrugged. "All I have is bagels. I hope you like them."

"Sure."

"And coffee. I need to grind the beans, but it should be ready in a few."

"Definitely coffee." I glanced around the living room. To my left was the wall facing the alley on one side of our building. A couch was situated in front of the windows with their blinds closed. It faced a huge TV mounted on the opposite wall. The TV was on, newscasters talking soundlessly with a lot of facial expressions while the previous day's market results slid across the bottom of the screen. Against the adjacent wall was a long desk — a simple plank with wheeling drawer units that fit underneath. There were two very expensive-looking dark red desk chairs with mesh backs curved to perfectly fit the human spine.

On the desk were two large computer screens. They were both on, cluttered with seven or eight overlapping windows showing charts and numbers. The lines and bars on some of the charts were moving of their own accord. I felt a slight headache. I could not comprehend how this would at all be something I wanted to do even for four minutes a day, much less four hours.

We moved toward the couch. Victoria gestured at it, offering me a seat.

From my perch on the end of the couch, I could see part of their bedroom. It was dark. "Where's Rafe?"

"I sent him out for the morning."

"Out where?"

"Just out. I'm going to walk you through everything. Part of what's so exciting about day trading is that it's a perfect job for women. We don't need to answer to a guy telling us what to do." She laughed. "I'm as successful at this as he is, and there's no sexist bullshit to deal with. No harassment, no men explaining how to do the job *correctly*." She smiled. "It's one of the true feminist jobs of the future. The playing field is completely level. It's really frustrating that more women haven't taken to it."

"How do you know they haven't?"

"Just a guess." She held my gaze for a moment. "A lot of

women are intimidated by analytics. Just saying." She gave me a smile that was the epitome of condescension.

I wanted to argue that I was not at all intimidated, but left her bait untouched.

After a moment, she turned and went into the kitchen. The sound of coffee beans grinding erupted from the kitchen. The refrigerator door opened and closed several times. I thought about getting up and taking a closer look at the computer screens, but I doubted the information would make any sense, even close up. I wasn't intimidated, just bored with an excessive focus on numbers. People are so much more complex than numbers, and therefore more fascinating and entertaining.

I turned my attention to the TV. The blonde woman and Hispanic man were having an animated conversation about the tech industry and the companies that were due to announce their quarterly results within the week.

Their words popped up in the closed caption box, sometimes with odd misspellings.

I hate watching closed caption. My attention can't avoid flicking back and forth between the words and facial expressions, trying to match the words to the shapes of their mouths. Half the time, I feel like I miss parts of the conversation because my attention is scattered.

Victoria returned carrying a tray bearing toasted bagels, two mugs of coffee, a dish of whipped cream cheese, a small bowl of fresh dill, and a plate with glistening, jewel-red slices of salmon.

We ate, and she talked about how she usually began her day looking over and analyzing the results of the previous day. She and Rafe worked side by side but completely independently. *Completely.* They each had their own pool of cash. After the markets closed, they bounced strategies off each other, and during trading, they used the other to moderate an excess surge of adrenaline that might lead to untenable risk, but their decisions were their own. It was a bit of a game, really, seeing who came out ahead each day, each week, each month.

His results were more erratic, beating hers dramatically some days, far below hers on others. Most months, she was slightly ahead. *To be honest,* she said, *her profits exceeded his most years,* but she *tried not to make a thing out of that.*

She liked the challenge of it, the tension of not knowing what was going to happen from one minute to the next. She liked the ability to scoop up profits and put some aside. Her goal was to keep her nest egg constantly growing.

She liked being faceless and nameless, a silent ghost crawling through the wires of the internet, making money without having to answer to anyone. She liked the satisfaction of knowing her results beat others' and that all the knowledge she acquired and skills she developed went to benefit her future, not a giant corporation. She and Rafe weren't owned by anyone.

When we'd talked in the past, she'd always made a point of this. "It's so freeing."

"I can see that."

"I mean, you might like taking photographs," she said. "You might get energy from your clients and feel satisfied about helping them and all of that, but at the end of the day, your boss is in charge. And he owns your work."

"He's a good boss."

"And always a *he.*"

She laughed. Bitterly, I thought.

She stopped abruptly. "Have you ever worked for a woman?"

"Yes." I thought about this. I had, but Tess was never the top dog. She answered to men, and even though I worked for her, my life and career choices and even my daily work had been controlled by the men around and above her.

Other than Tess, I'd always worked for men. I honestly hadn't given it a lot of thought, and now, I wondered why that was. There were plenty of women in positions of power, and yet, somehow that's where I ended up.

I saw Victoria's point. If you looked around the Wall Street trading floor images flashed on the TV screen from time to time, it seemed to be mostly men. How many women were ghosts like Victoria, quietly making money and taking charge of their destinies?

It was a very seductive thought. But it was still gambling. I couldn't get past that. Still, it might be that I should make a choice — the thrill of manipulating people or the thrill of manipulating numbers. The latter could be a means to an end, a temporary detour.

13

When I sent a text to Joe, I wasn't sure whether it was because I liked talking to him, wanted his body, or needed my tour of the house so I could start narrowing down the possibilities of where the key might fit. It might have been all three, but if it was, which was the primary desire? I didn't like not knowing my own mind.

He responded immediately with an offer to send the limo to carry me out of the city. We could enjoy a dinner that was *a little nicer than microwaved ravioli.*

I left work early and went home to wait for the limo. I did not need the curious eyes of my co-workers or other people I rode with in the elevator watching me get into the back of a rather ostentatious limousine. It was glamorous and luxurious and a thrill, but not something I wanted to explain.

Since Joe had promised a dinner *worthy of a Michelin-starred chef,* I wore a short black dress and high heels. Not the little black dress I'd worn to Jim's dinner party. That dress was now decaying in landfill. I'd thought about donating it to a second-hand store, but I didn't want to deliver the bad karma of it to a stranger. If I'd taken two minutes to think about it, I would have burned it. I closed my eyes and imagined flames chewing through synthetic fabric, curling it into ash, leaving no evidence it had existed. But maybe decay was a more fitting end for it.

When I was dressed except for my shoes, I pulled an old hairbrush out of the bottom bathroom drawer. It was the kind that had a flexible rubber base holding the stiff plastic bristles. The rubber pad slid into the handle along a groove on either side. I worked the bristle pad free, placed the old-fashioned key inside the cavity and re-attached the bristles. It looked secure, and when I shook it, there was only a slight sound that could pass for a loose piece of plastic. I dropped the brush into my messenger bag along with a small zippered cosmetics bag and another pouch that held lingerie and a hair clip.

The ride out of Manhattan was as fantastic as every other ride I'd taken in that amazing car. It would be easy to get used to. It was so much nicer than a taxi or Uber, not just because of the comfort, but because I didn't have to provide any directions or suggest a change of course. There was no need to keep my eye on the meter or rate the driver on an app. I could disappear inside my head, knowing I'd arrive safely and without incident.

After three trips now, Dirk and I had become nodding acquaintances. This time, he called me Ms. Mallory instead of simply, Miss. I didn't like the formality, but when I suggested he call me Alexandra, he smiled and opened the car door for me. The next time he spoke, asking if the temperature was to my liking, he called me Ms. Mallory.

Riding in that car was like being in a sensory deprivation tank. It was utterly silent unless I chose to turn on music. The sounds of other cars were nothing but soft whispers, and the feeling of tires moving over uneven pavement was little more than a gentle shifting of position.

Joe met me at the front door with a long kiss. He lifted my bag off my shoulder and carried it to the entryway bench. He slipped my leather jacket off my shoulders, picked up the bag, and carried both to a walk-in closet tucked behind the staircase. "Dinner will be in the dining room in about thirty minutes."

"So formal." I meant his tone, but the entire thing, really. "The dining room is huge."

"The lighting will solve that."

I wasn't sure how. I smiled.

"How was your ride?"

"Perfection."

"Good." He smiled. "Would you like a martini? A glass of champagne?"

"How about that house tour?"

"Why don't we do that after dinner. You don't want to rush it, do you?"

"Then a martini sounds delicious."

He left me in the living room, seated in front of the fire. He returned a few minutes later with two martinis.

Even more than the previous time, he seemed settled into the house, as if he were the de facto owner. I took a sip of my drink then put the glass on the table. "How long will you be staying here?"

"Not sure."

"You seem settled in, as if you own the place."

He laughed. "I'm comfortable here. It's been my home for almost five years."

"And the chef doesn't have a problem making dinner for you when you're not his boss?"

"Of course not. We've worked together for a long time. He likes preparing meals, he doesn't want to just sit around collecting a salary for nothing."

"When, exactly, is the brother supposed to arrive?"

"Just before Christmas, I think."

That still wasn't exact, but I accepted it. "What's taking so long?"

"I'm not privy to that information."

"Hmm." I picked up my glass and took another sip. I crossed my legs and shifted my back against the couch. "It would be easy to get used to a place like this."

"It's too big," he said.

"If I had this much space and money, I'd lay it out differently, but it's still nice."

"You haven't seen all of it, how do you know you'd lay it out differently?"

"The parts I have seen."

"What would you do?"

"This room is too large, unless you're having a party."

"I agree. It's almost a lonely feeling. It's designed for a lot of people, and without them, you're aware of how alone you are."

His description was excessively melancholy, but the calm of the vodka prevented me from splitting hairs. "Something like that," I said.

"Why are you so curious about the house?"

"I'm always thinking about the house I plan to build someday. So I like looking at houses, collecting ideas in my mind, deciding what fits my taste."

"You must be a planner."

"Not with everything. Just my future house."

He laughed. "I'm the opposite. I figure when I get to the point where I want a home, it will evolve from wherever I am in my life at the time."

"But you won't know what you like."

"I think I will." He put his hand on my leg, firm and affectionate, but not possessive. Warmth spread across my skin, following the path of the martini as it moved through my bloodstream. "When I was a little kid, I cut out magazine pictures of houses and furniture I liked."

"So this house you're building is a very long-term plan."

"It is."

"When is all this going to happen?"

"When I have enough money."

A woman pushed open one of the double doors connecting the living and dining rooms. "Dinner is ready."

Joe introduced us — her name was Nell. I assumed she was the woman who lived in the house to do cleaning. She had long, perfectly straight dark blonde hair scooped into a tidy ponytail. She wore a black sleeveless dress with a white apron tied around her waist. She didn't look like she was dressed in a serving uniform, more like it was her own dress and she just happened to be using a white apron, which is really so impractical, but it's nearly always the choice. Even butchers wear white aprons, which strikes me as disgusting and pointless. Maybe they want to show off all that blood, who knows. Maybe butchers all have a little masochistic streak, and they want to make the point that satisfying your hunger is a brutal business.

We followed Nell into the dining room. The chandelier was

turned down low, casting a soft light across the white tablecloth. At the near end of the table, there were two place settings framed by an arrangement of six candlesticks of varying heights. The white candles were burning, the flames steady and strong and the candles smooth without a single drop of wax.

Seated on the breakfronts on either side of the table were abstract metal sculptures that were wound with white fairy lights. The sculptures were bookended with more tapers in candlestick holders that matched the silver ones on the table.

Light flickered off the walls and made the room seem small and cozy despite the long table with its sixteen chairs.

I was seated at the head of the table, and Joe was to my right.

The dinner was beyond amazing.

We started with eggplant rolls stuffed with feta cheese in a light tomato sauce. This was followed by baby octopus on top of endive salad with shaved cheese and sliced cumquat. The main course had the creamiest whipped potatoes I'd ever eaten in my life, grilled Brussels sprouts, and salmon that was so fresh it tasted like it had been pulled from a stream behind the house. It flaked with a fork and at the same time was so moist it wrapped itself around my tongue like cream.

Dessert was cheesecake with a chocolate drizzle.

My body felt as if every flavor was absorbed fully and completely into my cells, satisfying them as if they'd met the nourishment they were designed for. Along with all these heavenly tastes, we drank a silky bottle of Cabernet Sauvignon.

It was so incredibly delicious, I wasn't sure I needed sex to complete the evening. More pleasure seemed impossible.

14

Joe poured a single shot of brandy into two glasses. "Something to sip during our tour."

I felt a little loopy from the martini and the wine, not to mention the rich, superbly prepared food that acted like a drug to my senses. I couldn't stop talking about how good it was, so the drug filled my ears as well.

After we'd finished, we'd gone into the kitchen, and I'd gushed my appreciation all over the chef. The chef was close to my height. His head was shaved to a light brown bristle, and his face was shaved clean. He didn't have that day-old stubble that's so fashionable and sexy. And it is sexy, except when it's not. Only some men can pull it off. Joe, who could pull it off, had a bit of that and I was strangely drawn to it, despite the roughness when we kissed.

Brandy is not my favorite drink, but it seemed fitting after the dinner we'd eaten. A complement to the flavors of our meal, encouraging them to linger, although that was probably my imagination.

We went into Jim's study first. It was on the opposite side of the entryway from the living room. I'd seen this room, spent part of my life in this room, recalled every detail. I wasn't prepared for the chill that ran through me as I crossed the threshold. Even the brandy, hot inside veins already heated by Joe's presence and the food and wine, couldn't keep my bones warm.

I was certain I sensed Jim's presence. I felt his cool, utter dismissal of me as an object he could acquire, or not, as he chose. A silly Barbie doll who was marveled at for actually having a brain and an opinion and something to say. An object he could touch and grab. And I don't think I read too much into that. In fact, I think I gave him the benefit of the doubt early on, more than I should have.

Part of the sensation came from all those photographs of Stephanie's daughter. They were still there, scattered like gulls resting on the shore, across the top of the cabinet below his bookshelves. Seeing them now that I knew who the woman was, now that I knew how Jim had taken possession of her life and turned it inside out caused the chill to continue rippling through my blood.

There was also the memory of my confidence when I entered the party and my effort to be professionally polite by agreeing to stay for a final glass of wine, not knowing I'd left the door open for his brute assault.

It's impossible for a room or a house to have a mood or the lingering presence of someone who spent a lot of time there, whether that person is still alive or not. It defies logic. It's the sort of semi-supernatural thing I often heard when I was growing up. I resist that idea, and yet, there it was, sending spasms of cold to the core of my body.

And I'd had those sensations before. Possibly it's some sort of projection of your own memories combined with familiar furniture and objects, the resurfacing of the physical essence of your experiences. In a house or building one has never entered before, it's possible the brain might pull odd fragments from the memory banks and relate them to what's in front of you.

Maybe. Or maybe I'm wrong.

Either way, the room had a powerful effect on me. I wanted to get out of there but didn't want to share my train of thought with Joe. He would assume the alcohol had gone to my head.

I edged toward the doorway.

"Don't be so anxious to move on. I thought you wanted to see it all."

"I've seen this room. Several times."

"You haven't seen this." He crossed the room and opened a door that I'd assumed led to a closet housing the networking devices for the property. He gestured for me to join him.

I put down my glass on the desk. This had the effect of reclaiming my sense of superiority over Jim Kohn. It reminded me why I was there — to take the upper hand in death as well as in life. The room had nothing to do with me. Already my memories were dissolving. If I didn't entertain sensations in my imagination, they would fade faster.

I walked toward Joe and met him near the open door. He stepped inside the room, and I followed.

It was a richly carpeted den that held several leather armchairs and a matching couch. The lights were dim, so the tiny spotlights on the artwork glowed brighter. The paintings were lifelike portraits of nude women. There was a large round coffee table in the center of the ring of chairs. In the center of that was a black granite ashtray. Lying beside it was a sleek lighter made of sterling silver with red lacquer sides.

Along the back wall was a series of four glass doors in oak frames covering shelves that displayed open boxes of cigars.

"It's like a store," I said.

"Hard to believe, isn't it. And notice there's no stale cigar smell. It has its own, custom-designed ventilation system."

"With enough cigars to entertain his buddies every weekend if he'd lived to be eighty."

He laughed. "Maybe not that many, but almost."

I walked to the glass cabinets and surveyed the contents. The labels and various sizes meant nothing to me, but I had no doubt they represented the best in the world.

After that, he escorted me through the rest of the first floor, most of which I'd seen during the dinner party. Once again I saw the library, an entertainment room that was furnished like a small theater, a room with a pool table and its own bar, the outdoor patio, and the breakfast room.

The second floor was mostly bedrooms — six of them — all with their own sitting room and full bathroom. And by full, I mean spacious door-less showers and large bathtubs with jets. There was also a workout room that I'd seen during my self-guided tour. It too had a bathroom complete with a shower featuring three shower heads.

Jim's bedroom was at the end of the main hallway. It was larger than my apartment. In addition to the king-sized bed, the walk-in closet with a wall of mirrors, the alcove with armchairs and a window seat that looked out over the lush back yard, the enormous bathroom with a full jacuzzi tub and a shower large enough for three, the bedroom had two small rooms attached. One held a large TV and a love seat. The other had a table for four and a kitchenette.

If all of this had been in the basement, I would have thought he was one of those extremely rich people preparing for a dystopian future, stocking everything you'll need to be entirely self-sustaining for two years. In his case, he was probably one of those who had an escape plan to a vacation home on a remote island, the helicopter or plane on call, the bags packed.

By the time we started up the stairs to the third floor, my brandy glass was empty. Joe placed both our glasses on a shelf built into the wall of the staircase. This staircase wasn't as grand as the sweeping stairs that curved up from the first floor, but they were nice — angled with a landing halfway up.

I'd already seen Joe's suite. He opened the door anyway to show me my bag had been taken from the downstairs closet and placed on a narrow table near the entrance. My stomach flipped when I saw it, once again aware that people were moving about inside this house, very much noticing my presence, while I never saw them except when they wanted to be seen.

There was no reason to think anyone had looked inside my bag. And I was confident the key was snug in its hiding place, but there's something unsettling about other people touching and moving your things when you aren't aware. Especially something as personal as the bag you take absolutely everywhere.

My jacket hung from a wood hanger on a coat rack near the bathroom door.

"Who moved my things?"

"Nell, probably. Maybe Ed. Just trying to be helpful."

I nodded. I wished I had that brandy glass in my hand.

He pointed out three other suites, all opening off the single hallway — Nell's, Ed's, and one that was obviously uninhabited. As he opened the door to the unoccupied one, I smelled air scented with almonds. The furniture and bedding looked brand new. Between the two suites that overlooked the backyard, one of which was Joe's, there was an alcove with huge windows that opened outwards, secured with a center latch. Beneath them was a window seat large enough to hold two people comfortably. I imagined it was a quiet, peaceful place to sit on a summer afternoon, the windows open wide, listening to the birds.

Joe suggested I get comfortable while he went down and refilled our brandy glasses. As we moved closer to his door, I glanced toward the end of the hallway. There was a door slightly wider than those that led into the suites. "Where does that go?"

"Storage." He put his hands on my shoulders and brushed his lips across mine. "I'll be right back. Do you want anything to eat?"

I shook my head.

"Water?"

I nodded.

I wanted to look inside the storage room, but that had the potential to sound both slightly demented and extremely nosey. There would be time, later.

15

I woke at one-fifteen with a parched mouth.

Joe was turned on his side with his back toward me. His breath was deep and soft, a peaceful sound that made me want to burrow deeper under the covers. I ran my finger down his spine. He didn't move. His breathing remained steady. I placed my hand on his hip and squeezed gently — still nothing.

I slipped out of bed and put on the shirt he'd been wearing the night before. I buttoned it down to my thighs. I walked into the sitting room and poured water from the pitcher into a cut crystal glass. That's when you know someone has money to burn — when they drink water from a glass that costs upward of seventy-five dollars.

I drank the entire glassful which woke me further, cleared my head of brandy, and brought the storage room to the front of my mind.

There was something about the dimensions of the house that didn't line up. Knowing where Joe's room looked out onto the yard, the location of the patio and the rooms that were below his along the rear of the house, that storage room was pretty damn big. Larger than his suite. Even if Jim Kohn was a holiday freak and had a hundred and fifty boxes of decorations stacked inside, there was more going on than simple storage.

Of course, it was possible he kept old furniture, things from the past, but he didn't strike me as a guy who would hang onto used furniture.

I pressed gently on the handle of Joe's exterior door. I moved the door back quietly and stepped into the hallway. Dim lighting came from a recessed channel along both sides of the ceiling. There was enough light to allow me to walk easily along the hallway and see where I was going, but not enough to get a good look at the storage room door.

If it was unlocked, I could easily step inside. If it was locked, and Joe woke up, there was nowhere for me to escape to. I stood for a moment, trying to imagine what he would say if he caught me snooping. I didn't know him enough to call it, but I had to see inside that room.

I walked quickly along the thick carpet to the door. The handle had a lock after all. I pressed down. It remained locked into position. I moved my hand away.

Standing on my tiptoes, I ran my fingers along the top of the doorframe, hoping for a key. Not only was it empty, the entire length of wood was completely free of dust and grit. Nell and the woman who worked with her were obviously very thorough.

Surely Nell had keys to all the rooms. Of course, so did Joe.

I turned and walked back to his door, trying to decide whether it was worth the risk to go through his pockets. I paused outside his door, my mind flipping back and forth as if I were turning over cards, looking for the right match.

"What are you looking for?"

Startled, I moved to my left to see where the voice had come from.

Nell sat on the window seat. One of the windows was open several inches. I was surprised I hadn't felt the breeze. On the seat tucked up close to her crossed legs was a small ceramic ashtray. She held a cigarette between her fingers, close to the open space between the windows.

She gave me a cat-like smile. "I said, what are you looking for?"

16

I walked toward Nell, giving her a sleepy, friendly smile. "Can I bum a cigarette?"

"Are you sleepwalking?"

I laughed. "No."

"Are you lost?"

"No."

"Then why were you trying to open that door?"

"Curiosity."

"You should learn to mind your own business."

I shrugged.

"Does Joe realize you're out here prowling around?"

I laughed. "I'm not prowling. I was just curious." I moved toward the window seat. "I could really use a smoke."

"Smoking isn't allowed in the house. Except for the cigar room."

I stared at her.

"And if you're curious about this, too..." she held up her cigarette. "I'm right next to the window."

"I can still smell it."

"I'm an excellent cleaner. There won't be any odor in the

morning. If two people smoke, it's impossible to be rid of the odor."

I gave up, but now I was really craving a cigarette. For a half second, I thought about making my way down to the cigar room, which was not locked, unlike the storage room, even though there were thousands of dollars of cigars in that room.

I started back toward Joe's door.

"I want to know. Why were you trying to get into a place where you're obviously not supposed to be? The door is locked for a reason."

I had no doubt about that.

"You're a guest here. It's not very polite to be trying to get into places that are private, where you don't belong."

"I was just curious. That's all. It's not a big deal."

"I wonder if Joe would see it that way."

"Should I wake him? You can ask."

She pushed her free hand through her hair which was loose but still ironed smooth as glass. She took a drag on her cigarette. She turned and exhaled through the opening.

I didn't want things to end with Joe when they were off to such a good start, but if she wanted to sabotage me, it was her choice. Possibly, he wouldn't care. I moved closer to her again. I softened my face and my posture. "I didn't mean to get off on the wrong foot."

She gave me a tight smile. Her eyes remained hard, evident even in the muted light. She took another drag on her cigarette and immediately blew the smoke directly into the gap between the windows. She held her cigarette close to the open space and let the smoke drift out into the night where it moved slowly away from the window.

"Are you going to stay working here when Mark and his wife move in?"

She shrugged. "It's not up to me."

"Sure it is."

"No, it's not. They'll decide that."

"Well, you can decide to leave now. *That's* up to you."

She gave a short laugh. She put the cigarette to her lips and inhaled gently and slowly, keeping her gaze fixed on me. She no longer seemed quite as hostile. More curious than anything. Like me.

"You know, I could really use a smoke. Do you mind giving me one? I'll take it outside."

She reached behind the cushions and pulled out a box. She flipped open the lid and held it out to me. I slid a cigarette away from its companions. Of course, I had no way to light it. She might not be as hostile, but she wasn't going to help me out. At all.

I had cigarettes and a lighter inside my bag. I'd only bummed one of hers to keep the conversation going while I worked to calm her ruffled feathers and her territorial feelings about a house that didn't belong to her. It was strange because it sounded like she wasn't at all certain she'd even be living there in a few weeks. Why did she care so much about preventing me from smoking?

If I went back into Joe's room to get a lighter, she'd see that I was playing a game with her. If I returned the cigarette, however...

I handed it back to her. "Thanks anyway. It's too cold outside. And I don't have a lighter. I'll have to tap into my self-control. If I have any." I laughed.

Instead of returning it to the pack, she left the cigarette

lying alone on the bench. I couldn't tell whether she was debating whether to relax the arbitrary belief that the smell of one cigarette could be eradicated, but two would linger indefinitely, or if she just didn't want to be bothered placing it inside the box.

I crossed my arms and leaned against the corner of the alcove. "How long have you worked here?"

She inhaled and stabbed her cigarette into the ashtray. She placed the one she'd given me beside it. She blew smoke out the window, then pulled it closed and locked it.

"Joe is a good guy. Don't take advantage of that." She slid off the window seat and went to one of the rooms on the opposite side of the hall. She opened the door and disappeared inside. The door closed with a loud click.

17

Stephanie was appalled that she'd put it off this long. Thanksgiving was a few days away, and she hadn't said a word about it to Eileen. Of course, Eileen was caught up in her own world. She probably didn't realize one of the most important holidays of the year was barreling toward them. It was the sole holiday when the country actually pretended to be a religious nation, giving half-hearted thanks for the abundance of food, and possibly their families and jobs.

Ever since Eileen had been in that degrading relationship, she no longer cared about anything spiritual. Still, she'd always liked Thanksgiving. Stephanie should be encouraging her straying daughter to celebrate the holiday fully. Eileen might actually eat something nourishing. Get some more protein and bone-padding carbs into her body.

But the other thing was more important. Right now, Stephanie had to make that the priority — the trap for Alex.

Besides, what did one day really matter? If Eileen ate Thanksgiving dinner, she would restrict herself to celery and water and chicken broth the following day. For all Stephanie knew, Eileen might purge. So many of those models did.

How else to keep your bones more prominent than your flesh?

Telling your daughter she wasn't welcome to Thanksgiving dinner in her own home was cruel and ungodly. Stephanie knew that. She wasn't being the best mother she could, tossing her daughter out on the sidewalk, but it had to be done.

Nothing was more important right now than taking her rightful ownership of that photography job. And the only way to do that was to provide an opportunity for Trystan to see he'd made a mistake hiring Alex. A terrible mistake. The previous attempt at exposing Alex's flaws had failed spectacularly. Stephanie had been shown up as a liar. And she was not a liar. Her plan failed, and she'd damaged her reputation. This dinner was the first step toward reclaiming it. This time, she would be more subtle.

It was only five a.m. Her coffee mug steamed on the table in front of her. Down the hall, the shower was running. Eileen would be finished in ten minutes. She would come out to the kitchen for her boiled egg and a cup of green tea. She claimed the green tea helped her lose weight. Stephanie shivered. She wanted to cry, so she forced herself to shiver again in an effort to subdue the tears.

On weekday mornings, while Eileen ate her egg, Stephanie took her own shower. Finished with her egg, Eileen would retreat to her bedroom and lay out seven or eight outfits on her bed, trying to make her choice for the day. It was a ridiculous amount of effort. Besides, most of her clothes looked exactly alike. A lot of black. Tops with varying necklines and sleeve lengths, but all the colors devoid of life — beige, cream, white, black, dark brown, taupe...

By the time Stephanie was ready for work, Eileen would be waiting to reclaim the bathroom to begin the process of styling her hair and smearing layers of cosmetics on her face.

"It's cold." Eileen stood in the kitchen doorway. Her long, dark hair was wet and twisted into a coil. It hung down the center of her back where it was leaving a slowly spreading damp spot on her pink terrycloth robe. It was the only soft-colored garment she owned, a gift last Christmas from her mother.

Stephanie sighed. "It's cool, yes. But you wouldn't feel so cold if you weren't so underweight."

Eileen made a scoffing sound and moved past her mother. She turned on the faucet, filled the kettle, and plugged it in. After running water into a pan, she placed it on the stove. She turned and opened the refrigerator door.

Stephanie coughed softly. "So, Thanksgiving is next week..." Her voice sounded strange, slightly false. She wasn't sure Eileen had heard with her head buried in the refrigerator. She raised her voice. "Thanksgiving is next week, and..."

The refrigerator door slammed with a heavy thud. "I heard you the first time." Eileen held the single egg over the pot of water. She pulled a serving spoon from the ceramic jug, placed the egg on it, and lowered it into the water before turning on the gas. "I'll eat turkey, you don't have to nag me about it. I can cut myself some slack for holidays."

"That's not..."

Eileen's tone was sharp. "I *said* I'll eat turkey." The kettle clicked off. She spooned tea leaves into the infuser. "I suppose it will be just the two of us..." She paused, and her voice trembled. "...since I have no one to share it with."

That was all the impetus Stephanie needed. No one to

share it with indeed. What was Stephanie, sautéed liver? "I assumed you might get together with some of your modeling friends."

Eileen laughed, the sound like a small dog issuing a yelp of displeasure.

"Since you all like to watch what you eat," Stephanie said.

"Don't be like that. I need to eat deliberately for my career. And it's actually quite healthy. Most people eat far more than they need. It's the cause of half the health problems you see."

"About Thanksgiving…"

"What are you trying to say?"

"I've invited Trystan and my co-workers to dinner."

"Oh. I guess that's okay. Not ideal, but I can live with it."

"I'd prefer it if you made other plans."

"What?" Eileen carried her mug to the table. She placed it across from Stephanie and returned to the stove to watch over her egg. She laughed. "Are you telling me you're kicking me out of the house for Thanksgiving? I'm not invited to your holiday meal?"

"I didn't know…I assumed you'd have plans."

"I don't have plans. Usually, mothers want to spend holidays with their daughters."

"We can do something on Friday. Maybe we can do some shopping."

"Friday is not Thanksgiving. We don't need to do something to make up for you disinviting me to dinner."

"I'm sorry. I didn't think you'd care."

"I'm practically a grieving widow, and this is how you decide to treat me?"

"You're not a widow by any stretch of the imagination. And I hope you're not grieving for a man who dumped you!"

"Well I am, okay?" The water boiled with a loud, steady rumble, hard eggshell rattling against the bottom. Eileen turned the knob to lower the temperature.

"You didn't put enough water in the pan," Stephanie said.

Eileen shoved her hands in the pockets of her robe. "It looks like I'll be enjoying my Thanksgiving dinner at a soup kitchen."

"Well, you're thin enough to pass for homeless." Stephanie regretted the words even as she was speaking them. Each word echoed in her ears, mean and petty. But how did her daughter, whom she adored with every fiber of her being, who she prayed for on a daily and nightly basis, who she'd give her soul for, manage to make her feel like such a piece of shit? She didn't often use such language, never spoke it out loud, but the word came into her head because that's how she felt. She'd dedicated her life to meeting Eileen's needs. Stephanie had been the one to pick up the pieces after Jim Kohn gutted Eileen like a fish. "I'm sorry."

"Whatever," Eileen said.

She felt as if they'd gone back in time. Eileen was a sour, argumentative fifteen-year-old and Stephanie was treating her like a child. But she behaved like a sulky teenager. Why didn't she have plans with all these great friends she supposedly had in the modeling industry? All those friends who'd taken the place of people she'd met at church when she was a teenager, friends from her college youth group?

Eileen's life was Godless. No wonder she looked so gaunt. No wonder she cared about nothing but her appearance and money. No wonder she didn't have a decent man who loved her.

Of course, neither did her mother.

Stephanie picked up her mug and drank her coffee slowly and steadily, hardly pausing to breathe. "I should get ready."

"I'll find something to do. Don't worry about throwing me out onto the streets."

"I didn't mean to kick you out. I need to do this for work. It's important, and it could make an important difference in my future there."

"Fine."

Stephanie left her dirty coffee mug on the table. Now, she was acting like a fifteen-year-old. But let Eileen pull more of her own weight for once. There wasn't even that much to pull. Eileen could put the mug in the dishwasher.

The petulant attitude did nothing to ease her guilt.

18

Instead of falling into a comfortable sleep with my body fitted along Joe's spine, I lay on my back and thought about smoking. Smelling that smoke and watching it slide through Nell's lips had woken an intense craving.

I got out of bed again and drank another glass of water. I peed. I climbed into bed and lay on my back again. I placed my hands on my belly, taking long, slow breaths. Finally, I fell asleep, but at quarter to five I was awake, and I knew that was it for the night.

I went into the sitting area and angled the shutters so I could see out onto the vast stretch of backyard. The night sky was dissolving into charcoal gray, partially lightened by the nearly full moon. I could see pathways through the garden that would provide a perfect trail for running. There was also that fabulous exercise room one floor below me. Why hadn't I thought to bring workout clothes? I suppose that would have been assuming too much, settling into this house where I was a dubious guest because it didn't belong to the guy I was having sex with.

Once the brother showed up, it was unlikely I'd be invited back.

At most, I had a few weeks to figure out how to get into that storage room, or to revisit the rooms I'd seen in a more leisurely fashion, trying to find a home for the key. It was possible there was a cabinet in the cigar room that I hadn't noticed. Other candidates for a locked closet or cabinet were the library and Jim's study. How would I get time to check out those rooms when I spent every minute with Joe?

"You're up early."

I turned at the sound of his voice. "It's my usual time."

He came up behind me and put his arms around my waist. He rested his chin on my shoulder. "When do you need to leave?"

"Soon. By six or so, but I can be a bit late to work."

"Come back to bed then."

I went.

A little more than an hour later he packed me into the limo. The car was beginning to feel like it belonged to me. I imagined that was how he felt about the house after all those years of being responsible for all the details of what was going on inside. I turned in my seat and stared back at the house as the car pulled out of the drive. My estimate had been accurate — the placement of the windows which I could now identify by room suggested the storage room was quite large.

I faced toward the front.

Maybe the best approach was to find out more about Joe, find out what he wanted out of life and where his ethical boundaries lay. Instead of trying to sneak around, I could enlist his help. Not by telling him about the key, of course.

But he already knew how Jim had behaved toward me. He obviously didn't have an excellent opinion of the guy, so there might be a way to…

I sighed. There was no way. In order to look around the house more closely, to get access to that room, I'd have to provide some sort of reason. And my mind was empty of reasons except for the key.

I could resort to drugging him into a deep sleep. Not the most respectful thing to do to a guy who treated me like a queen in every possible way, but it would work. It was easy. Except now that I knew Nell was prone to post-midnight wandering, I'd have to be even more careful.

I closed my eyes and let my head settle against the beautifully contoured seat back.

Part of me wished I'd never taken the key. Wanting to find out what it unlocked was eating me alive. Looking at it every day, feeling its weight in my hand, caressing the cold metal, and tracing my finger along its seductive lines was consuming me.

It just did not go with the classically modern design of Jim's home. It didn't fit with his ultra-sleek office. It didn't fit *him*.

Maybe it was only decorative, but that didn't fit either. And he certainly didn't seem like the type to carry extra weight and bulk on his keyring for sentimental reasons.

When we reached my apartment building, it was after seven. The street was starting to fill with activity, and there were a few curious looks as I climbed out of the limo. A sleek black car double-parked, a driver opening the back door, wasn't a common sight in my neighborhood — less than common. I'd never seen a limo anywhere in the ten or twelve-block area around my apartment.

Dirk closed the door. "Joe wanted me to ask when you'd like to return."

I looked at his impassive face. "I haven't thought about it."

"He suggested this evening."

I liked being with Joe. The luxury of it all was also quite nice, but spending two hours or more riding in and out of the city every day was taking a huge toll on my running. It was also taking a toll on my equilibrium. Nothing about that house or the area around it fit with the rest of my life. And yet, I wasn't inclined to invite Joe to my place. What for? Inside that near-mansion, I ate food prepared by a highly rated chef instead of takeout or salads, I slept in a luxurious bed in a soundless room... "This evening is good. Seven."

"I'll let him know."

"Do you get tired of driving in and out of the city like this?"

"I'm paid to drive."

I nodded. "Did you drive Jim to his office every day?"

"When he stayed at the house."

"How often was that?"

"Weekends. Occasionally a few nights during the week."

"He had an apartment in Manhattan?"

"Yes." He closed the door and started to walk back toward the driver's side.

"What will happen to you? When Jim's brother gets here?"

"We'll find out soon."

"Are you worried?"

"No." He didn't smile or frown, just spoke the word and held my gaze.

"Thanks for driving me. I've never experienced anything like this."

"My pleasure." He waited by the car until I was inside my building.

The first thing I did after the apartment door closed behind me was slip out of my shoes, strip off my dress, and pull out a bag for overnight things. I was not returning home again in a cocktail dress and high heels. I showered and pulled on yoga pants, a sweater, and Ugg boots. I pried open my hairbrush, removed the key, and slipped it into the tiny pocket of my pants. I grabbed my messenger bag and went out. I climbed the stairs to the rooftop garden, relieved that I'd managed to enter and exit my apartment without seeing my neighbors. Of course, it was right in the heat of early trading.

The air was cold, and the sky was clear and bright. I lit a cigarette and inhaled deeply. After a few minutes, I balanced it on the edge of the ashtray, littered with six cigarette butts and four roach stubs. I pulled the key out of my pocket. I held it flat on my left palm and studied it as if I were begging it to tell me where it belonged. I kept it there in my open hand until my cigarette was gone.

19

Work was dull and the minutes dragged. With the Thanksgiving holiday so close, there were no photography appointments scheduled. I'd been spending my days reading new client profiles, which had their interesting moments, but a lot of the material was tedious information covering educational backgrounds and career advancement stories described with excessive detail.

The only good parts were the essays providing their self-analysis of weak areas in their lives and careers.

Reading the results of personality and aptitude tests was sometimes interesting — perfectionist tendencies, risk-taking propensities, and attitudes toward failure — but the multiple choice answers could also get dry. Over and over I read about people who wanted more, even though from all external views, they surely already *had it all*.

Mostly, I thought about the key and Joe and Nell, and how I would get some freedom inside that house. And that didn't include the lurking presence of the shadowy Ed whom I'd yet to even see, despite the fact he also had a suite of rooms there and laid the fires I enjoyed in the evenings.

The days were marching past. I had to take a risk, but I didn't even know what that risk would be.

At ten minutes to five, Stephanie appeared in my doorway. "Sorry to interrupt, but this is important." She put her hand on the doorframe and leaned forward slightly. "You haven't told me what you can bring for Thanksgiving."

"I could bring a pie."

"Diana is already bringing two pies. Didn't you see the email?"

I had, but I hadn't read it. This is what comes with obsession. Nothing else is able to fix itself in the brain when there's a single, continuous focus. Thoughts and conversations unrelated to the obsession drift away. My efforts at concentration were displaced by the key and trying to figure out how to get unfettered access to that house.

"The things we don't have covered are mashed potatoes, a vegetable, and another appetizer."

"I'll bring mashed potatoes."

"What about the other things?"

"If you want me to bring all of that, why didn't you just ask me?"

She stared at me as if I were dense. I couldn't figure out what I was missing. It didn't seem that complicated.

"And can you bring whatever you need to make martinis? Trystan is bringing three bottles of wine."

"Does anyone else drink martinis?"

"I don't know. But wouldn't that be nice for you?"

I shrugged. She seemed more concerned about the alcohol than the dinner. She didn't have ingredient specifications for the vegetable dish or the appetizer.

"Just tell me what you don't have covered yet, and I'll bring that."

"I told you."

"Stephanie, you're making my head hurt. Send it to me in email, so I have it on my phone."

"Sure. I can do that."

She disappeared. Two minutes later an email arrived listing the foods she'd already mentioned and *ingredients for martinis*. I supposed Trystan would enjoy a martini.

It seemed as if half the dinner had been dumped on me, but a meal like Thanksgiving does involve a lot of work. It wasn't fair for Stephanie to do all of it. She had to clean her house, stuff a turkey, wash the dishes after…

I hit reply on the email. *How many people will be there?*

She responded right away — *Just the four of us.* That was intriguing, although I'd hoped to meet her daughter. In fact, now that I realized I wouldn't get the chance to meet Eileen, it was clear to me that talking to her might provide some information about the key, if I asked carefully, vaguely, about her experiences in Jim Kohn's house.

I replied again and asked whether Eileen would be joining us.

Stephanie responded with an unadorned and therefore rather terse-sounding, *no.*

Late afternoon darkness had settled in, giving the office a desolate feel. All four of us were working, but there was a lack of energy in the air. The interruption from Stephanie had made me realize how little I was paying attention to what I was doing. I'd probably have to re-read half the material anyway, so why waste more time not absorbing it?

I locked my computer. When I stepped into the hallway,

the others' office doors were closed. I left without saying good-bye, eager to get home with plenty of time to pack before the limo arrived.

Victoria was waiting for me on the landing. She wore a flesh-colored dress with a jagged hem that brushed her calves. On her feet were matching ballet-slipper shoes. She looked like she was off to perform in a holiday dance.

"Going out?"

"Later," she said. She pirouetted toward me. "Come over for a glass of wine."

"I can't. I'm headed out myself."

"To see the mysterious new guy?"

I smiled.

"That means yes." She clapped her hands together.

Her enthusiasm sucked the life out of mine. Her clapping unnerved me with its borderline derangement. I unlocked my door and tried to ease my way inside my apartment.

"Did you give any more thought to what you learned? About day trading?"

"What do you mean?"

"You were so interested. I assumed you were thinking about getting into it. We could help set you up."

"It's interesting to think about, and the concept seems solid, but I'm not planning to take it up."

"You'd be really good at it."

"I'd probably be good at a lot of things. That doesn't mean I'm going to launch myself into all those possible career paths."

"But this one you don't need to go to school for. And you can make…"

"I know. I can make five times what I'm earning now."

"I just don't get why you want to be tied to a boss. Especially a male boss. I can tell you're independent and you don't like anyone telling you what to do. Why wouldn't you want to make the most of your time and energy while you're young?"

"I've already explained this, Victoria. I need to get going."

"Can you come over tomorrow? For drinks? Or dinner. We'd love to have you for dinner."

"I think I'll be gone all weekend."

"Where is this secret place you keep running off to? You need to tell me all about it. And him!"

"Then it wouldn't be a secret."

She laughed. "Maybe next weekend? Or will you be disappearing then, too?"

"Most likely."

"Okay. Then how about the night before Thanksgiving? That would be fun. We could have a Friends-giving."

That actually did sound fun. They were weird and oppressive, but so entertaining when they played off each other. "That's a good idea. Something non-traditional, right? Since there will be too much turkey on Thursday."

She nodded eagerly. "Fish. Maybe crab. Or lobster."

"That sounds fantastic. Do you know how to cook lobster properly?"

"Absolutely." She clapped her hands again. "We'll eat and party and…"

"And talk about things that aren't work-related."

She grinned.

20

Portland

The boys thought the basement was the superior place for hanging out. They were so convinced of its benefits, it seemed as if there was some deeper instinct that made them choose a place underground.

I wondered if they liked the idea of spiders and other bugs, and the suggestion of burial that comes with subterranean places. When they were younger, they were obsessed with monsters, with gruesome death and zombies. Knowledge of these things wasn't allowed in our house, but unless you're going to put your children in a plastic bubble and prevent all contact with other kids, they're going to learn all sorts of things parents would rather they didn't.

My parents went out of their way to block our minds from outside influences. They could have been more successful at this if we'd had a sheltered school experience, but there were no appropriate private schools in our area. They didn't want us to go to a secular private school that would *spoil* us with *elitist attitudes*, and they didn't approve of Catholic schools because their view of religion was much, much different from what the catechism taught. In their minds, the Catholic religion was nearly pagan with its rituals, cult-like because any group that didn't interpret the Bible like our church did was casually dismissed, labeled a *cult*.

With our spongy little brains outside of parental control for six or seven hours a day, we picked up things they weren't aware of. Their grilling and attempts to root out errors at the dinner table were mostly ineffective. Their rules and overbearing insistence on a world shaped by a literal interpretation of the Bible and their psychologically draconian punishments silenced us. We learned very early to tell them what they wanted to hear. They didn't know what they didn't know about our lives and the things we learned from other kids. It was a mistake they were blind to.

Despite the usual fights and battle for supremacy among siblings, my parents created a little army of children and then teenagers who stuck together and learned to say only what was acceptable. At least my bothers did. I had more trouble with this, but I still kept most things to myself.

The basement made my brothers feel like mad scientists. It was dark and solid. There were no permeable walls through which anyone could listen. Although the sounds of their voices floated up the stairs, the words they spoke couldn't be deciphered. They had near-total privacy.

On her second visit to our house, Carmen and I started the afternoon with cookies and two tall glasses of milk. We sat at the kitchen table while my mother asked Carmen about her family.

My mother picked up the plate that three minutes earlier had held two large peanut butter cookies. She put two more, slightly smaller cookies on the plate and placed it between us. She sat across the table and leaned her chin on the heel of her hand. "What church does your family belong to, Carmen?"

"St. Mary's."

My mother gave Carmen a weak, watery smile. She stood and went to the cookie jar. She got another cookie and returned to the table. She took a bite. Carmen stared at my mother's mouth, transfixed by the cookie crumbs embedded in her pale, barely-there lipstick.

To compensate for the extremely light lip color she used, which was the right choice for a modest woman of god, my mother applied two or three coats. Her lips were always somewhat wax-like. It was fascinating to watch them move, forming words, eating. They looked like something separate from the rest of her face.

"Do your parents read the Bible to you?"

This was one of our church's key objections to Catholicism — they felt there was not enough attention paid to reading the Bible. There was too much emphasis on what came out of the catechism, so how could people hear for themselves what god was telling them to do?

Carmen stared at my mother.

The front door slammed open, and Tom and Jake thudded into the front hall. The door slammed again. A moment later they entered the kitchen, moving quickly toward the plate of cookies my mother had already arranged for them. Beside it was a stack of plastic glasses in varying colors and a pitcher of milk.

Tom grabbed the plate of cookies.

"Slow down," my mother said.

They nodded but said nothing as Jake snatched up the cups and pitcher and they continued toward the door that led to the pantry, the mudroom, and the basement door. Their backpacks bobbed and jumped on their backs, stuffed with books and anything they wanted hidden from my mother.

They left the room and half a minute later the door to the basement opened and closed.

Carmen pinched a piece of cookie off the edge of hers and put it into her mouth. She spoke before she chewed. "Where are they going?"

"To the basement."

"You didn't show me the basement."

"That's the boys' private place." My mother leaned forward and smiled at Carmen. "Do you have Sunday School classes at St. Mary's?" She knew the answer to this, she just wanted to keep Carmen on the topic of religion.

Carmen held my mother's gaze. "Why?"

"Why, what?"

"Why is the basement private?"

"The boys need a place to play and talk about male things." Carmen's voice grew slightly louder. "Like what?"

"It's just for them," I said.

"Why?"

"Because that's how it is," my mother said.

"I want to see it."

"You'll have to ask them."

"That's dumb."

"Don't talk that way," my mother said.

"It's not fair."

"This is our home, Carmen. We manage things the way we think is best. We aren't criticizing how your family lives."

Carmen glared at her. I wondered if she knew my mother's questions about the church were not innocent and friendly. Those questions were looking for openings to criticize…in vague, kind words, of course.

"I want to see the basement."

"You'll have to ask the boys."

"Why don't girls have a place?"

"The attic is for girls, the basement for boys."

Carmen looked at me as if I were beyond stupid for choosing the attic. "You didn't show me the attic."

My mother curved her shiny, waxy lips into a smile. "After we're finished chatting you can see it."

We ate our cookies and gulped milk while my mother asked more questions about St. Mary's, all of which she knew the answers to, and all of which Carmen responded to with as few words as possible.

When my mother petered out, I led Carmen up the stairs to the third floor and then down the hall to the narrow staircase that led to the attic.

We climbed in silence.

At the top, she pressed up close behind me on the tiny landing. I could feel her warm breath on my neck. I smelled peanut butter and sugar. I opened the door and stepped inside, Carmen close behind me, still exhaling the sweet, nutty aroma into the air around me.

I remained by the door and let her walk past me so she could take in the room.

She looked out both windows — first toward the front yard, then out of the window facing down the hill sweeping toward the green belt. A bookcase was nestled under the eaves, and beside it, an identical shelf stacked with puzzles, coloring books and crayons, and a large wooden boat with carved animals depicting Noah's ark, although Noah and his family had gone missing. A few other toys from when I was younger were jumbled in baskets on the bottom shelf.

A golden barrel cactus that I'd picked out myself during a family trip to the nursery sat on a table under the front-facing window. The plant was covered in spikes that wove an intricate pattern around the green, flesh-like part beneath.

Carmen looked around the room, her head jerking madly as if she couldn't decide what she wanted to focus on first. She walked toward the cactus, touched the tiny spikes and yanked her finger away. She studied the pink spot on her skin where she'd pressed the pad of her index finger. She touched the plant again, pushing harder.

I saw what she was up to. "Don't hurt my plant."

"It's dangerous."

"Not if you leave it alone."

She stepped around it, sucking on her finger, and looked out the window. "You can see the whole street."

"Almost."

She stood there for a moment then went to the back window. "You can see into my yard."

When I didn't answer, she turned and looked at me. "You better not spy on me."

"Don't hurt my cactus and I won't."

After she'd looked through all my puzzles and books and tested the comfort of the couch, she asked whether she could bring a few of her toys to my house. "You can't play with them when I'm not here, but I could leave them on that empty shelf. It would give us more choices."

"I'm never bored."

"I might be. So I'll bring some over, okay?"

I shrugged. She pulled a puzzle off the shelf and put the box on the low table in front of the couch. It was a picture of the Moses parting the Red Sea.

In the end, I connected most of the pieces. She spent her time taking peeks at the cactus. I knew she was thinking about blood sisters and I wondered whether I should move the cactus somewhere safe until she got that out of her head.

21

The dinner Joe and I consumed wasn't as exotic as the previous one, but it was equally good. Delicious in its simplicity. We were served creamy potato leek soup and fresh sourdough bread accompanied by a ceramic dish of whipped butter. Dessert was a platter of seedless red grapes, imported cheeses, and flatbread. The meal was enhanced by an excellent bottle of Pinot Noir. Joe didn't mention whether it came from the cellar or had been purchased for our dinner. I didn't ask, but I did wonder how precise the inventory had been on that wine cellar.

After dinner, we watched a movie in the entertainment room, our legs wrapped around each other as we sprawled on a theater-style recliner made for two.

This time, because I'd told myself it was necessary, I woke fully at ten minutes to one. Joe was far from consciousness in what I was learning was his usual deep and soundless sleep.

Dressed in yoga pants and a long-sleeved t-shirt, my feet bare, I made my way down the hall and descended to the first floor. The foyer hall was icy cold on my feet even though the temperature in the rooms and hallways I'd passed through was pleasantly warm without being stuffy. I carried my cigarettes in one hand and my lighter in the other, although I hoped the fancy lighter I'd seen on the table would still be out so I could give it a try.

The old-fashioned key was snuggled up inside the nearly full box of cigarettes, in case I found a fitting lock.

I entered the cigar room and closed the door, which Joe had said would activate the filtering system. I settled on the couch.

The lighter was indeed in the same place I'd seen it the previous time. I studied it, wondering whether the room had been dusted, whether Nell, or whoever had cleaned, returned the lighter to its precise position.

Except for Joe slipping one bottle of wine, that I knew of, out of the cellar, the staff seemed to be operating as if Jim were still alive. Typical human behavior leads many people to slack off when they aren't closely observed and managed by their employer. That didn't seem to be the case here.

It was also possible Joe was behaving as he always had when Jim was out of town or staying in the city. For all I knew, he'd always had free access to the wine cellar. He'd certainly been familiar with its contents, giving the impression he had a personal connection to all those carefully selected bottles of wine.

I picked up the lighter, noting its position. Of course, I couldn't hide my presence because I didn't know where to empty the ashtray once I was finished. The thought of carrying a dish that looked like it weighed five pounds to a bathroom and flushing the evidence seemed awkward and open to the possibility of causing damage.

With a gentle press of my index finger, a tall, hissing flame emerged from the lighter. I played with it for a moment, testing its power, then lit my cigarette and returned it to its place on the table. I settled back and smoked, looking around the room for a home that accommodated the key.

Behind me were the glass doors protecting the shelves lined with boxes of cigars. The walls on both sides of me featured the nude paintings that had been the first thing I noticed when Joe led me into the room.

The furniture was beyond comfortable and halfway through my first cigarette I'd already made the decision to relax into it with a second smoke. All that was missing was a drink, but I was too comfortable to bother getting up to seek it out.

I let my thoughts drift and was partially into my second cigarette without even being aware I'd removed it from the package and deployed the fancy lighter again. I wasn't wallowing in gleeful thoughts of vengeance, but it was definitely satisfying to sit in Jim Kohn's well-appointed room, his investment in cigars left for someone else to enjoy, his perfect ventilation system removing my smoke from the air. I had a momentary thought that it would be fun to hang out and finish the second cigarette sitting at his desk with my feet propped up like some cliched fat cat from the 1960s. Instead, I focused on the pleasure of drawing in smoke and blowing it out in long, elegant ribbons.

The table in front of me was round with thick legs. There were no drawers beneath it, and the tables between the armchairs were equally lacking in receptacles that might be locked by an old-fashioned key.

An abstract metal sculpture hung on the wall facing me. I gazed at it and thought about the key. Why was I so determined to find out where it fit? What did it matter? It wasn't likely to reveal something titillating. There was no additional advantage to be had over Jim Kohn. That win was already mine. The key most likely fit an old box or trunk filled with meaningless papers and tattered objects from the past.

But if that was the case, why would he keep it on his ring? He'd had it nearby at all times. The question tormented me.

I put out my cigarette, picked up my things, and turned out the lights. I entered the study and turned on the desk lamp. I walked around the room slowly, looking closely for anything with an old fashioned lock. There was nothing. I turned out the lights and stepped into the foyer.

As I walked across the bone-chilling marble, I heard a voice from the second-floor landing. "You're making yourself quite at home."

I looked up. Nell was leaning over the railing. I thought immediately of Victoria and the way she leaned over the railing, watching me come up the stairs. They both had the ability to seemingly appear out of nowhere. Both of them seemed to want to control me in some way, but I couldn't figure out whether that was their desire with all women, with everyone they knew, or simply with me.

I shrugged and smiled up at her.

When I reached the second floor, she moved away from the railing, partially blocking my way. "What were you doing in Jim's study?"

"I wasn't in his study."

"I saw you come out."

"I was in the smoking room."

"It's not a smoking room. It's a cigar room."

We climbed to the third floor without speaking. I started down the hall to Joe's room. She grabbed my upper arm, her fingers as solid and strong as a leg iron. "What were you doing?"

"I was smoking."

"You shouldn't be."

"Joe said the room has a state-of-the-art ventilation system."

"It's not your room to use as you please."

"I wanted a cigarette."

"Then go outside."

"Why?"

"Does Joe know you're wandering around unescorted."

I laughed. "*Unescorted?*"

"Does he know?"

"Let go of my arm."

She released me.

I considered walking away, but if I could manage to maneuver her into chilling out, she might be helpful in getting me into that room at the end of the hall. If the key accessed anything in this house, it was most likely inside that room. "He's asleep. I wanted a smoke. You know how that is." I gave her a self-deprecating smile.

Her expression changed slightly, a micro-expression carrying a suggestion that she did know how that was, and maybe she was wondering why she'd never thought of hanging out in that exotic room. Trying to bat smoke out the window on a cold night was not the soothing experience that smoking should be.

"Just FYI, this situation is temporary." She gave me a smug

look, the whisper of connection between us gone before I could pounce. "None of us knows what our status is, and even if we stay working for Mr. Kohn's brother, we won't be entertaining guests that eat meals prepared by his chef and wander the house doing as they please."

"I'm aware."

"I just think you should be more respectful."

"I'll keep that in mind." I walked slowly toward Joe's room, my eye on the storage room door the entire way. As I entered Joe's sitting room, I turned slightly to give the locked door a parting glance. Then I looked back at Nell, still standing in the middle of the hallway. She couldn't stay up all night. Eventually, she had to sleep. I closed the door, knowing I could out-wait her.

22

Sitting near the window in Joe's room, looking out into the darkness, I waited, knowing that if I gave it an hour or two, Nell would fall asleep. While I sat looking at nothing, craving nothing, for once in my life, I thought about the keys Joe pulled out of his pocket each time he took off his jeans.

During the night, they sat in a wooden bowl on his chest of drawers. There were only a few keys, so I expected one of them was a master.

I'd definitely decided against checking his ethical boundaries to see whether I could enlist his help — there was no way to do that without revealing my possession of the key. Even if I had his help getting into the storage room, once I was inside, if I found the right lock, I clearly couldn't do anything without exposing the key.

The only chance to satisfy and subdue my obsession was to wait.

I was alert as if I'd just come back from a sunrise run. My body hummed with energy and my mind was eager without being impatient and bored. I relaxed into the pure feeling of anticipation.

At two-forty-five, I decided Nell had to be sleeping. While I'd been sitting in the dark, there hadn't been a sound from Joe's bedroom. I walked to the doorway and stood for a moment gazing at the outline of his body. He hardly moved. All I saw was the faint drifting of his shoulder up and down as he breathed. His head looked almost childlike on the pillows. I recalled his warm skin beneath the blankets, but shoved the thought aside.

I stepped into the room and took the keys. I felt each one, trying to find a feature that might suggest it was a master key. There were three keys and a car fob. None of the keys distinguished itself from the others.

I went to the outer door. I opened it gently and looked into the hallway. It was empty. I stepped out of the room, closed the door, walked quickly to the storage room, one key already pinched between my thumb and index finger. I stuck it into the lock. It refused to turn. I took a deep breath, telling myself not to rush, it would create unintended noise if I stabbed the next key at the lock and missed.

The second key slid into the lock and turned smoothly. I opened the door, glanced behind me at the empty hallway, slipped inside, and closed the door.

Darkness surrounded me. I rested one hand on the door handle and ran the other along the wall beside me. My fingers passed over a plastic switch plate and I pressed the button. The room filled with light.

It was smaller than I'd estimated. There were no windows. The wall opposite me was lined with floor-to-ceiling shelves containing small storage boxes. The two adjacent walls were lined with doors. I went to the first door on the left and opened it — a walk-in closet filled with women's clothes.

There wasn't enough time to investigate everything in detail. Given Nell's wakefulness, I had no doubt she might be out walking around or smoking in less than two hours. I closed the door and went to the next. This was also a walk-in closet. I began to realize that the center of the room was smaller than I'd expected only because the large closets surrounding it took up all the space I'd observed from the outside of the house.

One closet contained holiday decorations, one was filled with sports equipment. Assuming the other two closets along that wall also contained household storage, I crossed the room and started opening the series of doors on that side.

The first room was a decent-sized photography studio. There was a tripod with a Canon camera attached. Large lights with metal cones surrounding the spotlight-sized bulbs sat in both corners. The carpet was thick and the color of cream. In the center was a soft leather love seat, also cream-colored. A few light brown pillows were scattered across it.

The next room contained a desk with a computer, an expensive-looking printer, and a scanner.

The third room held nothing but an enormous old-fashioned armoire. Dead center in the armoire door was a keyhole. I pulled the key out of my pocket, inserted it, and turned. The door swung open.

Inside were narrow wood trays like drawers. I tugged gently on one of the middle trays. It slid toward me. It was filled with eight-by-ten photographs of Stephanie's daughter. The woman whose photographs still lined the shelf in Jim's study, the woman whom he'd tossed out of his life after breaking her spirit and damaging her soul, according to Stephanie.

These photographs were nothing like those in his study,

which looked like a cross between professional advertising shots and appreciative depictions of a man's fiancé.

In these images, Eileen was nearly naked, in some, completely naked, but they weren't erotic in any way. They showed her huddled on the cream-colored couch, her head bent forward in a pose that suggested she was defeated and weak. They showed her sitting in a corner on the floor, hugging her knees, her hair obviously unwashed, mascara smeared across her cheekbones. Some were unvarnished close-ups of every inch of her body, exposing dark, unruly hairs missed during waxing, blemishes and moles, and a faint smear of cellulite on her upper thigh.

It was a documentation of her flaws — physical and emotional.

One of the drawers was filled with pictures of her crying, her mouth distorted by sobs of…I wasn't sure what. Her eyes were blurred with liquid, her cheeks streaked red and damp. I hadn't known there were so many ways to capture human despair. All of them were raw and managed to make her sadness look ugly instead of creating empathy.

Each successive drawer had more of the same, some even more degrading — poses with her legs spread wide and her genitals swollen, several of her bending forward, the camera angled up between her legs, again without any erotic effect.

The last tray contained photographs taken outside of the studio. In these, she was dressed like a worn out hooker, posing in the dark in various alleys and outside of bars around New York City.

I wasn't prepared to take the pictures with me. And I really didn't need to. There was no point, they were embedded in my memory. The question was, why had they been taken?

Was Jim the photographer, or someone else? And was Eileen worried about their existence? Did Stephanie know?

I'd replaced a single obsession with questions that had the potential to torment me even further.

23

The storage room was dark again, the armoire locked, the door into its dedicated room was closed. I stood close to the door into the hallway, waiting for my eyes to adjust, although it wasn't possible for them to accomplish much. Without the ambient light from windows, I was enclosed in utter blackness. I rested my fingers on the door handle. It had a simple button lock.

In the next few seconds, I needed to open the door, reset the lock, step into the hallway, avoid letting the latch click too loudly as I closed the door, and get myself into the vicinity of Joe's suite without being seen. There was no way to prepare for the risk. I needed to figure out what I would say if anyone was out there.

I leaned against the door, hoping I might hear the softness of a footstep on the carpet or a door opening, even breathing, anything to tell me to stay where I was. But the longer I waited, the closer the clock ticked toward sunrise, the greater the chance I'd be seen. Once Joe woke, he'd go looking for me.

I let my thoughts wander over the worst possible scenario.

It wasn't as if I'd be searched. They'd never know about the key to the armoire. I might lose my welcome in the house, I might lose Joe. But even those were maybes. In the end, nothing could truly threaten me.

I pressed on the handle and opened the door. The hallway was empty. Keeping my head turned toward the stretch of hallway, I turned the lock and carefully closed the door. A few more steps and I'd be home free.

A deep sigh came out of me when I was once again standing outside Joe's door. The house was filled with silence. I leaned my head against the doorframe and calmed my breathing so I could enter his room with equal stealth.

The sound of another door opening shocked me back to an upright position. I held myself still and watched the door to Nell's room swing wide. A man stepped into the hallway. He was tall, with short dark hair, clipped up the sides of his head. I couldn't see his face. His shoulders were thin but broad and he had long legs. He wore jeans, navy blue Vans, and a loose-fitting dark green t-shirt. The extra fabric did nothing to conceal those very broad shoulders.

He closed the door behind him. He didn't look in my direction. Obviously familiar with his surroundings, he walked toward the staircase and disappeared from sight.

I went into Joe's room, returned the keys to the wooden bowl, and peeled off my clothes. I slipped into bed and turned onto my back. I closed my eyes and let my breathing slow.

It was possible that Nell's lecture about entertaining guests had been directed at herself as well as Joe. It was equally possible the man leaving her room was the shadowy Ed. The man had walked confidently, sure of where he was going, not at all concerned with being seen. His lack of interest in his surroundings suggested he was headed somewhere specific.

The desire to find out more, to put Nell on the defensive, was strong. I considered getting out of bed again and knocking on her door. And yet, at this point, why did I need to speak to her? What did it matter who was in her room? I'd found the home for the key. All I needed to do was figure out what, if anything, I should do about those photographs. Nell didn't play into it at all anymore.

Lying in bed, I regretted not taking them. I was too startled, and then too focused on being seen carrying them. There aren't many things as annoying as knowing after the fact that a risk was not that at all.

Sleep wouldn't come. I turned on my side, my back toward Joe. My thoughts spun more wildly, as if tipping my head sideways stirred them up. My eyes were open, unable to relax even to an unfocused gaze, much less allow the lids to fall closed. They strained to see something in the dark that wasn't there.

After trying a few minutes on my right side, I flipped back to my left. A moment later I got out of bed. I dressed and went into the sitting area. I pried open the hairbrush and returned the key to its hiding place. I slipped out the door and went downstairs.

The house was dark, although a chalky gray was beginning to seep in through a few narrow windows placed just below the ceiling that functioned like skylights, the glass opaque, providing natural light.

I walked into the living room. The fireplace was empty and clean. It seemed the fire was only set by request. I went into the dining room and then the kitchen. Both were spotless and devoid of human life.

Walking through to the breakfast room, I saw him. He was on the back patio, settled in an Adirondack chair. His hands were fiddling with something he held just above his lap.

I moved closer to the doors. It seemed too dark for him to actually see whatever he was working on. Likewise, I couldn't make out what he was holding, but he was constantly moving, manipulating it this way and that.

It was close to five-thirty. It was odd that he'd go outside without coffee or any type of beverage. The air was rather cold for sitting still to watch the sunrise. If he had work to do around the place, it was odd that he'd gotten up so early yet was not getting to it.

I opened the door and stepped outside. He turned. He settled the object on his thighs. A Rubik's Cube. I was so startled I didn't speak for a moment. Startled that he was trying to get it to work in the dark, startled that someone was drawn to that type of puzzle so early in the morning. And startled that he wasn't playing with a digital puzzle or game. Most people play games and work puzzles on their phones. I couldn't remember the last time I'd seen a Rubik's Cube outside of a game store.

I took a step closer. "Hi. I'm Alexandra."

He gave a single nod without looking at me. "I know who you are."

I curved one bare foot on top of the other, trying to keep at least one of them from freezing on the chilled, dew-covered flagstone. The position unbalanced me and with the slippery texture underneath, two feet were preferable. I moved my other foot back to the cold, hard stone.

He watched me fidget.

"Are you a friend of Nell's?"

He didn't respond.

"I've never solved a Rubik's Cube. Are you good at it?"

"Yep."

I suppose most people would have excused themselves at that point, taking the clear message he wasn't interested in talking. "Who told you my name?"

"Joe."

So he wasn't a friend of Nell's. Not exactly. This had to be Ed, but clearly he didn't care whether or not I knew who he was or what his position was in this odd collection of people drifting in the wake of their boss's murder. I suppose it would be difficult when you worked in someone's home to have the man suddenly disappear and leave you not only potentially jobless, but homeless. Yet none of them seemed driven to take control of their circumstances. They were suspended in time, waiting for the new guy. Even Joe. "Do you always come out here and do your puzzle at sunrise?"

He scowled.

Or at least it seemed that way. Still, I didn't want to give up. There had to be something that would crack loose whatever was blocking the flow of words that most people provide when they're asked the right questions, given a chance to embellish themselves. "I'd love to go for a run on the property. Do you think that's a problem?" I didn't care whether it was a problem. Who would it be a problem for? But there's nothing like asking advice or permission to soften up most people.

"Not a problem. As long as you don't run on the lawn. It damages the roots of the grass."

I nodded.

"Smoking and running don't usually go together," he said.

"Not usually, but I limit my smoking."

He laughed. He didn't tell me what he found funny in that statement. Maybe that most smokers don't limit themselves very effectively. I smiled. "Do you prefer to be left alone?"

"That's why I'm sitting out here."

"Okay. Well, nice meeting you. Except I don't know your name."

"Ed."

"Good to meet you, Ed. See you around." I went inside and returned to Joe's room. At least I had my bit of information, but for someone who worked there, he was strangely aloof to a guest in the house. Of course, I wasn't a proper guest and so I suppose I didn't count.

24

I spent all day Saturday at the house and slept there again. As Nell had pointed out, this was temporary. I wanted to relish as much luxury and sex as I could before the landscape changed and Joe and I moved out of each other's lives.

After I'd taken a short run in the garden that morning, it started to rain. The rain poured down in alternating bouts of buckets followed by delicate droplets misting down all day long. We watched movies, we sat in front of the fire, ate homemade pizza, and napped naked.

The entire time, thoughts of those locked up trays of photographs drifted in and out of my mind. Did Joe or the others know of their existence? Who was the photographer? Jim was the obvious choice, but there were other possibilities.

Finally, it dawned on me that Jim had to be the one who'd taken and printed the photographs because he'd kept the key to the armoire close beside him. But the others, Joe for sure, knew the studio was there. They'd seen the closet of women's clothes, the desk with the computer equipment. Were they socialized to lack curiosity about their boss's activities?

But that wasn't entirely true, because Joe said he'd been

watching when his boss was pawing me. He knew the guy was a sleaze. He knew the storage room existed and that it wasn't just a storage room. Even if he'd never witnessed a photography session, he surely must think it was odd to have a studio tucked away inside a locked room.

The circling questions and fabricated explanations, none of which fully satisfied me, made it hard to concentrate on the movies we were watching. I wanted to ask Joe, but I liked what we had with each other. It was easy and thrilling, and I didn't want to make it complicated. I didn't want to end it abruptly, which prying was apt to do.

While we ate dinner in the candlelit dining room, feasting on steak and grilled squash, he suddenly put down his knife and looked at me. "You seem like you're not really here. Bored already?"

"Absolutely not." I gave him a dramatic air kiss.

"Then where's your mind? Work? Holiday planning?"

"I met Ed this morning."

"Nice evasive action."

"I'm not being evasive. I meant to ask you about him."

"If you say so."

"He was playing with a Rubik's Cube."

Joe laughed. "Yeah, he loves that thing. I think he believes it makes him look smart because he can always get it worked out."

"He was doing it in the dark. Not trying to impress anyone."

"Some people like to impress themselves."

It was an interesting point. I turned it over in my mind while I sliced off a tender strip of beef. I put it in my mouth and chewed.

"Do you know you have the same look on your face when you eat as you do when you come?"

I smiled. "Doesn't everyone?"

"Not that I'm aware of."

"How well do you know him?"

He shook his head as if he was dislodging water from his ears. "Ed? As well as you know anyone you work with."

"And live with."

"Not really. We all keep to ourselves when we're not working. Why are you so interested?"

"I'm a curious person."

"So I've heard."

I took a sip of wine. I moved my chair away from the table slightly, turning so I could see his face more clearly, shadows from the candles making it look slightly unfamiliar. The flicker gave the impression his expression was shifting wildly. "You've heard...?"

"Don't sound so nervous."

"I'm not nervous." That was probably a lie, but I didn't take time to think about it. "Where did you hear?"

"Nell said you were wandering around in the middle of the night. Checking out the cigar room."

"What else did she say?"

"That's all."

I didn't believe him. She wouldn't have casually mentioned something so unimportant without having a point she was trying to make. If she thought I was only pursuing meaningless curiosity, she wouldn't have said anything to Joe. Talking to him about me meant she wanted to make trouble for me. Or at least what she thought was trouble.

With a slight nudge from me, our conversation drifted to

other topics. I wanted to know more about Ed, and Nell, for that matter, but I needed to think through what she might have said beyond mentioning my late night prowling. I needed to think about whether there was quite a lot more going on in this house than I'd realized.

I had no awareness of when Nell might have spoken to Joe. As far as I could recall, he and I hadn't been out of each other's presence for more time than it takes to pee, flush the toilet, and wash your hands.

Did they communicate by text, even while living in the same house? The place was large enough. If they did, why? Were they closer than he'd let on? Did he already know she and Ed were together? He had to. But he'd said nothing to me. It wasn't important, I suppose, to explain all the ins and outs of each person who lived there, but it seemed like a natural thing you might mention.

He also didn't seem to think highly of Ed, given his comment about Ed trying to impress himself in the dark with his skill solving a puzzle that many people find impossible to master. It was clear that he thought Ed was both pompous and deeply insecure.

If all of them knew about the sickening photographs, what did that mean? Cold spots prickled across my skin despite the perfectly regulated temperature of the entire house. I'd thought Joe was into me, but maybe there was more to it. What the hell could it be? I felt like I'd fallen into a massive cube-shaped puzzle of my own. Four people, one dead. Or was Eileen the fourth, and Jim had been the puzzle master?

My head ached from thinking about it.

After Joe and I had sex, which quieted my brain for a while, but only a short while, he fell into his silent, self-contained, motionless cocoon of sleep. I lay on my back. My eyes were closed, but my eyeballs strained to see something that was completely obscured.

Finally, I thought of the only thing I could do. Next week, I would arrive early at Stephanie's. There was a chance that showing up early would allow me to run into her daughter. Stephanie would hate me, she'd probably punish me with passive-aggressive behavior all day, but what did that really matter? The trick would be figuring out what to say to Eileen without mentioning my possession of the key.

Was she aware the photographs had been printed? If she did know, did she know they were locked up? I imagined she'd be frightened, knowing they existed but having no ability to get her hands on them without telling someone how awful they were.

She was the new key burning a spot in my brain. And Joe was now someone to be wary of.

25

The aroma from Victoria and Rafe's pre-Thanksgiving dinner filled the space between our apartment doors and drifted across the landing to the top of the stairs. It smelled of roasted garlic and the rich, spicy aroma of Chinese food. She'd obviously abandoned or forgotten about her interest in lobster.

Inside their apartment, the TV was turned off and the computer screens were dark. They'd placed candles on all the end tables and turned down the lights, so it didn't have quite the computer-rat atmosphere I'd experienced the last time I'd visited.

Their kitchen table was round with three chairs spaced evenly along its edges. A fat blue candle flickered in the center of the table. The fourth chair sat in a corner. On top was a grocery bag filled with canned and boxed food. I assumed it was a contribution for a shelter, but it looked like they weren't going to make it for Thanksgiving.

Rafe offered me a choice of red or white wine. I chose white without asking the variety. The scent from Victoria's pans said the tangy spices would be thrilled with white wine.

The chill would be nice, if nothing else.

Rafe and I sat in the living room. We sipped our wine and talked about Thanksgiving traditions. Rafe was of the opinion that the food typically served was too bland. Everything was white — turkey meat, potatoes, bread, even the stuffing barely made it to light brown. He thought gravy was disgusting, nothing more than dripping liquid animal fat all over your food. I pointed out that gravy could be made from a packet. He dismissed me with a wave of his hand.

Victoria was singing Christmas carols while she cooked. When either one of us approached the kitchen, she swatted us away saying she didn't want interference.

Our wine glasses were empty, and she was still finishing preparations. Rafe had moved onto his feelings about Christmas. I didn't mind listening to his rants. He was funny in his peculiar and curmudgeonly hatred of things most people enjoy.

The dinner turned out to be a full-on Chinese feast.

There were egg rolls and potstickers she'd made herself, as tasty and attractive as anything from a nice restaurant. This was followed by fried rice, Chow Fun with paper-thin slices of beef, cashew chicken with chili peppers to liven it up, and tofu in black bean sauce.

It was truly incredible. I felt I was eating in a high-end restaurant with a Chef born and trained in China who had expertly learned to modify the dishes to suit American tastes and biases.

The wine turned out to be a crisp Pinot Gris — a perfect complement.

Victoria wanted each one of us to talk about the things we were grateful for. I pointed out that it wasn't Thanksgiving yet. She thought that shouldn't matter. Besides, this was their Thanksgiving dinner. The following day they would be visiting a shelter where they'd cook and serve turkey and gravy and mashed potatoes to people living in a homeless shelter. Finally, she yielded. I expect she truly wanted me to have a good time. I was glad she didn't push.

I suppose I'm grateful for things, but I don't think in those terms. It sounds too much like obligatory gratitude that recognizes you shouldn't desire anything because you should be grateful for what you already have. At least that was the spin on *gratitude* when I was growing up.

I appreciate what I have in my life — my job, living in New York, my skills, and of course the people I know and all the amazing experiences I've had. But I want more. I always want more. And I don't think that's a bad thing, even though my parents did. They considered me greedy and yes, ungrateful.

Wanting more is human nature.

Ask anyone, no matter who they are or what they have — there is something they want.

When you stop wanting, you're dead.

Victoria thought my explanation was weird.

Rafe agreed with me wholeheartedly. "This is why we keep talking to you about sticking your toe into the day trading waters," he said.

I stabbed some rice noodles and a slice of beef. I put them in my mouth and let the flavor run across my tongue and around the insides of my cheeks. I chewed the soft, comforting noodles. When I was finished, I took a long swallow of cold wine.

"It's obvious you're a person who wants so much more," he said. "We've seen that from the get-go. I really don't understand why you're so squeamish about it. I mean really, even if day trading *was* a little like gambling, which it's not, not really, because it takes skill…"

"Gambling takes skill," I said.

"No. Games where you bet on your skills aren't technically gambling," he said. "True gambling is a slot machine or roulette. No skill required. Cards? That's entirely different."

I shrugged.

"If you don't think you'd enjoy the actual work, even though Vic and I agree you'd be fantastic at it, why don't you let us invest a bit on your behalf."

"No thanks."

"Not a lot. Just so you can see what happens, how incredible the return is. A hundred bucks."

"Nope."

He laughed. "I'm sure you can spare a hundred bucks. What do you spend on cigarettes a month?"

"None of your business and completely unrelated."

"You don't have a hundred bucks to spare? What do they pay you to take pictures?" He pushed his chair away from the table. He poured water from the pitcher at his left and drank half the glass.

"It doesn't matter what I have. I'm not going to gamble it on a bunch of corporations."

"Invest."

Victoria went into the kitchen. She returned with a new bottle of wine. She refilled our glasses and remained standing, clutching the bottle by the neck. "We really like you, Alex," she said.

"Thanks."

"We want to help you."

"I don't need help."

"You said you want more. You're always wanting more," Rafe said.

"We can tell you're curious. You're interested but don't want to admit it," Victoria said.

I sipped my wine.

"I was thinking," she said. "Why don't we put up a stake *for* you. Our money, our risk. We'll show you how quickly it can grow."

"No matter what you show me, I imagine the opposite can also happen."

"You have to try it. I could have made an investment on your behalf without even asking you, but why don't we do this? We'll show you the data to illustrate your return. So you'll know it's real."

I was tired of them pestering me. Why wouldn't they let it go? Sometimes, it seemed as if they were running a pyramid scheme and they needed me to join at the bottom layer so they could advance to the next level. What did it matter if it was their money or mine? I didn't want to take money from them. The thought repulsed me.

"We'll invest five hundred dollars for two weeks. When we realize a return, you can have the profit. No skin in the game. All upside."

"I don't want your money."

"It won't be our money. It will be yours."

"Only in your mind."

"Let us do it. You have nothing to lose."

I did have something to lose. Several things. My self-respect. My autonomy.

"Think about it. We can talk after the holiday."

I took a sip of wine and considered eating another potsticker, but I was full and on my way to finishing my fifth glass of wine. It was clearly a good time to return home. I had to get up early to whip up all the food that Stephanie demanded. We'd been told to arrive at noon. There would be plenty of time for a run and cooking if I got up at my usual time, but one more glass of wine and the functioning of my automatic body clock were at odds.

Victoria refused my offer to help clean up the kitchen. She said the best thing I could do would be to allow them to make an investment on my behalf.

I'd never known anyone so eager to give money to someone else. There was something deeply unsettling about it.

26

The apartment looked lovely. Stephanie had dragged the coffee table into Eileen's bedroom and closed the door. This gave her plenty of space to expand the dining table to its full size. Now, the table intruded into the living room as if it was reaching out its arms, asking her guests to gather around it. Even without the coffee table, there were still three end tables for people to place their drinks and appetizer plates while they chatted before the meal.

It was going to be a slightly disconcerting gathering with her and Diana consuming little to no alcohol, Trystan behaving like the gentleman he was, and Alex being her lush-y self. But that was the whole point. She'd spent money and time on that turkey and scrubbed, dusted, and vacuumed the place to a sparkle. She was giving up part of her four-day weekend in order to spend time listening to Alexandra's aggressive opinions and watching her preen, all so that horrific side, the true side of her would be fully exposed to Trystan.

He'd probably never even seen any of that behavior unless she did it in front of clients. But Stephanie guessed that

Trystan was the one to take the lead in those meetings and Alexandra managed to keep herself subdued. She didn't know that for a fact, but it was her guess.

Trystan wasn't stupid. If Alex didn't tone herself down around clients, surely he would have already seen what she was really like and decided she wasn't the right fit for his consulting team. He didn't realize he'd invited such a ruthless person into their midst — viper wasn't too strong of a comparison.

Stephanie was not a fool. She knew exactly what that woman was — a manipulator. If Alex had a soul at all, it was calcified. Stephanie smiled. No one like that could hide her true nature for long. Unpredictable social events had a way of bringing out different facets of a person's character. She was confident her Thanksgiving dinner would be a tremendous success on that front. A few martinis and Alexandra's filters, what few she had, would fall away.

There was so much to be thankful for.

Even if Eileen was still a wreck, at least that man was dead — a cause for incredible gratitude.

Putting Alex aside for a moment, Stephanie had a decent job. She had a good boss who just needed a slight push to realize he had a blind spot that required removing — more gratitude. Diana might become a better friend once Alex was out of the way and she too realized how much better their work environment had been before Alex literally took over.

She stood by the front door and admired the room. A clear glass bowl filled with brilliant red and yellow leaves decorated one occasional table, and the other had a grouping of three orange candles.

The table was covered with a yellow cloth she'd bought for

this occasion. Her white plates with gold trim glowed on the yellow background like brilliant white suns casting bright splashes of light around them. Beside each plate was a yellow cloth napkin. The flatware was laid out and tiny white cards, folded in half, stood like small tents with the names of her guests. She would be near the kitchen, Trystan would be at the head of the table, with Diana to his left and Alex at his right.

In the center of the table was a thick glass vase filled with water. A candle shaped like a pumpkin floated on the surface.

She'd lined up the serving utensils to the right of her place, and wine glasses for Alex and Trystan and herself. She would have a glass of wine to be polite. Maybe two. The Bible did not forbid drinking wine. She was never sure why some traditions ruled it out. What God found offensive was drunkenness. The affliction of modern society. It seemed like everything was built around alcohol — sports events, parties, even brunch wasn't really brunch without mimosas, Bloody Marys for breakfast, wine with lunch. Had it always been that way, or was the use of alcohol increasing? Still, a few small glasses of wine were something to be enjoyed. Just because other people abused it, didn't make wine itself something to be shunned.

Trystan would appreciate her tasting what he'd selected to complement their dinner. She smiled and tugged on the corner of the tablecloth — a gentle adjustment to smooth out the wrinkle that had formed beside Trystan's plate.

The aroma of roasting turkey filled the apartment. The turkey had been in the oven since five that morning. Her guests would arrive at noon, and the meal would be served at one. She had three hours and not a lot left to do. She felt relaxed and in control.

Only the final touches remained — mixing the cranberry sauce and wiping down the bathroom after their showers and…her brain slipped gears…

Eileen was vague about her plans, but she was prepping her hair and face as if she was headed out for a photo shoot under two hundred-watt spotlights. She'd promised to leave by eleven. Stephanie was ignoring Eileen's tiny pouts and the sad look that infused her eyes. This was healthy. For both of them. They needed to spend time away from each other. A single mother and her daughter were too tightly knitted. Some cracks had emerged, widened. But that was temporary now that Eileen's ex-lover was dead. Time apart would relieve the pressure causing the cracks. It was important to have other friends.

The way Eileen was behaving about one silly dinner made Stephanie wonder whether Eileen felt closer to her mother than ever, despite the damage caused by that man. It both warmed her heart and frightened her. All women wanted their daughters to feel tightly connected, but no mother wanted her child crippled because she failed to venture outside of her mother's embrace.

She moved away from the door. She needed to get herself dressed and ready. She needed to make the green bean casserole, and she needed to create a playlist that was long enough to last for several hours.

The bathroom door opened. Eileen came out, her face made up, her wet hair wrapped in a towel.

"I need to take my shower," Stephanie said.

"You're the one kicking me out for the day, you'll have to wait a few more minutes."

"Please stop with the guilt trips."

"It wouldn't be a guilt trip if you didn't feel guilty." Eileen smiled. "So I guess I have that to be thankful for. You do feel guilty for what you're doing."

"I told you it's a work thing. That's all. It's one day. One meal."

Eileen lunged into the living room. She grabbed her mother's shoulders and kissed her hard on her cheek.

"I know. It's just fun to see you get so wound up." She giggled. "So serious."

"Well, I don't think..."

"Relax. I'll be fine. We'll have our usual Christmas, right?" Stephanie nodded.

"Really, Mom. It's okay."

She put her arms around Stephanie and held on for a moment longer than required.

Stephanie's throat swelled, and tears pushed their way against that backs of her eyes.

"Happy Thanksgiving, honey. It makes me happy that you're feeling good."

Eileen didn't respond. A moment later, she had disappeared into her room, closing the door quickly and firmly.

Stephanie returned to the kitchen. She pulled four cans of green beans out of the cupboard and a can opener out of the drawer. She'd get the casserole put together and then hop in the shower. Maybe even do the cranberry sauce first. No sense doing all those messy things when she was wearing her nice clothes.

Besides, she wanted to stand in the warm, savory-smelling kitchen and think about the unexpected shift in Eileen's mood. Then, she would get her emotions under control.

But for now, she wanted to enjoy the tearful feeling of relief and hope that her daughter was coming back to herself.

27

To make sure I increased my chances of running into Eileen, I planned to arrive at Stephanie's apartment by nine-thirty. I imagined Stephanie's shocked and angry face. I imagined her possibly not answering the door, but I could always text her and let her know the food needed to be refrigerated.

Earlier, I'd gone for a short run, and by eight o'clock I had the potatoes peeled and cooked, ready for butter and half-and-half and mashing, and the carrots peeled and sautéed in butter and brown sugar. That left plenty of time for getting dressed and a leisurely Uber ride to Stephanie's apartment. I wasn't about to get on the subway with plastic covered bowls that I'd had to buy at the Duayne Reade because I only had the bare minimum of pots and crockery occupying my kitchen cabinets.

I made up my eyes with a coffee-colored shadow palette, chocolate liner, and dark brown mascara.

I chose a charcoal gray spandex and cotton skirt that felt warm and comfortable over black tights. I wore black boots and a black sleeveless top in case it was hot inside the apartment. I imagined it would be toasty with four people in a small space and an oven spewing heat onto a turkey for most of the morning. I'd wear a sweater under my jacket, just in case I'd called it wrong.

I twisted my hair into a messy bun. It was definitely messy since I didn't have enough length to hold much on the top of my head. Still, it made me look different than I did in the office, and that's all that mattered.

The Uber was still ten minutes away, as I'd asked for because I couldn't juggle all my dishes at once. I carried the potatoes and carrots to the lobby and left them on the side table where people placed found items. I ran back up for the shopping bag with the other supplies and my tray of not-yet-broiled, bacon-wrapped shrimp with cayenne pepper.

I locked the door and turned away from my apartment. At that moment, my elusive neighbor whose apartment door was directly across from the stairs was doing the same. He turned as I did. He lifted his hand in a half-wave.

Since my hands were occupied, I gave him a friendly smile. "Hi."

"Happy Turkey Day," he said.

I walked toward him. "Heading out to see your family?"

He shook his head. "They went to New Hampshire for the week, but I need to work tomorrow."

"Where are you eating your turkey?"

"At home."

I opened my mouth and let my eyes pop wide.

"It's no big deal. I can live without the carb catastrophe." He patted his flat belly.

The guy was a living advertisement for a gym, so I had no doubt he obsessed over carb quality and quantity like a lot of people who lift weights seriously.

"One day of carbs won't spoil everything," I said.

"True. But I'm fine. Looking forward to chilling. Watching some football."

"Why don't you come with me?"

He looked at me as if I'd just invited a stranger on a street corner to come to my house for dinner.

"It's just a work thing. My boss and two co-workers. That's it."

"Work? On Thanksgiving?"

I laughed. "It's a cozy group that lacks a few boundaries."

"That's okay. Thanks for the invite." He shoved his keys into his pocket but didn't make any move toward the stairs.

"You can't just eat a sandwich and drink beer in front of a football game. Come on. You'll make it a lot more fun. The woman hosting it is kind of...high-strung."

"And you're going to spring an uninvited guest on her?"

"She's very religious, so she'll welcome anyone. But not too in-your-face religious. Don't worry." I laughed.

"I don't think..."

"And there's only one man. You'll be doing me a favor. And the others. Balance matters."

He laughed. "Does it?"

"Yes."

"I don't know. I don't have anything to bring. I don't like being a mooch."

I held out the shopping bag. "Here. She wanted supplies for martinis. Carry this. And you won't look like a mooch."

He looked into the bag. "I could grab a bottle of vodka."

I thought of my potatoes and carrots in the lobby. "Okay. But I need to get down and babysit my other food." My phone buzzed in my jacket pocket. "My Uber's here. Come on, it'll be fun. Martinis. Turkey. Pie. Getting to know your neighbor."

"Okay. Why not. Share the Uber?"

"Yes. I'll meet you down there." With my free hand, I messaged the driver and started down the stairs.

I heard Kent's door open and close. Before I reached the last flight, his footsteps were thudding above me, the crunching and straining of the shopping bag filled with olives and bottles of liquor accompanied each fall of his feet.

I pacified the Uber driver, loaded my food into a box he'd conveniently provided in the trunk, and climbed in. A moment later, Kent was beside me. The thickness and denseness of him consumed the Prius. His knees pressed against the passenger seat back and his shaved head was close to the sloped roof.

"This is mixing it up," he said.

"You won't regret it. And don't worry about missing football, I'm sure she'll turn it on."

"It's not a requirement for the day. I'm more of a hockey and baseball fan."

I nodded. I had nothing to say about either one. I had only a vague idea of baseball teams and games and knew next-to-nothing about hockey. I explained my job and what we did for our clients during the short drive to Stephanie's.

Outside her apartment, we unloaded the food onto the curb. The driver took pity on us and let us have his box, assuring us it was easy to replace. And besides, the cardboard had absorbed the aroma of uncooked shrimp, so it was probably for the best.

The box was there so passengers could place their shopping bags inside to prevent them from tipping over.

They wouldn't want a new pair of jeans smelling like shrimp.

We carried the food to the door and rang the buzzer.

"Stephanie's voice came through the intercom crisp and suspicious."

"Who is it?"

"Hi. It's Alex. And I have a surprise."

"Alex?"

"Yes. Happy Turkey Day," I said.

"You're too early."

"I know, but I figured you're already cooking the turkey. And I have to mash the potatoes."

"I already allowed time for that. It doesn't take two and a half hours to whip potatoes."

"Well, here I am."

I heard a sigh, then silence.

"Helloooo? Are you there? It's cold out here."

"Why did you come so early? I'm not dressed. I'm not expecting you."

"I'll keep an eye on your turkey while you get ready."

"I told you to come at noon."

"Stephanie, I have all this food, and it's getting heavy. It needs to go in the fridge."

There was a long silence. Finally, the buzzer hummed and the door unlatched. Kent grabbed it, and we stepped into the foyer.

"I think she's going to be pissed when she sees a strange guy."

"She'll be fine. Trust me."

"She already sounds annoyed."

"She'll get over it. The whole point of Thanksgiving is getting together with people you don't know. The original

Thanksgiving, right?"

He shrugged.

We climbed the stairs, laboring under the weight of glass and ceramic and two pounds of boiled potatoes. I pressed the bell for her apartment and waited. Just as I'd hoped, a woman who wasn't Stephanie, who was young enough to be her daughter, and most importantly, who I recognized from the photographs in Jim's study, opened the door.

"Hi, I'm Alex."

"I know." She smirked. Her mother must have let loose her complaints about me. With my early arrival, it was probably justified, but I hoped she didn't believe everything her mother told her.

"This is Kent."

She stepped back and made space for us to enter. "I'm Stephanie's daughter. Eileen."

We exchanged pleasantries while she led the way to the kitchen. We unloaded the stuff from our sore arms onto the counter near the fridge. I opened it and rearranged the food to make room for my things.

Kent took the bottles of alcohol and olives and the shaker out of the paper bag. He folded the bag in half.

Eileen still stood in the doorway. She eyed the vodka and Kent. "This dinner is going to be more interesting than my mother led me to believe."

I smiled. "Do you have martini glasses?"

"Not that I know of."

"I'll run out and get some cheap ones," Kent said.

"Is anything open?"

"Liquor stores. Some of them have glasses."

He left Eileen and me standing in the kitchen. Half the

reason I'd invited him was to distract Stephanie while I tried to pry my way into Eileen's life, but I heard the shower running. Kent would be gone for twenty minutes or so. There was plenty of time to make a new friend.

28

"Do you want coffee?"

"Sure."

Eileen pulled the carafe out of the coffee maker. The aroma of hours-old coffee assaulted me. She filled a mug and handed it to me. "Cream or sugar?"

"No thanks."

She poured a glass of water, and we went into the living room. My mind raced, trying to figure out how I could quickly get her talking about the things I wanted to know. A virtual clock ticked at the back of my head. "I've heard a lot about you."

She laughed.

I smiled. "All good, of course." I took a sip of coffee, gritting my teeth to keep my lips from twisting at the sour taste.

"I doubt that," Eileen said.

"Why?"

"My mother isn't thrilled with my career choice and...I'm sure she complains about all of my *choices*."

I shrugged. "Some." I waited half a second. "Maybe you

need to get your own place."

She grimaced. "I do."

"Where are you looking?"

"I'm not, yet. Still trying to save up. Living on your own is expensive here."

"It is."

"Do you have a roommate?"

I shook my head.

"I'm just getting started with my modeling career. I've had some good jobs, but I have a long way to go. And I need a steadier income, obviously."

"Will your mother be upset when you move out?"

She took a sip of water. "Probably."

I waited.

She gazed at something above my head or behind me, I couldn't tell which. She put down her glass and ran her fingers through her silky hair. It was the kind of silkiness that came at a rather large salon price. A silkiness that looks natural and seems to speak to good genes, but can be bought as easily as a hair color you weren't born with.

"They say it's hard for mothers," I said. "When their daughters are hurt."

"So she has told you quite a lot about me."

"I guess that's normal for mothers — talking about their children."

"Is it?"

"Well…common."

We both laughed softly.

She gave me a grateful smile. "She didn't like the guy I was in love with." She paused, swallowing with a lot of effort. "She hated him, actually. And then…he was murdered." Her eyes welled up. "She hasn't been super sympathetic about it."

I gave her a very sympathetic expression. "That must have been terrible."

"It was. Is. It *is* terrible."

"What was he like?"

She picked up her glass and held it close to her chest. "We were broken up when he was killed, so I…it seems like I should be getting over him, but not yet. Him dying was such a shock, and…it almost made it harder."

"You still hoped you'd get back together?"

"We were engaged. I thought that…"

"It sounds so upsetting…so…*hard*. Did he live in New York?" The question was weird and abrupt, but she didn't seem to notice. People usually don't. As long as you don't slip into a full-on interrogation, they'll answer questions. People love answering questions. Most of the time.

"He had an apartment in Manhattan. And a gorgeous house about an hour outside of the city."

"Did you go there a lot?"

"I practically lived there." She crossed her legs, adjusting her leggings so the seam was straight down the inside of her calf.

"I love looking at houses. I'm always thinking about the kind of house I want someday."

She gave me a confused look.

I rushed forward, talking too much and too fast. "Maybe because I live in an apartment. And most of the time since college, I've been in apartments. So I always feel cramped." I thought about Sean's house. Even though the house was large and open and filled with beautiful furniture and art, I'd felt cramped there as well. Hemmed into my bedroom if I wanted any time alone.

Maybe that was why I thought constantly about having an enormous house of my own someday. I hate being hemmed in.

"I've always lived in apartments too. Jim's house was incredible. The gardens were gorgeous. The house was so big he had a staff. It was almost embarrassing."

"Having so much space?"

"No. Having people do stuff for you all the time, appearing out of nowhere and waiting on you, doing things you could do yourself. I never felt comfortable with that. I think you have to grow up with it."

"Were they nice?"

She laughed. "Why would you ask that?"

The sound of running water came to a stop. I had only a few more minutes alone with Eileen, and only a few more minutes before Stephanie found out about the extra place she'd need to squeeze in at her table. It was apparent she'd taken a lot of time to set up and arrange that table which was forcing its way into the living room like something that wanted to make sure this was all about togetherness and food. She was not going to be happy. "Just wondered. I was curious whether you become friends with a household staff, or if it always feels like strangers are watching you."

She took a sip of water. She glanced toward the table, as if she'd felt the intensity of my gaze there. She turned back. "That's a good question. It was sort of a mixed bag."

The bathroom fan shut off.

"I was thinking...I don't know a lot of people in New York," I said. "Would you want to meet up for a drink sometime?"

"Sure." She looked eager. Watching her face, I remembered Carmen and the intense, eager start of our childhood friendship.

"I have business cards in my bag. Show me which room is yours, and I'll leave one in there later."

She nodded. She seemed to get, and agree with, the unspoken suggestion that I didn't want Stephanie to know I'd be hanging out with her daughter.

She stood and finished the glass of water. As the bathroom door opened, Eileen crossed the living room quickly, edging around the table to get into the kitchen.

Stephanie came out of the bathroom, shot me an angry look, and disappeared into one of the bedrooms. I reached into the bowl on the occasional table beside me. I picked up two salted cashews and ate them.

As far as I was concerned, the rest of the day would be gravy. I had what I wanted, and I was quite grateful.

29

It wasn't until the turkey was carved and the platter passed around, the various side dishes scooped onto her guests' plates, that Stephanie felt a shimmer of gratitude. Or happiness, for that matter. It wasn't until they were all eating that she felt any peace of mind at all.

Once again, Alexandra had turned the tables on her. Stephanie couldn't believe how easily that woman got the upper hand and wielded it like a machete.

Starting with her arrival *hours* before she'd been invited, she'd shoved her way into the apartment as well as into a conversation with Eileen. She'd dragged a man she hardly knew herself, and who certainly had nothing in common with their workgroup, into the middle of Thanksgiving Dinner. In every way possible, Alexandra had managed to take control of the day. She'd upset every plan Stephanie had made and totally disrupted the flow.

Fortunately, there'd been enough food.

By the time everyone was eating, Stephanie had consumed two glasses of wine. She felt it humming deep inside her head. Blood thumped in her cheeks as if it were pooling along her cheekbones, and she had no doubt two red spots were blooming there. Of course, no one was looking at her, so it didn't matter.

It wasn't surprising that people loved alcohol. The reason she was feeling calmer now was solely the result of the wine, not because of any equilibrium on her part, or any Divine assistance in calming her upset.

Until this moment, her mind had spun furiously among each of Alex's many transgressions.

At first, Stephanie had assumed the early arrival was designed to unsettle her, to catch her flustered and unprepared and to keep her from pulling off a smooth and successful dinner. But when she'd stood in the bathroom, listening to the murmurs coming from Alex and Eileen, she hadn't been so sure.

When Stephanie and Alex had exchanged emails about the menu, Alex had asked whether Eileen would be there. She'd been told no. Did she come early so she could be sure of meeting Eileen? But why would she do that? What was she after? It was doubtful she was just being friendly. Alex wasn't a naturally friendly person. She was outgoing, sure. And she often made the first move in conversation, but she wasn't genuine. So what did she want with Eileen?

The last person Eileen needed in her life was someone like Alex. Eileen needed to get the modeling thing out of her system, and slowly, with her mother's help, make her way back to God, back to having friends with solid values, back to being involved in church where she could meet a decent man who didn't value money and sex above all the things that actually mattered.

Eileen did not need to be going out for a *drink* with

anyone, especially Alexandra Mallory. Alexandra was too old for Eileen, a different generation almost. Eileen did not need the influence of someone who appeared to lack any moral code whatsoever.

And then there was the uninvited guest. Alex had tried to put Stephanie on the spot, to make her feel guilty for failing to welcome him with open arms. The guy was nice enough. She didn't care for the tattoos or the aggressive muscles, or the shaved head for that matter. But he was polite. He'd helped her lift the twenty-pound turkey out of the oven. He'd refilled her wine glass without her having to ask.

Trystan would never do that. He understood that she drank very little alcohol. As she'd predicted, he was pleased she'd tasted his wine. He'd explained, bragged really, how he'd gone to a special shop and had an expert recommend the four wines he brought to the dinner. Far too much wine, although with the uninvited guest, it had turned out well.

Every time she looked up from her plate, the guest…Ken? No, Kent…was staring at Diana. He was almost salivating over the gorgeous black woman seated at the opposite side of the table, her hair like she usually wore it in a thick braid that formed a sort of crown around her head. She had on a sleeveless pale yellow top with lots of folds in the fabric, skinny black jeans, and black high heels. With very little adjustment to her clothing and an extra touch of makeup, she was able to look utterly festive and glamorous for the holiday.

Stephanie had spent an entire evening in front of her closet mirror trying to figure out how she should fix her hair and what outfit would make her look dressed up without suggesting she was trying too hard. But too hard for what? It was an age thing. In your thirties, you could casually throw on whatever you felt like and look fantastic and perfectly appropriate even when you were technically over- or under-dressed. In your mid-forties, the options were fewer.

Stephanie cut a piece of turkey, dragged it through a puddle of gravy, and placed it into her mouth. The salt and fat and the flavor of unpretentious meat settled her mouth after the bite of red wine. She picked up her wineglass and took a small sip. She needed to slow down with the wine. Ahead of time, she'd planned maybe two glasses, and now she knew she would be wanting a third before the dinner was even half finished.

Voices swelled and faded around her, everyone seeming to talk at once. Were they, or did the wine make each voice seem louder, more insistent, layered on top of each other?

Trystan was talking about plans for his winter ski holiday in the Swiss Alps. The others were recounting their experiences with skiing, wishing it was a sport they'd participated in more than any of them had. Kent interrupted to ask whether Trystan had tried snowboarding. He hadn't. Diana talked about how she'd skied a lot in high school, but once she moved to New York, it fell off her radar. Alex said she'd tried it once and wasn't opposed to trying it again, but she would need lessons.

The sounds rushed past like a freeway of words. Stephanie was stalled at the end of the onramp, unable to merge into the flow, afraid of being run over or her car slammed and spun around by the rapid movement of so many voices and words. So many words. They almost became senseless. Besides, she'd never been skiing. There wasn't much to say.

30

With every single part of the meal, Stephanie had tried to convince me I should have a martini.

For some reason, I didn't feel like it. There hadn't been a cocktail hour before dinner, just a general scrambling around to put out food and fill wine glasses. People ate the bacon-wrapped shrimp and tasted the French wine Trystan had opened the minute he arrived, but everything was somewhat haphazard.

That, plus the crowded room and the maneuvering required to get around the table and into the kitchen wasn't the kind of setting that made me think longingly of a drink that's filled to the rim of the glass.

By the time I'd gorged on turkey and stuffing, mashed potatoes and sweet potatoes, soft, comfy vegetables, and pumpkin pie with foamy whipped cream, a martini sounded entirely uninteresting.

I'd had several glasses of wine, so I wasn't sure why I was explaining my lack of interest to myself. There was no need for an explanation. I wanted to go outside and feel cold air against my swollen, over-heated skin, maybe smoke a cigarette, more than I wanted a martini.

It was possible Stephanie had killed my desire with her constant pestering. It seemed as if she knew only one thing about me — that I liked martinis. And she was convinced I couldn't enjoy Thanksgiving dinner without one. As if that was all I ever drank, as if I couldn't manage without. She seemed overly disappointed when I refused.

The table was filled with orange- and white-smeared plates, half-empty coffee cups, and wine glasses.

Stephanie suggested we settle in the living room. She went to the kitchen and returned carrying a tray stocked with bottles of flavored sparkling water. She offered a choice to Diana and took one for herself.

"Now. Who wants a martini?"

No one spoke.

"Alex?"

"No thanks."

"Why not? You love them!"

"I'm fine, thanks."

"You'll have one if others do. Trystan, doesn't a martini sound nice?"

"No thank you. I'll have a bit more wine I think." He stood and started toward the kitchen. He paused in front of me, caught my eye, and took the glass I held up to him.

"What about you, Trent? I mean Kent." Stephanie giggled as if this mistake was the funniest thing she'd heard all afternoon. Her face was pink from the stuffy apartment and more wine than she was obviously used to.

"Another cup of coffee, if you have it."

"Of course I have it. But this is a party. Coffee isn't any fun."

Kent smiled at her and replied as if he were speaking to a child. "Coffee sounds good. Thanks."

Stephanie whirled around in an attempt to turn toward me. She lost her balance and grabbed onto Trystan's sleeve as he passed by. He stumbled. The glasses he was holding by their stems in his left hand rattled against each other.

"Oops." Stephanie giggled.

Kent looked at me, a slight pleading in his eyes. It seemed he was done hanging out with my co-workers. Done with five people in a living room that was adequate for three.

Trystan returned and handed my glass to me. He perched on the arm of the couch.

I raised my voice over the others. "Should we watch football?"

"No," Stephanie said. "The holiday is not about football. It's such a shame people would rather watch bulky men wrestle and toss around a ball instead of interacting with each other."

"It's tradition," I said.

She shook her head. "It's not tradition. It's an escape." She smiled. "If you show me how they're made, I can fix a martini for you."

"I don't want one."

"But you love martinis."

"I do. But I'm not in the mood."

She laughed, the tone shrill and borderline hysterical. "How can you not be in the *mood*?"

I took a sip of wine.

"Your friend even bought martini glasses. Just for you…"

"That wasn't necessary."

"…because you love martinis. I feel like you're being a little bit rude. I planned them for you."

I was not going to argue with her about something so ridiculous. What was her problem? She was acting as if the success of her dinner rested on my topping it off with a martini.

Stephanie stomped her foot. "Alexandra. You're really upsetting me."

Everyone stopped talking and looked at Stephanie. Trystan put down his wine glass. A look of concern, or possibly shock at her childishness creased the edges of his mouth.

"I'm not doing anything," I said. "Why are you so upset because I don't feel like having a drink? The wine is delicious. I'm perfectly happy."

"Because I'm trying to honor your wishes."

"It wasn't my wish at all. Just because I like something doesn't mean I need to have it every day. Let it go."

"I bought glasses." Now her voice wavered on the edge of tears.

"Kent bought the glasses," I said.

"I meant I'll reimburse him of course!"

"Give it a rest," Diana said. "This is getting boring."

It wasn't just getting boring. It had been boring all along. What I really wanted was to get out of there for good. I took another sip of wine. What I wanted was a martini on the roof of my apartment building. Leaving behind the smell of gravy and sweet potatoes, the warm moist air filled with too many bodies too close to each other, the aroma of turkey fat resting over all of it.

Before the sun went down, I wanted to be drinking a martini on the roof with Kent. I could find out his perspective on my neighbors and breathe some freshly circulating air. I could ask him about the previous occupant of my apartment. With a drink in his hand, he might be more forthcoming. And I could relax without Stephanie breathing down my neck, elevating drinking a martini to a religious ritual.

I took a long swallow of wine and put my glass on the end of the dining room table. "Do you need help getting things pulled together? I'll get some of these glasses washed, and the guys can put your table back to its normal size."

Tears bubbled out of Stephanie's eyes. "You're trying to ruin my Thanksgiving. I don't understand why you're being so hateful."

Trystan moved across the room, stepping over Diana's legs that were stretched out in front of her as she nestled into the couch, watching everyone, looking as if she felt equally trapped in the small apartment, searching for the first opportunity to leave without being labeled rude.

"Dinner was great, Stephanie." Trystan put his hand on her shoulder. "Thanks for suggesting this. And for all your work."

"All I did was cook a turkey."

"That's a lot. And you made the table look festive...the, uh...the green beans..."

Stephanie sniffed.

"I think Alex made a good suggestion," he said. "Let's help you get this cleaned up."

"No." Stephanie's voice was harsh, rough. "Everyone sit down. We can watch football if you want. I have some potato chips. And I'll make dip."

"No one wants any more food," Diana said. She laughed. "I don't need any food until tomorrow. Saturday would be even better." She sipped her sparkling water.

Stephanie marched across the room to the TV, staggering, then making her movements more forceful to cover up the wobble. Diana looked at me and shook her head gently. I wasn't sure whether the expression on her face was one of sadness or disgust. Maybe only pity.

Stephanie grabbed the remote from its place on the stand and powered on the TV. She clicked through the channels until she found a game. She moved to the side and handed the remote to Trystan.

She clapped her hands once. "Now. Who wants a martini?"

31

After handing the remote to Trystan, who held it as if she'd given him something she'd retrieved from the sludge running along a gutter, Stephanie made her way back to the armchair beside the TV. She gripped the back to steady herself and flopped down. She was honestly surprised she'd made it.

She could no longer recall how many glasses of wine she'd consumed. She closed her eyes, but that made her brain feel as if it were spinning inside her skull. She opened them quickly and tried to focus her gaze on the wall above the people seated across from her.

Being tipsy, drunk even, was disgusting. She was so ashamed, but it was too late now. There was no way to remove the alcohol from her bloodstream. It had to find its own way out. A large part of her wanted them to leave. They were all behaving badly, but she couldn't let them walk out. Not before she found a way to provoke Alex.

She tried to think what they'd done to upset her so much. Maybe it was just Alex. That had started it. But the others had joined in. She felt them staring at her, Trystan looking concerned or sympathetic or shocked or...she couldn't tell what it was, but his face looked funny. Different. And that guy from Alex's apartment building. She'd welcomed him into her home, and he'd repaid her by pouring too much wine into her glass and otherwise spending the entire meal staring at Diana with a look of unfiltered lust. He ate and drank her food and did little to help prompt a worthwhile conversation.

In fact, none of them had been very good conversationalists. Their so-called dinner table conversation had consisted of casual chit-chat about weather and work and sports. There was nothing meaningful. None of them had asked anything about Stephanie's life. They hadn't even mentioned the murder of one of their clients. That at least would have made her feel better, reflecting on how good God had been to remove him from her daughter's life.

She'd always thought her colleagues were more interesting than this. What was wrong with them? It was probably the addition of a stranger into their tight-knit workgroup. Alex's fault. Again.

The annoying voices of the football commentators hammered at her left ear. Her guests sat in silence, staring at the screen, sipping their drinks. She'd known this would happen if they turned on a game. It always happened. People sank into a fog of mindless preoccupation. No one really cared that much. They were simply numbing themselves. No one even bothered to discuss the action on the field.

This was what Thanksgiving had become across the entire country, and it was unbearably sad. How had football edged God out of the picture? Tears welled up in her eyes. She allowed her lids to close for a moment, despite the spinning in her head. She could not let tears drip out of her eyes in front of them. Not that they'd notice, with their eyeballs glued to the screen.

She thrust herself out of the chair and lunged across the room. She grabbed the remote where it lay on a table beside Trystan. She fumbled it like a wobbly football and dropped it.

Trystan put his hand on her hip. "Careful there, Steph."

She wrenched away from him. "Don't touch me."

"Sorry. I…"

"There's no *sorry*. Do not touch me. Ever." She bent down and picked up the remote. She pointed it at the TV and pressed the power button. The screen went black, the voices and shouting fans died instantly. A glass thudded on a coaster. Someone coughed.

"It's Thanksgiving," she said. "Football is a national disgrace. Violent and meaningless. The opiate of the masses." She turned to face them. She held the remote against her breastbone like she was positioning a mic in preparation for speaking to a large crowd. "When I was a little girl, we went around the table and said what we were thankful for. I gave thanks during our prayer today, but I haven't heard about your blessings."

"Dinner's over," Alex said.

"We were remiss. You go first. What are you thankful for, Alexandra?" She stretched out the name as far as her tongue would allow. Alexandra seemed to prefer the male version of her name. There was some hidden meaning in that, Stephanie was sure of it. "You're certainly not thankful for martinis."

"God," Diana said. "Enough about the martinis."

"I tried to do something nice for her, to make her feel at home, and she was completely ungrateful. So, Alexandra, tell us what you *are* thankful for. Your job? Your health? Having a group of people that welcomed you to New York?" She gestured toward Diana and Trystan. "Let us know, instead of acting like you're entitled to all the blessings in your life."

Alex smiled. "It sounds like you have it covered, so I'm done."

"I want you to say it."

"I'm not religious."

"You can still show gratitude. God is sending blessings into your life whether you acknowledge Him or not."

Trystan stood.

From the corner of her eye, or maybe just by instinct, she felt him move toward her.

"Maybe you're grateful that I allowed you to show up three hours early, sabotaging my plans to get ready for the day. Or maybe you're grateful that…that…" The room tilted slightly. Her stomach felt uneasy. She pressed the remote hard against her bone as if trying to bruise herself, hoping the discomfort would take her mind off whatever was going on along the length of her intestines. "I know! You're grateful that my daughter was so kind to you. She acted like your friend, even though you're much too old for her." She laughed. The sound of it was unpleasant. It had a cackling quality, but that was okay. It was a full belly laugh. Laughter was good for the soul. "Much too old."

Alex laughed. She put her wineglass to her lips. She stuck out the tip of her tongue and ran it along the edge of the glass like a moth that drank through a straw-like proboscis instead of a human tongue.

"I'm grateful for an excellent team," Trystan said. "You…" He moved around so he was facing Stephanie, his arms stiff at his sides, clearly wanting to grab her and place one of his hands over her mouth to shut her up.

He turned. "…Diana. Alex."

Kent nodded wisely as if he'd had a hand in choosing the team.

"What are you nodding at?" Stephanie said. "We're complete strangers to you."

"Why don't we go into the kitchen and get some of the dishes cleaned up?" Trystan jerked his head toward the table as if he expected her to follow like the little lap dog he wanted her to be.

"I prefer to spend time with my guests. It's rude to abandon your guests and start cleaning. Your guests feel like they need to help."

"We're happy to help," Trystan said. "It's a joint effort. No one expects you to do all the work."

"Is that right?" She laughed, cackled, again.

"Come on, Steph. Let us help. I'll make coffee," he said.

"I already made coffee. And stop calling me that."

"A fresh pot. Doesn't a fresh cup of coffee sound good?"

"Why do you think I need coffee?"

"I don't think you need it. I'm just suggesting we should relax, have a bit of coffee, help you clean up, and then get going."

"The day isn't over."

"It was a terrific meal," Diana said. "We had a really good time, but we're all tired."

"I'm not tired," Stephanie said. She could not allow this to end. It was all wrong. Backwards. She was the one who'd had too much to drink, and Alex was sitting there smug and in control, gloating over Stephanie's lack of decorum. It was humiliating, but she couldn't stop herself. She was so angry. All this anger, burning inside her, whipping her tongue to life so that it spat out things she hadn't realized were even inside of her.

Diana stood. She moved across the room and positioned herself beside Stephanie. "Let us help you."

"I don't need help."

"I think you need more help than you realize," Alex said. "You aren't used to having so much wine. You'll feel better if you move around and…"

"I don't need your advice!" Stephanie's voice rose. This was wrong. Alex was supposed to get drunk, she was supposed to expose her rotten core to Trystan. He was supposed to reconsider his decision to hire her.

Alex's voice was sharp. "Stephanie. Calm down. You're drunk."

She could have handled that. She really could have, somewhere, beneath the alcohol, the Spirit of God was still making His home in her heart. He forgave her, even though it hadn't been her fault. But He forgave her for saying things that weren't nice. Although was that true? She wasn't sure because she could no longer remember what she'd said. She felt hot and sweaty and sick to her stomach. She wanted to cry over her spoiled Thanksgiving dinner, and over her failure to put Alexandra in her place. Why wouldn't God help her with that? Surely he hated Alexandra equally.

Stephanie could have handled Alexandra's condescending words…the ugly, unfair accusation…if the next thing hadn't happened — Alexandra giggled.

As if she'd been planning it all along, calculating velocity and distance and calibrating her aim, Stephanie threw the remote directly at Alex's smug little face.

She missed. Which made her even more furious, although

it was probably a good thing she'd missed.

The remote hit Kent instead. It glanced off his brow where it left a dark red mark. He lunged to his feet. He looked like a gangster — all those tattoos, that shaved head. She trembled, afraid of what he might do. He looked very angry. He started toward her.

She backed up, stumbled, and crashed into Trystan. He grabbed her waist, preventing her from falling. It didn't matter, even if he was trying to be nice. He had not been nice. He hadn't given her the job she deserved, the job she'd earned. He'd succumbed to the dripping sexuality that came off that woman, and he was on his way to destroying their company with his carnal choice. Stephanie struggled out of his grip and turned to face him.

The look of disgust smeared across his face was clear to her now. She raised her hand, knowing what she was going to do, knowing she shouldn't, but not caring, because it was all she wanted.

She smacked his face. Twice.

32

No one spoke after Stephanie slapped Trystan. The sound of bone hitting flesh echoed in the small space. Diana took Stephanie's wrist and wrapped her arm around her waist. She led her out of the living room. The silence continued, then broke as the bathroom door closed with a loud click. A moment later, the vacuum of sound was filled by the echo of Stephanie's esophagus spasming and vomit splashing into the toilet water.

A moment later, Trystan and Kent went to the table. Trystan eased his way around it and into the kitchen. He turned on the water in the sink. Kent removed the floating candle centerpiece, placing it on one of the end tables. He rolled the tablecloth like a burrito, the soiled napkins inside.

I dug a business card out of my bag and slipped out of the room. I opened the door leading to Eileen's bedroom. I placed my card beneath her pillow.

After that, I helped Trystan and Kent clean up the dishes and cut the turkey off the bone. We stored the meat in plastic bags — enough turkey for Stephanie and her daughter to feed themselves for a week. I wiped down the counters, and Kent and I removed the extension pieces from the table, leaning them against the kitchen wall.

By this time, Diana had returned, informing us that Stephanie was lying down.

We took the remains of the food we'd brought and stepped out of her apartment as a group.

Diana turned the button lock and closed the door. "I hope she'll be okay without the deadbolt."

"She's fine," I said.

"Well, not fine." She laughed, then looked slightly guilty.

"I meant it's safe. It's daytime. And her daughter will be back this evening."

Diana nodded. Downstairs, we said good-bye. Trystan crossed the street and began walking toward the building about fifty yards down the block where his car was parked. Diana ordered an Uber, and Kent and I ordered our own.

Neither of us said anything until we'd settled into the back seat, dishes stacked around our feet. "That was different," he said.

"Probably more traditional than football."

He laughed. "She only had four or five glasses of wine."

"She doesn't drink much," I said.

"Maybe she'll give her martini glasses to you."

"Not interested."

"You don't want cheap glasses from a liquor store?"

"Nope."

The car sped along relatively empty streets. "I could go for a martini after all," I said. "In a nice glass. How about an early nightcap? On the roof?"

"Sounds like a good way to wrap up the day."

While I put away the dishes of leftover food, Kent went

into his apartment and returned with a pitcher of ice. We took the bag of alcohol up to the roof and mixed our drinks up there since it was easier to carry the bottles and olives up there than it was to maneuver a glass of swaying liquid up several flights of stairs.

As we raised our glasses filled with glistening vodka and vermouth toward the sky and each other, the sun was sinking, disappearing behind the skyscrapers. "I'm thankful to be out of there," Kent said.

"I'm grateful as well."

We laughed in unison and sipped our drinks. The sun disappeared, and the sky turned a dark, rich blue. It was cold, but we were wrapped in scarves and thick coats.

I lit a cigarette. Kent declined. I inhaled and blew out the smoke, slowly and languidly. The heat and claustrophobia of the day eased out of me, and my thoughts drifted toward Eileen, wondering how many secrets I might extract from her over several drinks.

"That cast of characters must make your job a minefield," Kent said.

"Not really."

"Stephanie is seriously unbalanced."

"Just too much wine, I think."

"It's more than that. There's a lot of repressed something going on in that woman."

"True. But that doesn't make her unbalanced."

"It wouldn't take much."

The sky darkened. We sipped our drinks and let our gazes move away from each other, toward the barren trees in pots placed at perfect intervals around the roof garden. Concrete planters with withered stems and dead blossoms and missing leaves looked as if they just wanted to be rid of their contents, stripped clean for winter. Our attention moved up and rested on the sky where a few stars revealed themselves.

"How are you liking New York?"

"It's great," I said. "I like the energy."

"Everyone does. If they don't connect to that feeling, they hate living here and can't wait to escape."

I put the cigarette to my lips and drew smoke into my mouth. "So where did the former occupant of my apartment escape to?"

"Back home."

"He didn't feel the energy?"

He shrugged.

"Where's home?"

"Ohio, I think."

"What made him leave? You said he loved the apartment."

"I think I told you, I'm not sure of the details."

I laughed. "It sounds like you do know details, you just don't want to say what they are. If it's a secret, I'm good at keeping them."

"I don't know if it's that..."

"So there are details you're not saying. Don't you think I have a right to know if there's an issue with my apartment?"

"There's no issue. It's a good apartment."

"Not that good, if he rushed out of here carrying secret grudges."

"I didn't say it was a grudge."

"It was the first thing that came to mind." I inhaled again and held the smoke for a moment before letting it slip through my lips like a secret making its way into the open air. "I'm not going to tell anyone. And obviously he's not coming back." I pulled the stir stick out of the liquid and ate two olives, one after the other.

"Excellent olives," Kent said.

"That's not a very adept way of changing the subject."

"Large, meaty olives are key, otherwise they're just decoration. Peanut-sized olives add nothing to the experience."

"I agree. But maybe it's just the supersizing of everything. In old movies, the olives were tiny, and the glasses were smaller."

"A nation of alcoholics," he said.

"That's a dark view."

"Maybe."

"So if there's nothing wrong with the apartment, and there doesn't appear to be, and you don't want to tell me why Nick left, which means it wasn't anything to do with his job or personal life, I can only conclude the reason was you or one of the other neighbors."

"You can conclude whatever you'd like."

"Was there trouble with Victoria and Rafe?"

"That's a leap."

"Is it? They're troublemakers."

He pulled one of the olives off his swizzle stick and studied it, avoiding looking at me. "And you're not?"

"And *you're* not?" I said.

"I'm usually chill."

"So am I."

He laughed.

I ate my last olive, regretting that I'd rushed it, but longing for salt to counter the alcohol.

He was still smiling, his face dark even in the faint glow

from the lights around the planters. His teeth gleamed, polished clean by vodka and vermouth.

"Did Victoria hit on him, and Rafe got pissed?"

"Something like that." He took a sip of his drink.

"Well, what's the big secret."

"I think I'll have one of those." He picked up the cigarette box. He pulled out a cigarette and fired up the lighter. "It's not my place to talk shit about the people who share your wall."

"Is there shit to talk?"

He inhaled and said nothing.

"Should I be concerned?"

"You already are, so what do I have to add to it?"

He was right, but it didn't satisfy my curiosity. His refusal to say made me think I'd been right to think it was some weird kind of sex game between Victoria and Rafe. The way Rafe came onto me and then didn't, the way Victoria seemed unmoved by the things he said to me, and even occasionally encouraged him.

I wanted nothing to do with it. But I was still burning to know. I wondered whether another martini would get Kent talking.

33

Portland

Making friends requires revealing facts about your life, letting others peak inside your world, giving them access to your very mind. From what I've observed throughout my life, friends, and lovers become entwined with each other by slowly pulling back each successive curtain, first revealing preferences in taste and their casual thoughts about the world. Then they open the next series of drapes to expose unpleasant memories and situations that have damaged them and made them hide parts of themselves from the world. From there, they go deeper, tunneling into the very depths of their souls.

For many, this is a painful process. They fear their private thoughts and weaknesses will be used to inflict even more pain. For me, it's something else entirely — I don't want anyone to think they know who I am. I don't want them to have power over my life. I don't want them to find out things that might send me packing off to prison for the rest of my time on this earth.

I don't have wounds per se. Not like other people, those who are embroiled in and driven by feelings of love and hatred, confidence and shame, sentiment and regret. I have no problem telling a new acquaintance selected pieces of my life, just to be friendly, to exchange information, as long as those revelations don't touch on something that might put me at risk.

Of course, you can fabricate the stories of your past and people will feel you've become friends. You can say whatever you please and no one will ever even wonder whether it's the truth or not, as long as you don't get too dramatic about it.

I unreel a certain amount of fiction to keep people in my life without putting myself at risk.

For the most part, I don't go out of my way to make friends, but people seem to want to become friends with me. It's a natural thing, I suppose — human beings seeking each other out, interested by the new and the novel. I certainly fit the latter category.

That's how it was with Carmen. She was so infatuated with me and my life, it sometimes seemed that she wanted to move into my house with me. Of course, she didn't know what my house was really like. From her perspective, it simply looked interesting and very different from her own home.

She'd hardly spoken five words to my father. She didn't know the punishment that came with holding unacceptable views on god and the nature of the world. She talked willingly to my mother, never having to worry about the consequences of saying something displeasing, never considering that her words might cause trouble, free to speak whatever passed through her mind, walking out the door at dinner time.

I wasn't sure if Carmen was drawn to me alone, or if she

liked that I had siblings, or that she simply liked my family because we were different from hers. She was interested in our rules. She was intrigued by our religion that was more complicated than her own. An only child, she was fascinated with the idea of other children occupying a house together, children who shared the same parents and every moment of their lives.

As she'd promised, she showed up at my house with a few additional toys to enhance what I had to offer. The first was the game of Operation, which she found thrilling and I found tedious. I had a steady hand which made removing tiny bits of plastic from narrow slots an easy task. I hardly ever touched the tweezers to the metal edges of the slot that buzzed and meant you lost your turn. Carmen's hand trembled with the pressure of the delicate extraction. She was constantly yielding her turn to me. For her, the game held her interest as she had to work so hard to keep up with me.

I grew tired of winning, but every day it was the first box she wanted to pull off the shelf.

Next, she brought a Gameboy. She said I wouldn't be allowed to have it overnight. It was too expensive. It had to be kept safely at her house. This game was more fun, but only one person could play at a time. She was eager to share it with me, then she began complaining that I was ignoring her.

After we'd been playing together every day for nearly two months, she showed up at my front door on a Saturday morning carrying a black leather case with protective metal covers on each corner. It was the kind of suitcase women used in the nineteen-fifties and sixties to carry their cosmetics when they traveled. Two clasps held the lid down, and a padded handle was tucked into a cutout space on the top of the lid. When the clasps were undone, the top lifted up to reveal a mirror. Inside the case itself was a tray. Makeup could be stored in the tray and in the space below.

Carmen wouldn't let me touch it until we were settled in the attic with the door closed.

She sat with her legs angled out and the case pressed against her inner thighs. She gripped the handle with both hands, making sure I couldn't sneak up on it and open it before she was ready.

I scooted closer to her feet. "What's inside?"

"Do you want to be a beautiful lady?"

"I never thought about it," I said.

"Every little girl thinks about it."

"How do you know what every girl thinks about?"

"My mother told me."

"How does she know?"

Carmen glared at me, her eyes glassy, the whites showing around the iris, the anger at my stupidity clear.

"She doesn't know what I think about," I said.

"All girls think the same. They all want to be pretty. They want boys to think they're pretty."

I waited to hear more. I wondered whether Carmen was so dumb she believed her mother could actually know what thoughts were swirling around inside of someone else's skull, silent and completely hidden from the world. Unless Carmen, and every other girl on earth, told Mrs. Mitchell what they were thinking, she couldn't possibly know. Therefore, she was lying to her daughter.

This made me slightly less interested in spending time with Carmen. She said things that surprised me. I liked playing games with her, I liked that she helped me spy on my brothers from the attic window, but I wasn't sure I wanted to hang around with someone who believed every word her mother said, someone who didn't think about what was true and what was simply made up by adults who wanted to be in charge of everything, including the inside of your head.

"There are lots of ways to make yourself prettier," she said.

"I think I look okay the way I am."

"You don't. You have to be alluring."

This was a word I'd never heard. "What does that mean?"

She sighed. "It means you have to make yourself look special so boys will pick you instead of other girls."

"Pick me for what?"

"For their girlfriend. Their wife."

"I don't want to be a girlfriend or a wife."

"Someday you will. We have to practice being adult women."

"I don't."

"Why are you arguing with me?"

"Because you sound like a robot. You're just saying what your mother says, and I don't think it's true."

"Don't argue. If you want to see what's inside the case, you have to stop arguing."

I made a face at her.

She seemed to take that as agreement. She unsnapped the first clasp. It sprang up with a loud click. She undid the second, still holding onto the handle with her free hand. "Are you ready?"

Before she lifted the lid, I couldn't have said what I expected, but it wasn't what I saw. Inside the top was a rectangular mirror surrounded by a ruffle of fabric. Below was a tray divided into sections. One section that formed about one-third of the tray was filled with gold tubes of lipstick. Shiny gold, and matte-finished gold. Some with filigree work where the cap joined the base of the tube. I'd seen lipsticks like these in department stores. My mother only owned two lipsticks. They came in plastic tubes, both filled with waxy missile-shaped sticks of pale pink.

As I gazed at the tubes of lip color, I realized I'd expected to see toy cosmetics, the hard plastic kind that enable girls to pretend they were applying makeup, or at the most, play lipstick with its garish shades of bubblegum pink and cherry red.

"Is this your mother's?"

"Yes."

"She lets you play with it?"

"She doesn't know I have it."

"She will when she sees it on your face."

"It won't be on my face." She plucked a tube of lipstick out of the row of gold cylinders and removed the cap. She twisted the base, and a magenta stick rose up like a flower growing in time-lapse photography. She extended her hand toward my face. "Open your mouth."

"I don't want any."

"You have to."

"No."

"You'll look so pretty."

"I don't want to."

"Color is necessary to enhance a girl's face."

"Is that what your mother says?"

She nodded.

"Then put it on your own face."

"I brought it for you."

"Show me what else you have."

She twisted the lipstick down and replaced the cap. The other large section of the top tray was filled with brushes of various sizes. The smaller sections contained hair clips, tiny plastic disks with clear lids exposing various shades of brown powder. Carmen pointed at the disks. "These are for your eyebrows."

I ran my fingertip along my eyebrow.

I'd seen women wearing lots of makeup. Not at my church or in my house, obviously, but on TV, some of my teachers and the mothers of other kids at my school.

I wouldn't tell Carmen, but I wanted to put the color on my face to see what it looked like. The idea of re-shaping my appearance, the thought of smoothing powder and cream across my skin like my face was a blank sheet of paper and I was creating a drawing seemed interesting. But if my parents saw a single streak of color on my face, there would be a punishment of some kind.

After showing me the rest of the contents of the case — creamy and powdery cheek color, bottles of liquid the color of her mother's skin, eyeshadows and mascara, she opened the magenta lipstick again. She touched the lipstick to her bottom lip and smeared it in a ribbon of color about half an inch wide. She smiled at me and returned the lipstick to the case. "Next time, we'll both make ourselves pretty. I'll bring cleaning pads. No one will know."

I was tempted. I wanted to see the colors on my face, but I didn't want Carmen touching me. I wanted to do it myself.

34

New York

Kent appeared to have more immunity to martinis than I do.
A second drink did not get him talking about our neighbors.
Every attempt I made to turn our conversation in their
direction was blocked by his stubborn interest in my co-
workers or stories from his past, his job, questions about my
past, my job.

It was clear from the tired look around his eyes that he was
getting impatient with my less-than-subtle effort to get him
talking about the neighbors. Despite the vodka flowing
through his veins, he wasn't going to discuss things that he'd
decided to keep to himself.

The more he refused to let the conversation turn naturally
toward our shared acquaintances, the more certain I was that
he was keeping back something I needed to know. The
former occupant of my apartment had an experience with
Victoria and Rafe that not only drove him out of the
building, it drove him out of New York City.

I couldn't imagine what it might be and I couldn't decide

whether I should be more concerned than I had been. Maybe viewing them as quirky people who simply wanted to insert themselves into my life had been a mistake. Maybe there was a lot more to it than that.

Kent was so determined to avoid saying anything about them, I began to wonder whether he was slightly afraid. I began to wonder whether I should be less cavalier in my view of them. They were very aggressive. They seemed to want something from me, and I'd brushed them off as a bit of harmless entertainment. Was I wrong?

Still, even if I was, I can take care of myself. What could they do to me? I couldn't imagine a situation where they would chase me out of New York. The only thing that would make that happen would be the discovery of my connection to Jim Kohn's death. Surely my predecessor hadn't been a killer who was found out.

If Rafe and Victoria were so terrible, why wasn't Kent concerned with warning me? He seemed to like hanging out with me. We'd laughed about the Thanksgiving dinner. He wasn't pissed that I'd invited him to such a dull, lifeless, and energy-sucking afternoon around an overcooked turkey. He'd wanted to drink a martini together. And then another. We were sharing cigarettes and stories from our past and our jobs and yet there was this thick wall of mud that enclosed the one thing I wanted to know.

It made no sense. I was starting to consider whether I would need to seduce him to get to the truth. But even that might not work. Whatever he knew about Nick's flight from New York remained locked inside.

We sipped our drinks and finished the pack of cigarettes. Finally, we said good-night.

35

The following morning I put Kent and the former occupant of my apartment and my weird neighbors out of my head. I sent a message to Eileen and asked when she wanted to meet for a drink. She responded immediately, and before the sun went down on Black Friday shoppers, I was riding the steamy, standing-room-only subway to the Flatiron District.

We met in a slick, crowded bar. All of the women in the room appeared to be quite like Eileen. Some had long expensively blown out and styled hair that had the look of something that was designed for a movie set. Others wore short, expensive styles with wild tangles of curls, exotic combos of blonde and bronze hair color, or chic super-short cuts that showed off some of the most stunning facial bone structures on the planet. All the women were tall. Even perched on stools or sitting in lounge chairs, their long slender legs and long fingers revealed that when they stood, nearly all of them would be taller than me.

The room was more brightly lit than most bars — a place to be seen more clearly. The light was intensified as it reflected off walls that featured mirrored panels as well as the white ceiling from which oversized bulbs dangled like so many bubbles floating in a glass of champagne. The furniture was all soft camel and white leather and light creamy wood. Along the left side of the room was a bar made of glass. It allowed patrons to look down and see women's elegantly crossed legs and designer shoes perched on bar stools or trying to root themselves to the floor.

Eileen rose out of a low-slung leather chair and waved at me. I worked my way past the clusters of furniture and people to an alcove with two matching chairs and a narrow table between them. The table was the height and length of a coffee table, but only a foot wide, enough to hold a few drinks and one of those long appetizer plates that's often used to arrange Asian dumplings and garnish in an artfully curved line slicked with red chili oil.

She moved toward me and gave me a hug, her fingers light on my back, her arms not touching me. Her scent was hard to pin down. It made me think of limes.

We settled into the chairs, and a server appeared immediately. Eileen was already drinking a glass of champagne. I ordered a martini. I glanced at the small menu. "Should we get an appetizer?"

"Go ahead. I'm not hungry, so whatever you'd like."

The server suggested flatbread and caviar, and I accepted her choice.

"Do you come here a lot?"

"All the time. They offer over fifteen champagnes by the glass, which I like."

Clearly, she bought into the promise of champagne carrying fewer calories than a glass of wine. It explained the crowd of models. Even the men looked like models, wearing self-conscious clothing, their faces as beautiful as the women's. "It looks like a model hangout."

She glanced around the room. "You're right."

"Are they all models?"

"A lot of them."

"That seems strange."

"Quite a few agents have offices in this area."

"And there are fifteen champagnes by the glass."

She laughed. "You know."

"All women do."

She picked up her glass and sipped. Her face was smooth with expensive makeup, her skin pale with a soft glowing rose below her cheeks that looked entirely natural, unless you play around with makeup a lot, which I do. Her brows were perfectly arched and brushed into a smooth curve. She wore light gradations of shadow around her eyes and brown mascara. Even so, her eyes stood out from her face like living creatures in their own right. Her hair was dark and fell in layers around her cheeks and jaw and curved around her neck in waves that looked to be strangling her.

She touched the edge of her glass to her cheek. "How was the Thanksgiving dinner?"

My martini arrived, and we toasted each other. Right behind the server who had placed the drink on the table without a single drop slipping over the edge, came another person carrying the plate of flatbread with its dark, earthy beads of caviar. He placed the caviar beside my drink.

I broke off a piece of flatbread and spread a smear of caviar across the surface. I put the entire cracker in my mouth. After I'd tasted and chewed and swallowed, I spoke. "It wasn't nearly as good as this."

"This is one of a few places that offers sustainable caviar."

So, she did occasionally indulge in food. That was good to know.

"My mother wouldn't say a word about the dinner."

"She didn't want to tell you she got drunk and passed out."

Eileen ran her fingertips across her forehead as if checking for moisture. "She doesn't drink, or rarely."

"I know. But she did. Kent kept refilling glasses, and she wasn't paying attention."

"I wouldn't expect her to tell me. I imagine she's embarrassed and feeling guilty. Was she a fun drunk or sloppy?"

"Angry. And sloppy. She puked."

Eileen made a face. "Nice way to impress your boss."

"Was that the purpose of the dinner?"

"What else would it be?"

"I wasn't sure. I thought she was just being friendly."

"My mother isn't normally friendly for the hell of it."

"You don't get along?"

"Do you?"

"Get along with your mother or mine?"

She gave me a coy smile, trying to suggest she'd planned my confusion. "Either one."

"I'm not close to my mother. We see the world differently. And I suppose I would say the same for yours."

She laughed. She held up her glass and studied the rising bubbles. "Tell me more."

I didn't want to tell her more. In fact, I didn't want to talk about anyone's mother. I wanted to find out about those photographs. I took a sip of my drink and nibbled on another piece of bread, loaded with more caviar this time.

She studied her fingernails and spoke without looking at me. "You don't want to talk about her?"

"No."

"Fair enough. I can see why you'd be edgy. She's your co-worker, and you don't know me at all. Who knows what I might pass back to her."

"Something like that."

"I won't, though. I'm not close to my mother. We're at war, really. A religious war. In some ways, I blame her for Jim. For his murder."

"Isn't that a bit of a stretch?"

"If we'd still been together, he wouldn't have been in a hotel with a hooker, or whatever she was. And if I hadn't been raised in such a repressive atmosphere, maybe he wouldn't have left me."

"Is that why you think it ended?"

"He wanted me to have more drive. He wanted me to be successful. He was beyond successful, and he wanted an equal partner. I was so saturated in guilt, it was impossible to throw my entire self into my ambition. I couldn't put myself out there. I couldn't let go and pose with the kind of abandon the photographers want. Guilt has a way of sticking to your skin, and the smell of it seeps into everything you do. Sex, especially. Your work. How you interact with other people." She let out a long, deep sigh. A sigh that seemed heavy with guilt.

I wondered at the difference between us. It sounded as if our mothers were similar. And I had the bonus prize of a father who was a pro at creating situations designed to inflict guilt. And yet, I had none. I'd been immune to the rules and stories pumped into my brain.

"What do you feel guilty about?"

"I'm not even sure. Just for being me, I suppose. It's not really a feeling. I question every single thought and decision because it might be *wrong*. Whatever *wrong* is." She laughed. She took a long swallow of champagne. "How did we get onto this topic? Do you want another drink?"

"Sure."

She flagged down the server and ordered another drink for both of us.

"Do you feel guilty being a model?"

"I did. Not as much now anymore, because I love it so much. I love changing how I look. I love acting out different scenarios. But I can't let myself go like I should. That's the guilt part. And Jim believed in my potential, he was more passionate than I was in some ways. And when I couldn't...he tried to help me...but it didn't work out."

"Tried to help you?"

She waved her hand beside her ear as if she were brushing away the sound of my question. "Nothing. It's all in the past. We're over. And now he's dead. It doesn't matter. I'm trying to focus on getting where I want to go and not letting my mother or her ideas or the past get in the way. It's all I have now."

Looking at her face, I knew that his help involved those locked up photographs. I tried to think how I could get her to mention them without seeming to pry, without hinting I knew of their existence. "Do you feel like things were settled between you? That you can move on without being tied to the past?"

"You sound like the therapist I saw."

I laughed. "Far from it."

"Yes, I feel settled. I'm going to be more successful than Jim ever dreamed of."

"Why was he so concerned with your success? That seems unusual."

She shrugged. "As I said, he wanted us to be equals. Equal in ambition. Equal in status. He knew what I wanted, and he played off of that. Tried to push me to what he knew I wanted. He was big on that — meeting your potential."

"Did your mother tell you he was a client of ours?"

She nodded.

"He still had your picture in his office when I met him. Right before he died. It might still be there."

"What picture?"

I described it.

"I suppose he still has a lot of pictures of me." She shivered. She picked up her glass and took a sip.

36

With questions left unanswered regarding Eileen's awareness of the photographs locked inside the armoire, and my potentially dangerous or at least malevolent neighbors, I decided I would escape to see Joe. The thoughts occupying my mind added up to a sensation of drowning in things that were none of my business, but at the same time, seemed like they were brushing up against the edges of my business. I needed a break from my own brain.

It was cold, the sky covered in clouds that looked and felt as if they would bring snow, not that I knew anything about how an impending snowstorm behaved. It was just so cold, the coldness of the earth itself seeping up through the soles of my boots, the wind cutting through wool and cotton and fleece. The air smelled cold. I hadn't looked at a weather forecast, so I had no idea whether a storm was coming, but there was something pent-up about the atmosphere that made me think I might be close to experiencing my first New York snow.

I'd taken trips to the mountains to go sledding when I was a child, so snow wasn't completely outside of my experience.

A few inches of snow occasionally fell on Portland, Oregon, but not the thick winter wonderland snow of New York. I'd never woken to a yard draped in white, never taken a long walk with it falling around me.

New Yorkers seemed willfully disinterested in snow except in knowing how it might impact their commute and the creature comforts of heating and electricity. But I believed they liked it more than they let on or they wouldn't have chosen to make their home in a city that was blanketed with snow seven or eight days a year.

I didn't tell Joe I was coming. Every indication I'd had was that he was always glad to see me. And I wasn't in the mood for the drama of a limo pulling up at my apartment. During daylight hours, the limo attracted all kinds of stares, snarky looks, and occasional comments about the one percent or paid escorts.

I silently laughed at the voices, just loud enough for me to overhear. The voices were obviously raised with the *intention* of letting me hear, while pretending they were talking quietly to a companion, not wanting to be heard at all. It was a game that I'd lost interest in. I just wanted an anonymous ride in an Uber.

When the Uber was a few miles from Jim Kohn's house, I sent Joe a text and announced my arrival. He responded with a winking emoji. I wasn't sure how to interpret that but assumed it was an overall positive reaction.

As the Uber pulled up, the gate opened. The front door was standing ajar when I stepped out of the car. I climbed the steps slowly, feeling for the slick presence of ice. It was mid-afternoon so ice was unlikely, but I didn't want to end up sprawled on the bottom step, looking up at a slate gray sky while I tried to catch my breath and felt the results of cold concrete slamming against my bones.

After my bags were settled in Joe's room, he suggested a walk around the gardens. "…before it snows."

"Is it supposed to snow?"

"That's what they're saying. The temperature's hitting twenty-seven tonight. And rain is coming…that usually means snow."

"I wouldn't mind walking in a snowstorm."

"Watch what you wish for. It looks romantic in the movies, but it's not always as magical and blissful as people think."

I doubted that, but I expected I'd find out soon enough.

We headed toward the back of the property, our gloved hands holding onto each other, our feet moving with a similar cadence.

We talked about Thanksgiving. Mine full of contention, his low-key. The chef had prepared lobster for Joe, Nell, and Ed. They'd eaten in the breakfast room and watched football.

"Does Ed do his Rubik's Cube while he watches football?"

"He does it all the time."

"I wish I could make those things work."

"Why?"

"Because most people can't do it."

"And you need to prove you're better than most?"

"No."

"Then why do you care?"

"I like knowing I can do difficult things."

"And most people not being able to do it makes it difficult?"

"I think so."

"It's mindless entertainment. Feeling you've accomplished

something when what you've accomplished is meaningless."

"Lots of things are meaningless," I said. "If you really stop and think about it."

"Now we're discussing philosophy?"

"If you say so."

He quickened his pace, and I kept up. "It's pointless," he said.

"I know. But it's interesting."

"Have you tried?"

"No."

"It's a false assumption to think that completing a pointless puzzle indicates anything about your intelligence."

"You sure have a lot of opinions about something you consider meaningless."

"I don't have a lot of opinions. I have one opinion. It's a waste of time."

"Or does it bother you that Ed is wasting time working at it?"

"He's not as smart as he'd like to think he is."

"I think I hit a nerve." I tugged gently on his arm.

He stiffened, and I felt the rest of his body, rigid and dragging at my forward momentum.

"I thought we were walking."

"We are." The drag of his weight continued.

"You seem pissed."

"I don't like people who have to make themselves out to be better than everyone else. Especially when they're not."

"And you think that's what I am?"

"I have no idea what you are."

He didn't say this with affection. It sent a chill along the upper edges of my arms that went beyond what the weather was causing. He seemed disconcerted by something I'd said, and I wasn't sure what it was. Surely talking about a cubist puzzle wasn't enough to cause a break in our fun, flirty relationship.

All I needed was a little snow to make it more interesting. We'd get lost in all the whiteness and build an ice hut where we could keep warm. I liked the idea of snow, of all the world being blotted out for a while. Roads indistinguishable from lawns and sidewalks. Houses took on a similar appearance with white roofs and sides and windows crusted with waves of powder and ice.

I understood why snow has taken on such a magical quality over the centuries.

Maybe this wasn't really about the twisting of a cube and the alignment of primary colors into a single panel. Maybe it was about Ed. Without the presence of an owner for the estate, with the new guy a complete unknown, was some kind of power struggle underway? "You think Ed pretends to be someone he isn't?"

He stopped walking. "Where did that come from? That's not what I said."

"Just a question. You seem awfully worked up about the Rubik's Cube."

"I'm not worked up."

"It's just a game. Why do you care if it's meaningless to you and important to others?"

He started walking again, his pace slow and languid as if he wanted to impress upon me that he really didn't care. "As I said, I don't like people who make themselves out to be better than other people."

"And Ed does that?"

"Yes."

"How so? Besides the cube?"

"Since Jim died, he seems to believe he no longer reports to me."

"He did before?"

"Yes."

"And now?"

"He doesn't do anything. I think we should behave as if we're still employed. We *are* still employed. We're responsible for this place. We aren't given comfortable room and board to sit around and play games all day. It's disrespectful."

"Disrespectful? Jim's dead. And you said yourself, he was…"

"We're still receiving paychecks. We're responsible to the person signing our checks."

If I'd wondered about his ethics, it was clear that his were precise and well-formed and not to be messed with. He wouldn't help me to prowl through Jim's possessions, even if those possessions were things that didn't belong to him — such as Eileen's image.

Suddenly, I wondered why I cared so much. The photographer, most likely, was dead. I was pretty sure the photographer wasn't Joe. If it was Ed, I cared even less. Eileen was a cool person to hang out with, but I didn't owe her anything. And she seemed to be aware of the existence of photographs outside of her control, aware that she was ripe for exposure, but at the same time, doing nothing to retrieve them. At least as far as I knew.

Was this all just my relentless curiosity run amok? Or was it the realization that someone, probably a man, had degraded a woman in front of a camera and kept the evidence for his own perverted interest?

I also wondered what Stephanie would think of those photographs.

37

I woke at two o'clock, as alert as if it were time for my morning run. My eyes immediately stretched wide open. The fog of sleep and dreams was cleared out as if my brain had been washed by cold water moments before I woke.

Whatever I'd dreamed of was gone. This isn't usually the case at two in the morning. Waking abruptly has a way of snagging your dreams so that you're left lying beneath the blankets in a state that's half reality and half something you feel you've deliberately made up.

And maybe we do...make up our dreams on our own. We've all been conditioned to think dreams assault us out of the subconscious, taking over our thought processes and drowning our lucidity. Maybe it's not that at all. Maybe we have a hand in it. During the day, we're frantic that we can't make sense of the world around us and so we carry that aggravation to its natural conclusion — creating more nonsense as if knowing we semi-purposefully invented it will make us feel that nonsense is a normal and acceptable state.

Maybe some part of our conscious brain creeps around picking up bits and pieces from the distant past, things we've seen on TV and experienced at work, childhood memories we assumed were buried, then deliberately creating something that entertains and confuses and terrifies on alternating nights. We want to escape into our own entertainment, so we make it all up.

These are the kinds of thoughts that appear out of that immediate post-dream state.

I shoved them aside and turned onto my back. I stared into the darkness and tried to decide what I wanted to do. It was the sort of wakefulness that wouldn't be resolved by a simple shift in position and a relaxing of the limbs, leading to a return to sleep. I wanted sex. I wanted a cigarette. I wanted a martini. I wanted to go for a run. I wanted to dance in the snow drifts like a graceful doe. I wanted to look at those photographs again. I wanted too many things.

Waking Joe would get me the first, but his breathing was deep and easy, his mind obviously creating its own entertainment.

I folded back the covers and slipped out of bed. I pulled on my hoodie and yoga pants. After a glass of water and a few stretches, I opened the door to the hallway.

The armoire key was safely tucked away in my hairbrush again, waiting for an opportunity for me to study the photographs for some imagined insight as to their purpose. I thought again about Jim's *help* in eradicating Eileen's guilt; his perverse desire to humiliate her with a camera, sold to her as assistance in escaping from guilt.

If you pose in all sorts of ways that stir up feelings of shame, you'll be rid of the guilt.

I could almost hear him delivering that line of bullshit. I could imagine a lot of men saying that. Some men will say anything to get a woman to do what they want. So will some women.

I walked toward the staircase, keeping my eyes alert to possible opening doors, listening for sounds from the rooms I passed. The hallway was silent, the effect of solid wood doors and superior insulation more than a definite absence of sound. Anything could be going on beside me as I passed by, all of it pressed into silence by exquisite home design and construction.

I started down the stairs, thinking about the pack of cigarettes in my bag. I'd woken thinking I wanted one, but the thought left my mind, and now I was empty-handed. I paused. I retraced my steps quickly.

A few minutes later I was settled in the smoking room, my cigarette lit, my body comfortably curled up on the sofa. I longed for someone to talk to, anything that would keep my brain from spinning like an out-of-control carousel past the various things that leered and lunged at me as I spun past, demanding answers.

My first cigarette was a pile of ash, the second one half finished when the door to the smoking room opened. Ed stood in the entrance.

One hand held the edge of the door, the other was at his side, gripping the Rubik's Cube. Seeing him there, tall and gaunt, that silly puzzle clutched like a child's pacifier, was unsettling. Except for the cube, he looked like a creature from a horror movie. He wore a white t-shirt that was too short for his frame, exposing a line of reddish skin between the hem and the waistband of his unbelted blue jeans.

"What are you doing in here?"

I held up my cigarette.

"You don't belong here."

"Joe said it was okay."

"It's not."

I put the cigarette to my lips and inhaled gently. I held the smoke for a moment, watching him watch me, then blew it out slowly. "Are you pretty good at that?" I pointed the cigarette at his right hand.

"Put it out."

I smiled. "Do you want one?"

He glared at me.

"I'm really interested in your puzzle. I'm guessing you're an expert because you were working on it when I met you and here you are working on it again. You seem to practice a lot."

"I'm good, yeah."

"Most people can't figure it out."

He gave me a tight-lipped smile. "Because they lack persistence."

I nodded. It was clear he meant they weren't intelligent, but he wanted me to come to that conclusion without him pointing it out. "Why don't you sit down. Show me how it works."

"You can't show someone how it works. It's an art. Each person's subconscious has to learn to work it out. And if your brain isn't wired to think several steps ahead, you can't do it."

"Show me anyway."

He stepped into the room and closed the door carefully. I wondered whether he was thinking ahead to what might happen in the next several steps. I certainly was, even though I couldn't do a Rubik's Cube.

"Most people think puzzles like this are relics of the past. All the games are electronic now."

"This is true."

"But we exist in a three-dimensional world. Working on physical objects, things with dimension makes the muscle of the brain stronger."

I wasn't sure if this was true. I wasn't sure he was in a position to be an authority on the subject of brains and puzzles and dimensions, but we all have our opinions. Millions of people would disagree with his take on electronic games. "Interesting viewpoint," I said.

He scowled. "It's not a viewpoint. It's a fact."

I put my cigarette to my lips. As the smoke curled out of my mouth, I picked up the pack and held it out to him.

"I quit ten years ago."

"Didn't mean to tempt you." I placed the pack on the couch by my foot.

He crossed the room, picked up the pack, flipped open the lid, and removed a cigarette. I offered the lighter, then watched him inhale as if he'd been waiting for this moment for ten years. Quitting smoking is hard. It's not just the physical addiction. It's the pleasure of deliberate breathing, the beauty of smoke curling in the air, creating a painting with each exhalation. It's the habit, and the way that particular habit eases tension, the pure enjoyment of something to do when there's nothing to do.

He took the chair kitty-corner from me. He balanced the cube on one knee and enjoyed his cigarette for several minutes without talking.

"So are you going to show me the trick?"

"I told you — there isn't a trick."

I nodded.

"You seem to think this house belongs to you, that we

work for you."

"Do I?"

"This room, for example. And cruising around Manhattan in a limo that doesn't belong to you."

"I'm not cruising around Manhattan."

He took another drag on his cigarette while I lit a third.

"Once Mark arrives, you won't be welcome here."

"I'm aware of that." I wasn't sure that was the truth. Surely the staff living here had some allowance for guests as long as they were discreet. Otherwise, who would choose to live in a situation like this?

He stabbed out his cigarette, half finished. "What are you after?"

"Nothing."

He nodded. He didn't believe me, but he wasn't sure how to argue with my answer. He picked up the cube and twisted it several times, aligning more colors with their partners. It looked random to me, but that wasn't possible. There had to be a trick, or certain patterns to follow.

I was beginning to see Joe's point. Ed had mastered a puzzle that might take some persistence, but it wasn't chess, a game that changes every time you pick up a carved figure and move it to a new square. There were a finite number of ways .to complete the Rubik's cube. It was almost humiliating the way Ed clung to the belief that his constant manipulation of the colored squares of plastic proved superior intelligence.

I wondered what *he* was after.

38

I was the one to stand and pick up my cigarettes. I was the one to lead the way out of the room. But Ed had a set to his shoulders that suggested he'd won whatever battle we were fighting — I'd given up squatter's rights and was trudging back to where I belonged.

After slipping into Joe's room, I leaned against the closed door. I pressed my ear to the solid wood. Of course, it was impossible to hear anything, even another door closing or the whisper of footsteps.

I turned and rested my back against the door, pressing my spine against the wood.

While I'd been smoking with Ed, I'd come to a decision. I would take the photographs with me. He'd been right about one thing — I might not be welcome once the new owner arrived. I couldn't count on some benevolent gesture that allowed Joe and the others to host guests in someone else's home. Joe might be out of a job. The house might be sold. Anything could happen.

If I was going to get the photographs, it had to be now, before the sun breached the horizon.

I took Joe's keys' from their holding place and removed the old-fashioned key from its nest inside my hairbrush. I changed into jeans and slid the key into my front left pocket. I leaned against the door again.

The house felt silent, but I couldn't be sure without opening the door. What had woken Ed in the first place? Was he normally restless, often wandering the halls? It seemed that way. I'd never caught even a glimpse of him in the daylight, and now I'd encountered him twice in the pre-dawn hours.

I felt the shape of the key with my fingers, pressing it against my hipbone. I closed my eyes and tried to think. Not only did I have to get in and out of the storage room without being seen by the other midnight wanderers, I had to do it with an armful of photographs. I considered whether it was best to take my bag. If I were caught, the bag or an armful of photos wouldn't make any difference. If I weren't caught, the photos would be relatively safe. I could plan an early departure, snow or not.

I picked up my messenger bag and moved most of my things into my gym bag. I pushed those things to the bottom and zipped it closed. I slung the messenger bag over my shoulder and felt for the key again, reassured by its solid presence.

Returning to the door, I pressed my ear against it in another pointless attempt to determine whether the hallway was occupied. I held my breath. I imagined someone standing on the opposite side, ear pressed up against mine, breath held tightly inside a pair of lungs, wondering what I was up to.

I eased my breath back to its normal rhythm, trying to keep it shallow and as soundless as possible.

After several minutes of standing like this, my head ached,

and my shoulder was stiff. I stepped back, put my fingers on the handle, and pressed down. The door opened without a creak or even the click of metal in the lock mechanism.

The hallway was empty.

I stepped out and closed the door. I walked quickly to the storage room, inserted the key, opened the door, and turned to glance behind me as I stepped inside. I hoped that Ed was tired, that following me back to my room and watching me enter, knowing I'd likely had my fill with three cigarettes, had eased his mind for the time-being. I hoped Nell's soft, sleeping body, deep in her own dreams, had drawn him back to bed.

It was a lot of hoping, but in many cases, hoping works out surprisingly well. It's not a life strategy, but sometimes it's all you have. If I wanted those photographs, I had to rely on hope, as well as the unpleasant nature of three o'clock in the morning. It's a time when no one wants to be awake. Partiers usually crash by two, and most early morning commuters try to sleep until four.

Three o'clock is an hour for the dead.

Only medical and law enforcement professionals, mothers of newborns and shift workers lurk in the darkness of that hour.

I secured the lock behind me and went into the room that held the armoire.

The doors of the armoire stood open. The lock protruded like the stiff, distended tongue of a corpse. Most of the trays were partially pulled out. All of them were empty. There wasn't a scrap of paper on the floor or caught in a hinge.

I stared for several minutes. My mind blank.

All my thoughts and energy had been focused on escaping

the eyes of the others. I'd assumed so many things. I'd assumed only Jim knew about the photographs. I'd assumed the key was keeping them safe.

I'd assumed he was the photographer and that he had a purpose for them that was known only to Eileen. I'd assumed I would be carrying the photographs out of the house.

My first irrational thought was that Eileen had been here and removed them herself. Who else would want them? Unless someone wanted to sell them as porn, which they weren't.

I suppose they could fall into the dark edges of porn, the kind that likes to demean, drawing viewers who only find pleasure when women are pictured as objects to be battered and subdued and degraded.

The other possibility was blackmail.

Did someone want to destroy her budding career?

Or did someone simply want to hurt her?

The most likely candidate was Nell.

Jealousy?

Revenge for some unknown injury?

I closed the door and looked around the rest of the storage space. Nothing had changed since my last visit. It was possible other things had been removed, but none of them mattered to me.

I crossed the room and turned out the light. I opened the door and looked into the hallway. It was empty. I stepped out, closed the door, and returned to Joe's room.

Moving quietly, I let the bag strap slide off my shoulder. I pulled Joe's keys out of my pocket. Clutching them in one fist, I stretched my arms behind me to relieve the tension of holding myself tight, as if I'd believed that making my

muscles rigid might keep my body hidden from curious eyes.
I turned.

Joe stood in the bedroom doorway. "What are you doing?"

39

Proving for the ten-thousandth time that the mind is always on its own track, my first thought upon seeing Joe's naked body standing in front of me was that I definitely wanted sex. It had been my initial thought when I'd woken an hour or so earlier, and it rushed back with an intensity that made my breath catch. Why had I chosen a few cigarettes instead?

In the light cast by the sitting room table lamp behind me, he looked more smooth and sculpted than ever. I remembered his hands on my skin, his mouth on mine. I remembered falling asleep, my body humming with pleasure and my mind floating. I needed that feeling again.

His eyes were hidden by darkness, but his breath told me the question wasn't casual concern after waking to find me gone from his bed. His tone was hard and laced with anger.

"I went…"

"No bullshit. You weren't out for a cigarette or getting a snack or a drink. Not with your bag."

"I keep my cigarettes in…"

"Not with my keys."

I thought about unzipping my hoodie, distracting him by

getting half naked, but I guessed his reaction would be anger, not desire. And not the kind of anger that can turn quickly and easily to desire, but true anger at knowing he'd been manipulated.

"I wanted to check out the storage room. I didn't get what the big secret was."

"It's none of your business."

"Jim's dead. What difference does it make?"

"Is that the same level of concern and sympathy you have for all your clients?"

"I've never had any other client die. And I didn't...you know how he was with me." I moved toward the bed and sat down, hoping it would soften him.

He remained standing. I'd never known a man to be able to hold his dignity and express his thoughts while he stood naked and his partner was clothed. I was impressed.

"I invited you into this house, I invite you to enjoy all the privileges here, and you steal my keys and go sneaking around where you don't belong?"

"I didn't steal them. I borrowed them."

He turned and picked up his jeans. He shoved his foot into one leg then the other and yanked them into place. He zipped them with a ferocity that made me fear for the delicate skin of his penis. "I'm calling Dirk. He can take you home."

"In the middle of the night?"

"Yeah. That's his job."

"I'm curious..."

"Too curious."

"What I meant was, I'm curious why it's such a big deal. I didn't go digging through his study. I'm not trying to steal anything. I just wondered why the room was locked when nothing else is."

"It's not your place to wonder anything."

I laughed. "Not my *place?*"

In response, he grabbed his shirt and pulled it over his head. He didn't bother to smooth his hair like he usually did after he'd shoved it through a neck hole.

"You're awfully ethical about a dead guy who you know was a sleaze."

"I'm responsible for his things, for the entire property, until his brother gets here. Besides that, I don't want to be with a woman who sneaks around behind my back."

"Okay. But I asked, and you wouldn't tell me."

"Why do you even need to know? Also not someone I want to be with — sticking her nose in other people's business. Going where she shouldn't. Lying. I could go on..."

"You're making one small thing into something so huge. All I did was check out the room. We're good together. Do you really want to end that so easily?"

I felt him hesitate.

"I can't trust you," he said.

"And I can't trust you."

He folded his arms across his chest. We stared at each other, both of us recognizing a fresh flicker of desire. In my case, it was more like a surge, but I saw the same in him. It's funny how sex works like that. No one understands it. We're puzzled by couples who split up and then sleep together, by bosses and employees who cross boundaries, by people who hit on their best friend's spouse. The mind and every rational belief you have can insist someone isn't the right partner or the timing is not good, and yet, the body rules.

You can hate someone and still have that nagging,

unwanted longing for their body wash over you, driving you to say and do whatever it takes to get what it wants. I suppose that's why it's called hunger. Eating is the same way. The body demanding what it wants through a complex working of chemical reactions. Human beings can study the mechanics of how it works for decades, but knowledge doesn't change the firing neurons that will make you eat pizza when you know you should eat steamed broccoli without butter.

I touched the zipper of my hoodie and pulled it slowly down past my breastbone, lowering it to my navel. I stood and undid it the rest of the way.

Without saying a word, Joe was standing close to me, folding his warm hands around my breasts. "I'm so pissed at you," he said. "You're a conniving, lying…"

"I know."

We began kissing, and I felt him fighting with himself, wanting to push me away, and wanting to suck me up, all in a single surge of battling desires. His body won, of course.

Lying in bed after, he moved away instead of wrapping his arms and legs around me as he usually did.

He cleared his throat and closed his eyes. "I can't be in a relationship with someone I don't trust."

"Why not?"

His eyes opened, and he turned his head to look at me. I could see shock and confusion moving across his face, his expression shifting as he tried to figure out what was wrong with me. "Without trust, there's no relationship at all."

"But there's still good sex."

"That's all you want?"

"Why not?"

He turned on his side, his back toward me. I waited for

him to think it over. My stomach growled. I wanted coffee. Bacon and eggs. Or maybe toast with butter and breakfast sausages. I wanted to look outside and see whether any snow had fallen. I moved the covers, and he turned over again.

"I can leave," I said.

He sighed. "What were you looking for?"

"Nothing. I told you. I was curious about the big secret."

"I think you were looking for something."

"You can think what you want."

"I haven't been sure what you're after since you first showed up here."

"If you've never trusted me, what's the difference now?" I started to slide out of bed. He grabbed my leg and pulled me back. He rolled on top of me and started kissing me.

40

When Joe and I went down to make coffee and fix breakfast, nothing between us was resolved. He didn't trust me, and I felt the same. If he was so proprietary about that room, he must have known the armoire lock was broken. There was a chance he'd been the one to break it.

All the current occupants of the house were behaving oddly. Any one of them could have stolen the photographs. I could hang onto the key and no one would care about it now. None of it had anything to do with me anymore, if it ever had.

But still, I couldn't let go of it.

Unless Eileen had the photographs, and I didn't see how that was possible, someone wanted to hurt her with them. Someone wanted to carry on Jim's legacy of trying to diminish and control her. It was even possible that Jim had had plans for them and one of his employees had been privy to this and was determined to carry out his wishes. Why were the degrading photographs of her so important to him that he'd carried the key on his ring beside only a few others?

Joe set about making coffee, and I looked through the

refrigerator for breakfast foods. There was no bacon and only two eggs. We finally decided on waffles. He began mixing the batter, and I put out plates and utensils. Waffles are a one-person job, so while he poured batter and hovered over the waffle maker, I went into the breakfast room and stared at the backyard, letting the questions run on a repeat loop in my mind.

Twenty minutes later, our plates were wiped clean with only a thin covering of melted butter and maple syrup. We were on our second cups of coffee, the conversation flowing surprisingly well given the lack of trust and the crevice that had formed between us.

The kitchen door opened. From where we sat, we could see Nell. "Mmm, coffee." She went to the pot and poured herself a large mug. She raised her voice so it carried to where we sat. "Any waffles left for me?"

Joe called back that there was one in the warming drawer.

"Only one?"

Neither of us answered.

A moment later she came into the breakfast room carrying her lone waffle on a white plate. She'd smeared raspberry jam across the top. She sat beside Joe and drew her knife through the center of the waffle. "What are you up to today?" She gave me a large, phony grin, then glanced at Joe.

He turned away and picked up his coffee mug.

"Waiting for snow," I said.

"There's nowhere to go sledding around here."

"I wasn't planning to go sledding. I just want to walk in it."

"Isn't that sweet." She reached over and pinched my cheek.

I pushed my chair away from the table. I stood and went into the kitchen. I poured the rest of the coffee into my mug and took a sip. It burned my tongue, but I needed to do something. I needed a moment to think about that pinch and phony grin. It was clearly for Joe's benefit, but why?

I returned to the breakfast room. It was dark, the overhead lights hardly breaking the weight of the heavy, nearly black clouds pressed down across the sky, pushing themselves toward the windows.

I took my seat again.

"You should have made another pot of coffee," Nell said.

"I've had plenty. This is enough."

"I haven't."

"You can make your own coffee, Nell." Joe looked at her, then turned away quickly. He stood and picked up our plates, stacking mine on top of his. He left the room, and a moment later I heard his footsteps headed away from the kitchen.

"I didn't mean to chase him out of the room." Nell laughed.

I moved my chair back and started to get up.

"You can't leave me eating all by myself."

"I'm finished."

"You still have coffee."

I took a swig.

"Don't gulp it down just so you can get out of here. It's so rude." She laughed.

"I should…"

"You don't have anything to do but wait for snow. Remember?"

I settled back in my chair. It wouldn't hurt to find out more about her. The sudden switch from trying to chase me away to trying to pin me down was strange. I had no idea what any of them wanted.

"Do you think you and Joe will stay together when Jim's brother gets here?"

"I have no idea."

"You must have thought about it."

That didn't mean I was going to talk to her about it. At this point, I guessed we wouldn't. I wasn't sure we'd stay together after today. "I haven't really."

"Liar."

I shrugged. "If you say so."

"He doesn't have any money, you know. This house might look glamorous to you, but we're all paid normal wages. Don't think the trappings mean we're well off. And if you're thinking that we have a lot because of what we save on rent and food, wrong again. That's taken into account with our salaries."

"I'm not interested in anyone's money."

"Another lie. Everyone is interested in money."

"Of course. But not other people's money. I can take care of myself."

She smirked. "It's funny how you just showed up here. There's something not right about it."

I swallowed the rest of my coffee. I put my mug down on the table with a bit of extra force.

"I get it. You're done. But I'm not. You can humor me with a little company." She cut off a piece of waffle and put it into her mouth. A few clumps of jam clung to the skin just below her bottom lip. It made me think of blood. I licked my lips in an unconscious effort to be rid of it.

She licked her own lips but missed the jam. Now I had the urge to wipe it off. She'd pinched me, I could make the same unwanted move to touch her face.

I turned so I didn't have to see it.

"Where do you work?"

"I'm a photographer."

"*Where* do you work? I didn't ask what you did."

"In Mid-town."

"You don't like to give straight answers, do you."

"I would say the same about you."

"Fair enough." She drew the blade of her knife through the waffle, slicing neatly. As the section of pastry came away from the rest, it looked like a piece of pale flesh tearing off of a body, and the raspberry jam again took on the appearance of clotted blood.

I wasn't sure why my imagination was running wild with her food. Jam looks nothing like blood, and there was no reason for me to be thinking of such morbid things. The sky may have been thick with clouds, but the weather was anything but gloomy as they prepared to drop beautiful crystalline flakes of snow.

Nell tipped her head up toward me and smiled, jam wedged between her teeth. "What are you doing here, really?"

"Hanging out with Joe."

"But how did you get here?"

"Didn't Joe tell you?"

"I want *you* to tell me."

I tried to think about what he might have said to her. It seemed obvious he would have mentioned I was photographing her former boss. "I took photographs of Jim for an analysis of his style with clients and peers. He was a client of my company."

"What company?"

"It's a consulting firm. We don't have a name."

"Why doesn't that surprise me?"

"Not sure." I smiled.

"It must make it difficult to find clients when you can't even tell them who you are."

"We manage."

She returned her attention to the waffle, slicing off neat wedges and eating them carefully, chewing each bite thoroughly. All the while, even though her gaze was on her plate, I felt her intense awareness of me. She began to give off the sense that everything she was doing was a performance, even the way she cut and chewed her food.

"Would you make a pot of coffee, please. I'd really like another cup."

"I'm not familiar with the equipment."

"It's not a nuclear submarine. I think you can figure it out. It's the least you can do."

"Why is that?"

"Because I haven't told Joe to kick your ass out of here."

"What makes you think he would listen?"

She smiled. "The coffee beans are in the refrigerator."

The coffee in my mug was cold. It was to my benefit to keep her somewhat placid and friendly and giving out information.

Even though I didn't like what she'd said about Joe kicking me out and her supposed influence in making that happen, I needed any information I could drag out of her.

It's always better to know as much as you can about any situation.

I made the coffee.

When I returned to the breakfast room with two mugs of steaming coffee, her plate was wiped clean. Outside, the swollen clouds had finally released their overflow. Large, soft flakes of snow drifted to the ground. They looked as pure and beautiful and magical as I'd imagined they would.

41

I only drank half the mug of coffee. As snow began to settle on the flagstone and cling to the blades of grass and the leafless branches of the trees, I couldn't bear to stay indoors and watch the world re-create itself.

I went upstairs. Joe's rooms were empty, the bed made, the air smelling like almonds. It seemed polite to look for him, but it was entirely possible he was done with me, his desire for trust winning once his desire for sex and food had been satisfied and he could think clearly. Any moment the limo might show up, and I'd be escorted out the front door.

I changed into jeans and a turtleneck sweater. I shoved my arms into my jacket sleeves and pulled on the Doc Marten boots I'd packed, hoping and longing for a snowy path to walk on.

I hurried downstairs and back to the breakfast room. Nell's plate and both mugs had been cleared. The overhead lights were off. Nell stood near the door to the patio. She was dressed for a ski trip to the alps — complete with a pale blue snowflake-dotted sweater that was visible between the open sides of her white down jacket. She wore a knitted hat that matched the sweater, white leather gloves, and bona fide snow boots.

"Everyone likes to walk in the snow," she said.

She was probably right about that. I didn't mind going with her because who knew what other piece of information might trickle from her lips.

We went outside and crossed the patio. I turned my face up to the sky and let the snow fall onto my skin. The flakes were sharper and colder than I'd imagined. Snow looks so soft, almost delicate, the furthest thing from frozen water. Not frozen hard as hailstones, but frozen still.

"You don't have a hat or gloves?"

I shook my head, wanting her to be quiet so I could listen to the silence which was magnified by the insulating effect of snow. It had been falling for nearly half an hour, but the graceful descent was deceiving. Tree branches and shrubs, the ground and the exposed parts of the house already had a fine dusting of snow.

"You're going to freeze."

"I'll be fine with my pockets. I don't plan on throwing snowballs."

"It's still cold."

"I don't think I'll get frostbite."

We started across the yard, following the path that was still visible as it wound through gardens and around small circular areas of lawn.

Soon my hair was damp, and my ears were cold. I unzipped the pocket at the neck of my jacket and pulled out the hood. I lifted it over my head, and we continued walking.

"You and Joe seem pretty close," I said. "You've worked together for a long time?"

"Three years."

"Is he your manager, or how does that work?"

"All of us took our direction directly from Mr. Kohn."

That wasn't the impression I'd had from Joe, but I said nothing.

"What made you think he was in charge of my work?"

I shrugged. "Not sure. I guess I just assumed it."

"You shouldn't do that."

"Probably not," I said. "Have you met the other Mr. Kohn?"

"No."

"So you're still planning to take your chances?"

"I have options. But I'll wait and see what he's like."

"It would be hard to leave this place."

"Living where you work has its downsides."

"I know."

"I don't think you do."

I didn't contradict her assumption. We circled toward the swimming pool and stood for a few minutes watching snowflakes dissolve into the water. It looked almost ridiculous, seeing the drifts building up on the diving board. A pool and snow belong in two different worlds.

"Ed better get out here soon. The pool is supposed to be covered when it snows."

We walked around the end of the pool and entered a grove of trees. We wandered slowly through and emerged back on the vast expanse of lawn that ran to the edge of the patio. We stepped onto the white blanket, and I felt my feet pushing through a paper-thin crust onto the cold earth below.

Without warning, Nell took off running across the lawn. Adopting the change in her mood, I chased after her. She stopped and scooped up a handful of snow. She packed it into a ball and threw it at me. The snow plopped down and fell apart several yards in front of me. She laughed but looked decidedly unhappy with her failure.

Since she wasn't very good, it wasn't necessary to stick my bare hands into the freezing stuff and shape it into a defensive ball. I walked toward her, and she took off running again. I chased after her.

When I got close, she stopped abruptly and turned. I ran in a diagonal direction, and she ran after me, laughing wildly. Suddenly, she was close, and then she lunged at me in a full tackle. I fell to the ground, my face sinking into snow and pounding the ground below. She laughed and moved back several feet.

I tasted icy cold liquid and grass. I pushed myself to my feet and glared at her.

"I don't know my own strength." She giggled.

She was entirely aware of her own strength, and she'd overused it to make sure I had a painful, if not damaging fall.

I brushed snow off my clothes and rubbed my hands on my jeans, trying to warm them. I spit out bits of grass. I pressed my fingers gently along the side of my jaw. My chin had pummeled the ground like a tent stake being hammered into the earth.

I started walking toward the patio.

"Don't be mad," she said.

"I should get going."

"Dirk won't want to drive while it's snowing."

"I need to get cleaned up, so I'm ready when it stops."

"It could be hours. Or more."

I estimated that by the time I finished taking a warm

shower and changing clothes, Dirk would either be willing or I'd call an Uber. If no Uber drivers wanted to go out in the snow, there was always a cab.

"Don't be a spoilsport."

"I'm not. I just need to get going.

I walked as quickly as the snow would allow toward the house. When I was a few yards from the patio, I looked up. I must have felt something — that awareness that you're being watched, the animal part of your brain coming to life when you're no longer alone.

Joe stood at one of the second-floor windows in what I believed was the master suite. He was looking down at me, his expression impossible to see from that distance. I started to lift my hand to wave, but somehow I knew — he wouldn't wave back. I shivered and went into the house.

42

Stephanie had waited all weekend for Eileen to confess that she'd snuck out for drinks with Alexandra, but her daughter had remained stubbornly silent. It was Eileen's not-so-secret weapon. She knew she could control her mother by her refusal to talk. Since she was a little girl, Eileen had retreated into herself whenever there was conflict, leaving Stephanie to play a guessing game as she tried to discover what was going on, forced to wheedle information out of a tiny child. A monstrous adult woman pleading and pressing a little girl with wide blue eyes and dark, tangled hair — the appearance of an angel and the iron will of a dictator.

Despite Stephanie's offer of a mother-daughter shopping trip on Black Friday, Eileen had left the house before Stephanie had finished with her prayer time. It was further evidence of her willfulness and her crafty approach to manipulating her mother.

She'd returned home in the early evening, her breath smelling of alcohol and no offer of information about where she'd been or what she'd been up to all day. She was carrying a single small shopping bag from Macy's, so she obviously hadn't been loading up on Christmas gifts, or even taking advantage of specials to buy new clothes for herself.

There was no mention of who she'd seen, what she'd done for lunch, where she'd eaten dinner.

Stephanie was almost sure that Eileen had spent at least part of the day with Alexandra. The two of them had been whispering and cackling like best friends when Stephanie came out of the shower on Thanksgiving. They'd formed some kind of connection, and she had a feeling...no, she knew, she *knew* they'd met for drinks and a private conversation.

Thinking about Eileen spending the day shopping with Alex brought a flood of emotion to Stephanie's chest, pushing tears up to the backs of her eyes where they threatened to dislodge every time she mentally rehearsed the imagined scene.

Now, Eileen was in her room where she'd spent the entire afternoon. She'd been at the gym for over two hours that morning and refused lunch when she returned, saying she'd already had a smoothie. Some lunch.

Sunday was a family day. Yes, it was Stephanie's fault they hadn't shared Thanksgiving, and now, she regretted that decision with her entire being. But it was Sunday. They should at least be sitting quietly in the living room. If Eileen had a date or plans with friends, it would be fine for her to go out on a Sunday. But she didn't. She was fifteen feet away, her door closed, earbuds stuffed in her ears, lost in her Godless world, inaccessible to the person who loved her most, the only person who could help her reclaim her life.

Stephanie stood in the middle of the living room. She'd made sautéed chicken breasts, pounded thin and cut into strips, ready to be covered with a creamy white sauce. The green beans were nearly finished cooking, and the rice was steamed and fluffy.

It would have been nice to cook dinner together, but Eileen never offered to help, not these past few years. A lot of things would be nice. There was no point in focusing on something that simply caused more pain. She needed to keep her attention on the one thing she could control — finding out what Alexandra was up to, getting to the bottom of why she was trying to weasel her way into Eileen's life.

Why wouldn't her daughter condescend to come out and eat dinner? Surely she'd smelled the food cooking. Why was Stephanie forced to invite her to dinner in her own apartment? To beg, almost. It felt like begging. Asking for Eileen's company, always asking, always needing. While Eileen needed Stephanie for nothing but the bedroom she slept in. She shared half the rent and other expenses, making it quite clear this was a financial arrangement only, not something that indebted her to her mother.

She sighed, feeling the ever-present tears again.

No one told you this about children.

The adorable baby placed into your arms, the wonderful miracle that gazed up at you, locking eyes with utter love faded and then disappeared.

Eileen had adored her mother when she was small. She'd wanted to cuddle up for story time, and she'd kissed her mother full on the lips with her soft, sweet mouth. She talked constantly when she came home from school, describing every moment of her day, telling stories about what she'd learned, how she felt, and who she'd played with.

Then, in a single heartbeat, the teenager slammed the door

in your face, and it only opened a crack from there on out.

You poured your whole life into a child, and she took all of the pieces of your heart, turned in on herself, and you were left alone.

It wasn't that way for all mothers. But for many, it was. She had definitely been one of the unlucky ones.

She bit her lip furiously to keep the tears at bay. She marched into the tiny hallway and knocked on Eileen's door, harder than she'd intended.

"What is it?"

"Dinner's ready." Before Stephanie could think or even try to control herself, the words came out. "And don't you dare tell me you aren't hungry because a smoothie is not a lunch and you're not going to starve yourself to death on my watch."

The door opened.

"Don't be so pissy. I am hungry."

"Oh. Well…good."

They sat at the table and Stephanie served up the food, biting her bottom lip until she tasted blood when Eileen refused the *unnecessary carbs* in the white rice and rejected even a drizzle of butter on her green beans. She carefully dripped a single teaspoon of sauce onto her chicken.

Stephanie pushed back her chair and stood. "How about a glass of wine?"

Eileen looked as shocked as Stephanie felt at her unexpected suggestion. "Trystan left a bottle here at Thanksgiving."

"Half a glass would be nice," Eileen said.

Stephanie poured a few ounces of wine into two glasses and returned to the table. She lifted her glass. "To the most wonderful time of the year."

Eileen smiled and tapped the side of her glass against Stephanie's. They each took a careful sip, as if they were cautiously exploring this new landscape where mother and daughter drank wine together.

"Tell me about your weekend," Stephanie said.

"Not much to tell."

"Well, surely you didn't sit in the park and feed pigeons all weekend."

Eileen laughed. She poked a green bean with her fork and put it into her mouth.

After a few moments of silence, Stephanie felt her impatience swell once again. "Did you?"

"Of course not."

Stephanie prayed silently, pleading for help in keeping calm. "I want to hear what you're up to. I'm interested in your life."

"You don't approve of what I'm up to most of the time."

"That's not fair."

Eileen shrugged.

"Try me." Stephanie took a sip of wine and forced herself to smile gently, calmly, with genuine interest.

"On Thanksgiving, I went to a soup kitchen and volunteered my time. They were so grateful even though it was last minute. I really enjoyed the day. It was good to hear the stories of how people ended up on the street, to understand what their lives have been like. You'd be amazed."

Stephanie didn't think she would be amazed at all. She helped regularly in a homeless shelter. Possibly Eileen was unaware of that fact. She said nothing. She didn't want to stop the thin stream of words finally emerging from Eileen's lips.

"I did a bit of shopping. Got your Christmas gift." She grinned. "Had drinks with a friend and…"

"What friend?"

Eileen put a piece of chicken in her mouth and chewed. She seemed to take forever, working the meat into something she could swallow.

"Why so secretive?"

Eileen shook her head. She drank some water. "I'm not being secretive."

"Then why won't you tell me?"

"God, Mother. I was eating. Calm down."

"I'm sorry. I'm just interested, and it feels like you want to shut me out."

"If it feels that way, this is why. You get so worked up."

"I don't think I do."

"You do."

They ate quietly, taking tiny sips of wine, keeping their attention on their plates, avoiding meeting the other's eyes.

"So are you going to tell me?"

Eileen sighed. "One of the women you work with — Alex. We met for drinks. Are you satisfied?"

"Why?"

"*Why?*"

Stephanie took a deep breath. "Why did you have drinks with her?"

"Why not?"

"Did you invite her, or was it her idea?"

"What difference does that make?"

It made a huge difference, but she'd calmed herself enough to keep that thought inside of her head instead of blurting it out like she did with everything else. Maybe she could take a page from Alexandra on that front — not saying so much. Too much. But it was hard. And Alex was closed and cold. Stephanie liked to be open, to say what was on her mind. To be truthful. "What did you talk about?"

Eileen glared at her.

"Okay. Okay. I get it." Stephanie took another sip of wine. It was almost gone. She would not have another glass, but the desire was intense. She picked up her glass of water and gulped half of it down. "Be careful around her, that's all. Be very, very careful."

Eileen rolled her eyes.

"Don't be a child. I'm giving you advice born of hard lessons."

"Such as?"

"For once in your life, trust that I'm older than you and that I know a thing or two. I'll leave it at that." She finished her wine and plowed into her chicken. She'd already said too much. She refused to further antagonize her daughter simply because Alexandra had no boundaries. She would go directly to the source.

43

The snow had melted by the time I went to work on Monday morning. It was hard to get my mind back onto what I was supposed to be doing after four days off and all the food and sex and alcohol and various people parading through my life.

I opened my office door to find Stephanie sitting at my desk. I stopped in the doorway, my coat sleeve halfway down my arm as I'd started to remove it before I saw her beetle eyes boring into me.

"I need to talk to you," she said.

"You could text. Or email. You can even knock on my door any time during the day."

"Please sit down."

"You're in my chair."

She gestured toward the visitor chair facing my desk. I remained by the door. I dropped my messenger bag to the floor. I took off my coat and hung it over my arm. "What's up?"

"You need to sit down."

I stared at her. She stared back, and we held each other's gazes for nearly half a minute. Finally, she looked away. She pushed the chair a few inches away from the desk and folded her arms across her ribs. "Stay away from my daughter."

I laughed.

"I'm serious."

"She's an adult."

"A damaged adult, as I've told you. I never imagined, not in a million years, that you'd take advantage of my confidence like this."

"As I said, she's an adult. No one is taking advantage."

"You are taking advantage of me."

"How so?"

"I just told you. I shared my concerns about her life in confidence."

"What does that have to do with anything?"

"I told you she was vulnerable and you swooped in and tried to shove yourself into her life."

"So? Not that it's your business to know the private life of your adult daughter, but it seemed to me that she needed a friend."

"You are *not* a *friend.*"

"Look, Stephanie. I don't know what you're upset about, but Eileen is a big girl. We met, we chatted, we decided we'd like to chat some more. It has nothing to do with you. If you're worried that I'll talk about our interactions here, I won't."

"How do I know that?"

"You don't."

"Exactly. I don't want you talking to her, period. You have a cynical and pagan view of the world, and that's not the person I want her talking to and listening to."

"You can't do anything about it."

"Do you want to bet?"

Of course, I didn't want to bet. But I sort of did. Because it wasn't really a bet. It was a sure thing. What was wrong with her? Eileen was in her late twenties. Why did Stephanie think she could dictate her grown daughter's relationships?

Stephanie was like my father in a lot of ways. She was more neurotic than my father, but their views of the world and especially their beliefs that children were parental possessions, and that parents had some sort of divine directive to force-fit another human being's mind into a shape of their own choosing was the same.

"It seems like you believe you can tell her how to think. That you can think for her," I said.

"That's ridiculous."

"Then why are you telling me to stay away from her?"

"She's weak right now. She doesn't know her own mind."

"How do you know that?"

"I'm her mother. I know her better than she knows herself."

"That's not possible."

"Don't argue with me. I invited you into my confidence and my home, and you took advantage. You want something from her, and I don't like it. She doesn't need any more hurt in her life."

I wondered if Eileen would feel hurt if she knew her mother was talking about her weaknesses and flaws to her co-worker. "Please get out of my chair."

"Not until you agree you won't speak to her again."

"I'm not going to do that."

She stood quickly, letting the chair slide out behind her. "If you go anywhere near her again, you'll regret it." Her voice was shrill, her eyes wide. She reeked of fury.

I gave her a tight smile. I moved around the opposite side of my desk and sat down. As she walked to the door, I wondered what she thought she could do to keep me away from Eileen. It almost sounded as if she planned something malicious. Or violent. But the thought of her doing anything violent, anything more than throwing a remote control, was ridiculous. At least I hoped it was.

44

There was no way I was skipping the gym after the long weekend. I'd only gone for a single run in the past week, and my body felt flabby and soggy. The problem was, I wanted to skip the gym. I wanted a martini and something easy and satisfying to eat, like a hamburger, but the gym had to come first. And then a salad and a liter of water, not a burger.

It's remarkable how too many cocktails one evening leads to more cocktails the following evening and then the night after that and on it goes. The same with easy food. It's as if once those molecules find their way into your body, they start calling out for more of them to join the party. Begging, pleading, enticing. And on one level, that's actually the way the body works.

It was pouring rain, the romantic snow faded from my memory. This made it even more difficult to psych myself up for a visit to the gym, trudging along slick sidewalks and crossing streets where the gutters gushed with water that moved quickly enough to be considered a tiny river in the center of a concrete and steel city.

I clutched my umbrella with my right hand and tried to

juggle my messenger bag and gym bag on my left shoulder. The bags fought each other to swat at my hip as I walked as quickly as the other pedestrians and the rain allowed. When I finally reached the entrance to the gym, I felt I'd already had a workout.

Inside and wearing my spandex outfit, I shivered from the damp cold air as it touched my bare arms and upper back. I ran on the treadmill for twenty minutes to get myself warmed up, literally. Once my blood was pumping heat to my skin, I began the weight lifting circuit.

I spent over an hour, working each muscle group three or four different ways. By the end, my muscles quivered with exhaustion, which was exactly how I'd wanted them to feel. There's nothing like trembling muscles to wipe the desire for a martini out of my body.

I stood in the shower for several long minutes. I towel-dried my hair knowing it would probably get wet on the walk home.

As I entered my apartment building I collapsed the umbrella. Water ran off the fabric and formed a huge puddle just past the steps and another in front of the mailboxes while I unlocked mine and retrieved the mail.

My apartment was as cold as the gym. I turned up the heat, dropped the stack of mail on the dining table, and opened the refrigerator door.

The shelves were gutted. There was a large container of leftover mashed potatoes from Stephanie's dinner, a container of peach yogurt, and half a loaf of bread. I closed the door. I was starving and knowing there was no food intensified my hunger.

I dug around in my gym bag and found a power bar. I

peeled off the wrapper and took a large bite. As I chewed, I filled a glass with water. I drank half the water. Finally, my stomach stopped its screaming.

The mail was damp from the postman's walk through the downpour, the envelopes and leaflets sticking to each other. My mail was ninety-nine percent junk because I don't hand out my address. Usually, I glance at the stack to see if there are any interesting sales and then dump it into the trash, but I'd seen an official-looking envelope tucked inside the bright newsprint leaflets full of ads and coupons.

I wiggled the envelope out from the sheaf of papers. It was stamped in the upper left with a fancy, immediately recognizable logo beside the name and address of the FBI field office in New York City. The name on the envelope was Nick Ressler. I tossed the junk mail and left the envelope sitting in the middle of the table.

I emptied my gym bag and put my workout clothes in the laundry sack. I cracked open the bathroom window to let in the smell of the rain, so it would drift into my bedroom and give me a peaceful night's sleep.

The normal and natural thing to do was to draw a line through the recipient's address, write a note to please forward, and be done with it. But that return address and the neatly typed name in the center of the envelope, sitting perfectly aligned above my address, wouldn't let me go.

There had to be a way to leverage this either with Kent or even Victoria and Rafe to find out more about Nick and why he'd left so abruptly. I spent half a minute considering whether I might call the main number for the field office and try to find out what they wanted with Nick Ressler. But even thinking I could talk to someone who would provide any information was completely far-fetched. To have a thread of hope for making something like that work, I would need starting details, and I had nothing.

Kent would tell me to forward it. I had no idea what Victoria or Rafe might say. Suggest forwarding? Try to take possession of it? Tell me to destroy it?

I took the envelope into my bedroom and opened the bedside drawer. I dropped the damp, thin package inside and closed the drawer.

Starving now, and not at all up to battling the rain that had begun blowing at an angle, I heated the mashed potatoes and called that dinner. It wasn't the worst dinner in the world. It was probably healthier than a hamburger from a fast food place.

After that, I succumbed to a martini after all. I put on PJs and curled up on the couch with a blanket over my lower legs and feet. It wasn't at all cold inside my apartment, but the rush of rain and the sound of it splashing against the windowsill made me want comfort.

I played a few games on my phone and then let my mind drift back to Joe and Nell and the damaged armoire and missing photographs. I'd left the house in the limo, which might be taken as a positive sign, but Joe hadn't said anything about seeing each other again. Neither had he said anything about trust. We appeared to be in a holding pattern. Or maybe it was only me circling the airport, waiting for direction. Maybe he'd made his decision.

Seeing him looking out the window, watching as Nell shoved me to the ground, doing nothing, had sent a cold chill through me that wasn't caused by the snow that had scraped my skin.

I pictured each person living in that house, trying to figure out why they wanted those pictures. Whoever had broken the lock and taken the photographs hadn't just stumbled upon them. Not with a broken lock. The most logical answer was that all of them had known. Joe, because he so awkwardly tried to keep me from seeing inside that storage room, and Nell and Ed, because neither of them wanted me in the house at all. Really, all of them, because how could those photographs have been taken without the people who worked there being aware of what was happening?

45

Despite her promise to return with the makeup and cleanser, the next time Carmen arrived at my front door, she was empty-handed.

"Where's the makeup?" I spoke in a low voice to be sure my mother, always tuned into the slightest sound coming from her children's bodies, wouldn't hear.

"I couldn't bring it."

"Why?" I stepped back, and she walked into our entryway as she always did — looking around, wanting to see what coats or scarves were hanging on the hooks of the parson's bench or checking for new artwork on the walls, or most of all, hoping to see one of my brothers.

I closed the door and leaned against it, suddenly tired at the thought of another afternoon with Carmen.

She started up the stairs, then paused, waiting for me to follow. "You need to show me what's in your closet."

"No I don't."

She continued climbing the stairs. "I can't believe those

baby toys in the attic are the only toys you have."

"They aren't baby toys."

"Some of them are."

"I like them, and I'm not a baby. If I were a baby, I wouldn't have my own cactus."

She stopped again and turned to look down at me. She eyed me for a moment, surprised at my train of thought, maybe…realizing I was right and not wanting to admit it. "You don't have any other toys?"

"Just games for the whole family."

"I still want to see your closet."

We went to my room, and she walked inside. She put her hand on the closet doorknob.

"There aren't any toys in there."

"I have to *see*." She opened the door. She stepped into the closet and let the shirts and sweaters and dresses suspended from their hangers brush across her face.

"Get out of there."

She stepped out from under the clothes. "How come you don't have any Barbies?"

"They're not allowed."

"Why not?"

"Because they're frivolous."

"What does that mean?"

"It means they aren't useful."

"Toys aren't supposed to be useful."

"My father wants us to play with things that make us think about god. Toys that help us develop into good human beings. Barbies make you think about clothes and hair and how you look and being a model."

She stared at me.

I didn't know much about the Catholic religion at that age, but I was learning that they had very different rules. Mostly no rules at all, as far as I could tell based on the things Carmen said.

She turned and looked into the closet again as if she didn't believe me, as if she were looking for some secret that might explain such a strange notion about a toy. She closed the door. "That's dumb."

I smiled.

Her expression changed, the thoughts passing through her mind vivid in the reshaping of her lips and the widening of her eyes. She looked slightly afraid.

The following afternoon she arrived with a large pink, fabric-sided suitcase. It stood by her feet on the front porch where she'd left it while she rang the bell. She carried it up to the attic and placed it in the center of the floor. She closed the attic door and sat beside her suitcase.

"The Barbie rule is dumb." She unzipped the case and folded the cover to the side.

The suitcase was filled with Barbie clothes. Lying on top were four Barbies — two blondes wearing workout clothes, a redheaded astronaut, and an African-American doll dressed like a businesswoman. Beside them were two Ken dolls.

There was a white cardboard box filled with tiny plastic shoes and another containing purses and hair brushes.

I stared, transfixed.

"I have lots more Barbies so you can have these. Not forever, but for as long as we're friends. Even though we're not blood sisters."

"I don't think my parents will let me keep them."

"You said no one ever comes up here. How would they know?"

They wouldn't. I couldn't believe she could give away her Barbies. I also wasn't sure what I was supposed to do with them. Once you'd changed their clothes, then what? "I'm not sure…"

"You don't want them?"

"I do." I could see the fun of changing outfits, switching shoe colors and styles.

We spent the next two hours dressing and undressing the various dolls. The entire time, Carmen kept a running monologue of their conversations with each other. I was more enthralled by her voiceover than I was with the new experience of tugging sleeves the size of drinking straws over stiff plastic arms and combing synthetic hair.

It was as if Carmen had an entire world unfurling inside her head, separate from her primary self. Inside her mind, these plastic figures had names and families and problems. They talked about their friends, and what they wanted to wear, they talked about having colds and going to jobs, cooking dinner and taking naps and getting married.

I was stunned. I hardly said a word the entire time. Carmen didn't seem to notice. She was living in an alternate universe.

When it was time for dinner, we placed the dolls side-by-side on top of their heap of clothes. We zipped the suitcase closed, and Carmen advised me to *stash it* behind the couch, just in case someone made the trip up to the attic and wondered what it was…in case someone wanted to *snoop* through my things.

The next day was Sunday, and our family was busy with church and Sunday school, then an afternoon concert followed by the evening church service.

On Monday, Carmen wasn't at school. The next day, she returned looking perfectly healthy. She'd had an upset stomach on Sunday, and her mother wanted her to *take it easy* on Monday. I was stunned that parents allowed their children to stay home from school just to rest. I couldn't imagine my parents allowing this. In fact, we had to be coughing uncontrollably or running a fever to escape from school and spend a day lounging in bed, being waited on by my mother.

Carmen and I ate our snack at the kitchen table — apple slices smeared with peanut butter — while my mother lurked near the sink. When the plate was empty, we went up to the attic. She knelt on the couch and leaned over the back to pick up the suitcase. She turned and glared at me. "It's not here."

"It must be."

"It's not. Did you move it to your closet?"

I shook my head.

"Then where is it?"

"We could go to your house." We never went to her house. It seemed unfair, but she never invited me, and until that moment, I'd never asked, so I must have been content on some level with the imbalance.

"Who do you think took it?"

"If my parents did, I'd be in trouble, so it must have been one of my brothers."

"I thought they weren't allowed up here. They have the basement."

"It doesn't mean they don't come up when I'm not around."

"That's not fair."

"They do lots of things that aren't fair."

She glowered at me, angry that my family allowed unfairness to exist, I suppose.

46

New York

The letter addressed to Nick Ressler almost seemed as if it was vibrating inside my nightstand drawer, reaching its fingers into my brain and fiddling with my dreams.

I dreamt I was standing on the steps of a stately courthouse. There were easily fifty steps between me and the massive Roman columns announcing its significance. I climbed the stairs, but each time I did, I somehow found myself a few steps from the bottom, once again looking up. I needed to get into that courthouse. There were important papers inside and it was urgent that I get to them before something else happened, although it wasn't clear what that something else was.

Finally, I was inside, arriving through no effort of my own, as you do in dreams. I was handed a stack of mail that I needed to deliver immediately. I flipped through and saw that all the addresses were blurred, so I had no idea where they were supposed to go.

I woke to the sound of a siren a block or two from my

building. The rain had stopped. The room felt muggy and cold at the same time. I opened the nightstand drawer and took out the letter. Before the end of the day, I needed to decide what I wanted to do with it. I wasn't going to commit mail fraud by keeping it to myself or destroying it.

What I couldn't decide was whether I should show it to Victoria, or simply mention its existence. I was intrigued by the shock value of seeing her unguarded face as I flashed it in front of her without any introductory explanation that allowed her to compose her features and consider her response. At the same time, I didn't want her to get her hands on it.

Outside, the sidewalks were already dry. I put on running clothes, grabbed my keys and phone, and headed out the door. I ran for two miles then called it quits. Usually running clears my head, but my mind was spinning so fast, I forgot to turn right at the Starbucks and was four blocks out of my way when I became aware of what I was doing.

After getting ready for work, eating the peach yogurt, which didn't satisfy me at all, and drinking two cups of coffee, which made me hungrier, I knocked on my neighbors' door. A small part of me hoped I'd be invited in for breakfast.

Victoria answered. I could see Rafe across the room, seated at one of the computers. It was strangely shocking to see him working. They talked incessantly about their day trading, but it had become almost mythological in its perfection as a path to financial freedom. So larger-than-life that the actual work of it seemed non-existent. The dream of it all had buried the reality that they went to their desks every morning just as I did.

The door immediately started to close. "Sorry, I'm really busy," Victoria said. "Unless you wanted to give me the go-ahead to make an investment for you?" She smiled, hope moving across her face and spreading to the roots of her spiky hair.

"No, just a quick question about the guy who lived in my apartment before me."

"Oh. I don't have time. Sorry. Come by after the market closes, okay?" She gave me another hopeful smile and closed the door.

As I moved away, I heard the sound of her door opening again.

"I might have two minutes after all," Victoria said. "If it's truly a quick question."

I turned back and faced her. "Do you have a forwarding address for the guy who lived here before me?"

"Why?"

It was not the answer she should have given. There were two answers for a person not hiding something — *yes*, or *no*. People often get stray mail after they've moved. No normal person would care a bit why a forwarding address was asked for.

"Did you get mail for him?"

"I tried to make this simple because you wanted it to be quick." I smiled. "We don't need to have an entire conversation. Do you have his address? Yes or no?"

"I'm just wondering why you want it. I think that's a natural question."

It wasn't, but... "I have mail to forward. I thought it would be more helpful than just scribbling *not at this address*. So it doesn't get delayed."

Rafe turned slightly in his chair. I couldn't tell if he was trying to listen or getting ready to signal her to stop talking and interfering with his concentration.

Her eyes narrowed. "Does it look important?"

"Isn't all mail important? Unless it's junk, and then I wouldn't be forwarding it."

"I can check for his address. Why don't you give it to me and if I can't find the address, I'll give it to the manager. He should have the contact info."

"No, that's fine. I'll just mark it to forward."

"But I might have it."

"I'll let you get back to work. Check if you have it and text it to me."

She stared at me. I could almost see the virtual gears turning inside her head, trying to think of a way to either find out more about the letter or get her hands on it.

I went back to my apartment door.

"You're kind of making a big deal out of a piece of mail. It sounds like it must be really important. It's not a check, is it?" She laughed, another bit of odd behavior in the circumstances.

"No."

"Do you know for sure?"

"Yes."

"Then what is it? Why are you being so secretive?"

"Do I seem secretive? I didn't mean to."

She cocked her head to the side. She grabbed her earlobe and rubbed it absently while she continued looking at me. Her eyes glazed over, staring past me. Finally, her gaze refocused on my face. "You can be really difficult, do you know that?"

"I've heard." I smiled.

"It's not funny. I'm serious. I'm trying to get work done. It's a very high-pressure situation here. And you're making a big deal out of some wayward mail."

"Am I?"

"Just give me the letter. You make it sound like it's some major thing. It's just mail."

"You're right. It is."

"Then give it to me so I can get back to work, and I'll check for his address later," she said.

"I'm wondering why you want it so badly. Since you have to work and all. You seem to be taking a lot of time trying to figure out what it is. I hope you aren't the kind of person who would open someone else's mail."

"Of course not. Just give me the damn letter."

"I'll ask the manager. It's simpler. You're right, he would definitely have the address. He would have had to mail Nick's deposit back to him. I'm not sure why I didn't think of that to start with."

"Because I'm right here. And I knew him."

"Sorry to bother you. Hope you have a productive day." I stepped into my apartment and closed the door. Victoria was still standing there.

I was happy with the way the conversation had unfolded but disappointed she hadn't offered breakfast.

47

Joe texted me: *We should resolve things.*

The message was simple. It could be taken two ways. The first was that he wanted to keep going as we had. The second was that he was the somewhat atypical guy who wanted closure on a brief fling.

I'd had the impression he thought there was more than just sex and good food and interesting conversation between us. But if that was the case, neither interpretation quite fit. Was he so genuine that he thought we were headed toward a serious relationship and he honestly needed to discuss what went wrong? The truth was, nothing needed to be discussed. He'd decided I wasn't someone he could trust. Why would that require closure?

I waited two hours before I replied. Not to be one of those girls, but because I wasn't sure what I wanted to say and I needed to say the perfect thing to get us back on a stable footing. Striking the right tone was tricky. His message seemed to have more behind it. Resolving things could mean a phone call. It could mean him coming into the city for a quick drink or even dinner. I needed to resolve things at the house where I had a slim, although dying chance of finding out who had broken into the armoire.

I closed my office door. I texted back: *I'd like that.*

In my mind, my message sounded vulnerable. It sounded like the words of someone he might be able to trust after all. And hopefully, it suggested more than a phone call. Of course, if he'd wanted things resolved with a simple phone conversation, he would have called already. I hoped.

He responded to my message with an invite to come over the following evening. For dinner. He would send the limo. It looked as if vulnerability had worked. I was pleased with myself.

Dirk was as inscrutable as ever, not giving any hint whether he knew that this ride was different from the others or giving any indication whether it might be my last. He didn't suggest in any way that my status had changed. He still held the door, called me Ms. Mallory, and wanted to be assured I was comfortable with the temperature and the beverages provided in the back seat.

Joe was waiting with the front door open when I arrived. It occurred to me that he and Dirk must be in regular communication regarding the car's location. Suddenly, being driven about felt less free and luxurious. Instead, it seemed slightly confining.

Dirk carried my overnight bag up the steps and handed it to Joe which made me feel even more controlled. Why hadn't I noticed this before? I felt like a package, handed off from one man to another. The pleasure of riding in a limousine was no longer something I could simply enjoy. Now, it felt weighted and slightly suspect.

We went up to Joe's room. There was a caution about him

as he removed my clothes and we fell into bed without talking, but otherwise, he was the same. He touched me in the same way, his desire was the same, and his playfulness wasn't altered by this dramatic lack of trust he'd experienced when he caught me with his keys.

After a while, the image of him standing at that window, silently watching me shoved to the ground, faded. I relaxed into things.

Nothing was any different as we showered and dressed. Going to the dining room was the same, as was the display of candles to make the room feel more intimate. We ate a feast of salad and pasta with grilled chicken followed by a board of cheese and miniature chocolates for dessert.

No one else was present. Even the chef kept out of sight as Joe went into the kitchen, carrying plates back and forth to the dining room.

We settled in front of another magically laid fire, each of us holding a glass of wine.

He stared into the fire. He placed his glass on the coffee table and leaned back, still keeping his attention on the flames leaping before us like dancers. "Did you take the photographs out of the storage room?"

I swallowed my wine, nearly gulping it as I tried to look preoccupied, distracted, my mind elsewhere instead of working to develop a credible lie. He'd asked the question in a very cagey way. Answering with a simple *no*, would be an admission that I knew about the photographs. Of course, he knew I'd been inside the room after the pictures were removed, but he didn't know I'd had access to the armoire before that, so how would I have known they existed?

My hesitation, caught off guard by a question I never

dreamed he'd ask because I'd assumed he knew who took them, made a lie more difficult.

Difficult, but not impossible.

"All I did was look in the closets and side rooms."

"You're deflecting."

"No I'm not. I said *all I did.*"

"You saw the broken lock?"

"What lock?"

He picked up his glass and took a sip of wine. He held the glass in front of him and turned it slowly, working the stem as if his aim was to keep the liquid level while the glass bowl moved around it. "I know you saw it."

I waited half a beat. "Oh, on the armoire?"

"Yes. *On the armoire.*"

I took a sip of wine. I crossed my legs and rested my glass on my thigh.

"So you did see it?"

"I said, *yes.*"

"But you didn't break it? You didn't remove the photographs that were stored inside?"

"I already told you."

"I didn't find them in your bags. But now that I know you can't be trusted...I've realized they might have disappeared earlier."

I let his obvious breach of trust go because all I wanted was to continue what we had for as many days as we had left. And I wanted those photographs. It was an almost impossible goal, but I had to keep trying.

I think he was waiting for me to get angry over his search of my bags which was far more egregious than borrowing a set of keys and checking out what I'd been led to believe was a simple storage room. His breathing seemed to slow and catch periodically as he waited for me to respond.

We sat there in silence, the flames waning as the clocked ticked forward. The score was even now, and we both knew that.

48

She should have done it the Monday after Thanksgiving. In fact, she should have done it the very next day. It would have been easy enough to call, or even text. Now, it was worse because she'd let several working days and multiple interactions with Trystan float past without acknowledging how she'd mistreated him and truly let him down.

It was obvious why she'd put it off — she was embarrassed. Talking about it would intensify her feelings of shame. And she was angry — at herself, at God for not helping her expose Alex, and at Alex, for a reason she couldn't fully explain even to herself. It was more than Alex stealing her job and more than Alex trying to corrupt her daughter even further.

In some ways, Alex had stolen Trystan's respect.

If Alex hadn't shown up early, if she hadn't brought an uninvited and unwelcome guest and then tried to make her feel guilty with all that nonsense about strangers at the first Thanksgiving, the whole day would have unfolded much differently.

Alex wasn't only a pagan, she was a vampire of sorts. She

stole everything that mattered, draining your blood and leaving you lifeless, turning you into a monster yourself.

The image of a vampire should have made her see how foolish and overly dramatic she was being, but it was oddly appropriate. This was not her imagination running wild and seeing things that weren't there — overdramatizing, as she'd been accused of. This was real — a serious threat to her life in every way.

But she was out of ideas for dealing with Alex. The woman was too strong, too powerful, too manipulative for someone like Stephanie to outwit. Alexandra was a wolf among lambs — the gentle, guileless believers — herself and Eileen. Yes, Eileen was still a believer. Deep inside. She'd strayed, but she could be brought back to the fold, if Stephanie could find a way to deal with Alex.

The first step was to ask Trystan's forgiveness. She couldn't get back into an intimate connection with God until she'd confessed her drunkenness. She'd already confessed to Him, but He'd made it clear she'd wronged Trystan and Diana. Both of them needed to forgive her before anything could move forward in her life.

Her prayers would be stalled at the gates of heaven until that was taken care of. The Bible was clear on that point — if you're standing at the altar and you remember you've offended your sister or brother, you should leave immediately and go to them for reconciliation. Only then could you return to the altar.

Trystan first, then Diana.

The office was dark except for the glow of her computer in the center of her desk. She liked it this way. It made the world seem more quiet, and she needed that right now. In another hour, the others would begin arriving for work, bringing noise and the energy of other human activity. Now, she had time to catch up on the comments in her Facebook group that focused on how to live as a Godly woman in a large city.

By the time she heard the outer office door open, the sun had come up on a crisp, clear morning. She'd finished two cups of coffee in addition to the cup she'd gulped down before coming to the office. The caffeine made her slightly jittery, but it also made her feel energized and ready for the task ahead.

Diana called a good morning greeting and went into her office, closing the door.

Maybe she should speak to Diana first.

She pushed her chair away from her desk. No. That wasn't right. Trystan was her boss. He was the one she'd spoken to so sharply, the one she'd...the memory of what she'd done was so horrifying she couldn't form the words to describe it in her own mind. She closed her eyes and took several slow, calming breaths, her jaw and hands and heart all trembling with asynchronous rhythms.

Moving her chair back to the desk and placing her fingers on the keyboard, she opened an email window and began composing an email to Alexandra.

Twenty minutes later the outer door opened. She heard the voices of Trystan and Alex as they entered the suite together. Her blood boiled at the sound of their laughing, friendly voices. No wonder people said that. It had always seemed so extreme — *she makes my blood boil* — now she understood. How did Alexandra manage to get Trystan alone so much of the time, twisting his mind to her way of thinking, flattering him? Most men were vulnerable to flattery, and Alex knew how to take advantage of that.

Maybe she should adopt some of the same tactics. In a godly way, of course. It might be a possible way to change the situation.

The two of them parted at Alex's office door. Neither one had said good morning to her. Trystan continued down the hall to his office. She heard Alex's door close but not Trystan's. It was perfect. Maybe God was taking an active interest in her life again. The simple intention to ask forgiveness had already partially restored the connection, causing things to flow in her favor.

She hurried down the hall, propelled by caffeine and her desire to get in there before he started work, before she lost her nerve, before Alex found a way to intrude. She didn't bother knocking on the open door. She walked in and closed it behind her. "Do you have a few minutes?"

"Absolutely." He smiled. There didn't seem to be any trace of negative emotion toward her, but it was difficult to tell with him. He was smooth. Always polite and professional. Now that she thought about it, she'd never seen him react with strong emotion to anything. Even when she'd slapped his face, thrown the remote, shouted at him...and yes, it had been a shout.

Her face grew warm as she recalled her sins. She sat down quickly.

"Are you okay?"

She nodded.

"What's on your mind?"

"I need to ask your forgiveness."

"For?"

"For my behavior on Thanksgiving."

He waved his hand at her. "It's all forgotten."

"I haven't forgotten anything. And I'd like to ask you to forgive me for…"

"There's no need."

That's what was one of so many things wrong with the world. No one thought forgiveness mattered. They didn't ask for it, they didn't even recognize when they needed it, and they mocked the idea rather than giving genuine forgiveness when it was asked for. They wanted to hold onto their grudges, they wanted to recount your sins and use them to attack you in the future. She wouldn't allow it.

"It's important to me that you forgive me for speaking so rudely to you. When you touched me."

"I was out of line."

"You weren't. You were being kind and I over-reacted. My ex-husband used to…"

Again, he waved his hand. "You don't need to explain, Stephanie. I shouldn't have touched you. And there's nothing more that needs to be said."

"Please let me finish."

He sighed.

She wasn't sure how to interpret the sigh. Was she wasting his time? Did he have an appointment? He'd said he had a few minutes. He was prolonging this by interrupting, and he was throwing her off course. "All I want to say is that I shouldn't have spoken like that. It was a harmless touch. And I was so, *so* wrong to slap you. I'm very sorry, more sorry than you can imagine. I'm asking you to forgive me for my terrible behavior, and for getting drunk, of course. That's not an excuse, but I shouldn't have gotten drunk."

"We all do it. I've truly put it behind me. The day was nice, and we all appreciate the effort you put into it."

She wanted to laugh. *All*, meaning him and Diana. Alexandra appreciated absolutely nothing. It was obvious in every word she spoke. It was obvious in her refusal to express gratitude, even on Thanksgiving Day.

"Is there anything else?"

"Will you forgive me?"

"Of course."

She smiled. Warmth flooded her heart, and the erratic hammering slowed as if God Himself was re-entering the space, making His home there, filling that organ with His presence and love.

She felt intense and overwhelming gratitude, and yes, love. Trystan was a wonderful boss, a wonderful man. She was so blessed to have him in her life. It wasn't the love of physical desire or human emotion. It was truly God's love transforming her. Although, he would be an easy man to love.

49

Eileen texted me, suggesting we meet again for a drink. I texted back that I was trying to get to the gym every day after work. She suggested I should join her as a guest at her gym. I agreed, eager to try a more luxurious place. It would be a welcome change from my gym, which offered the basics and didn't waste time or money on ambiance.

Her gym was not unlike the bar where we'd met — filled with women who looked like models. It was female only, but that didn't stop some of the patrons working out in full makeup and spandex tops that looked like evening wear.

Despite their slender figures and fancy outfits, they appeared to work out hard. The energy of their effort was palpable the minute I stepped out of the locker room. A locker room that resembled a spa with its two kidney-shaped hot tubs, a perfectly designed sauna made of gorgeous oak, several rooms where masseuses were booked almost non-stop, and showers and mirrors and sinks that would do justice to a four-star hotel.

We started on the treadmills so we could chat. It's not conducive to a good workout to talk while trying to maintain proper breathing and form for weight-lifting. And the equipment in most gyms is spaced in a way that doesn't allow for conversation.

We started up our machines and began walking.

"I normally run on here," she said.

"So do I. But we can use the incline instead, and put more effort into weights. Mix it up. It's the key to a successful workout."

"True."

Although the public setting might not have been the best for a deeply personal conversation, it did have benefits for asking her a direct question. Walking side-by-side, it might be easier for her to answer. She wouldn't feel the spotlight of having to look me in the eye while managing her feelings. And somehow, it didn't seem as forced.

I'd decided I didn't have time to let things take a natural course, waiting for her to share the dark experiences of those photo shoots. I needed to know about those images before Mark Kohn arrived to shake things up. I plowed right in — "It's a rather long story how I ended up in this situation," I said, "But I'm sort of seeing the guy who was chief of staff for your former fiancé."

She jammed her finger on the pause button. The machine stopped moving, and she turned slightly. "Joe?"

"Yes." I continued walking. I pressed the button to lower the incline slightly.

"How?"

"I said it's a long story."

"I need a long workout."

I laughed. "Okay, maybe the story's not that long. I'd gone to one of Jim's dinner parties to photograph him."

She nodded once, a single shake of her head.

"After he died, I felt I needed closure, so I went back to the house."

"Closure for what?"

I sighed heavily and somewhat too loudly. "He came on to me. Hard. Without an invitation. Attacked me, actually."

She nodded, several movements of her head up and down this time.

"It was...I didn't like how he made me feel. Not at all. And I guess I thought I would have some kind of victory over him if I went back and looked around his office. Not looked around, but just went in there and sort of...gave myself closure. Reminded myself that I was fine."

She nodded more vigorously. "That makes sense. So how did Joe happen?"

"You know."

"I don't know, but you don't have to say if you'd rather not."

I decided I should say. If I revealed something, it would pave the way for her own revelation. "He knew I liked martinis. It was pouring rain, so he made martinis. Then he showed me the wine cellar, and I kissed him."

She laughed. "You made the first move?"

"Sure."

"I just...I'm sorry. Not sure why I laughed. I was surprised. It's not funny, just...a surprise."

"It's a great house. He gave me a detailed tour."

"It is. Kind of too big, but gorgeous. And so much luxury," she said.

"I know. The kitchen is amazing."

"And the bathrooms. The cigar room!"

I slowed my pace slightly. "There's this so-called storage room on the third floor."

I could feel her body grow tight and her mood darken. Her feet thudded with more force on the moving belt beneath her. The sound of her breath changed into something feral.

"I saw the photographs."

This time, she didn't hit pause. She stopped the machine and stepped down. "I can't talk about this here."

"I thought maybe you were..."

"No, it's not your fault. I just can't. I can talk to you, I don't mind talking to you. Actually, I want to. But not here. Not right now." She climbed back on and restarted her machine, ratcheting up the speed. She began running as fast as it's possible to run on a treadmill.

Feeling her race beside me was unsettling. I was walking at a decent pace on the incline, but now I felt that her movements were so wild she was in danger of being flung off the machine. She would land with flying arms and legs right in front of me, and we'd both wind up with our ponytailed hair caught in the quickly revolving mat.

I started running as well, and even though we were stationary, I felt she was sprinting so much faster, she would be blocks ahead of me if we were outdoors.

Eileen's breathing grew hard and loud, so loud the two women on the machines to her right turned to look at her every minute or so. Sweat formed on her upper chest and along her arms. The front of her pink shirt was dark with moisture, and sweat was pooling in the small hollow at the center of her collarbone like a little cup of water.

I tried not to keep turning to stare at her, but she was so obviously upset, I wondered if she was going to break down crying or fall into a screaming fit right there. I had no idea what I would do if that happened. I might help her to the locker room, but then what? Surely I wouldn't call her mother, and I knew nothing else about her life.

Then it occurred to me she might be as unstable as her mother. We'd had several normal conversations. She was friendly and motivated and seemed relatively sure of who she was and what she wanted. But now I felt as if I'd ripped the skin off her face and exposed something raw and badly damaged, and I was left to take care of the mess.

If they were so disturbing to her, why had she let those pictures remain in Jim's possession? It's impossible for me to understand someone who allows other people to take such control of their lives.

50

Eileen's feet pounded the treadmill platform for over forty-five minutes. She looked like a woman running for her life. Eventually, she wound down and came to a stop. We moved to the weight machines, and she completed a circuit that clearly included heavier weights and more reps than her usual workout. I followed behind, impressed with the level of her commitment and her overall strength. She wasn't as strong as I am, but her ability was significantly beyond what you would expect from someone with such a slender frame.

We skipped the hot tub, sauna, and massage, opting for long, sweat-cleansing showers, enjoying the sensation of muscles worked to their breaking point. Neither of us felt the need to pamper our muscles as if they couldn't handle the load we'd placed on them.

"Now how about a drink?" She asked the question without the flicker of a smile, as if getting a drink was very serious business — on a level with the bench press — a workout that we'd put off far too long.

I agreed, and we went to an Italian restaurant that had a full bar.

Settled at a small table in the back, enclosed by walls covered with dark red paper and surrounded by hanging plants, we ordered pasta and a bottle of Zinfandel, and she told me the story of the ugly photographs.

Jim had been desperate for her to be an international success as a model. He'd always had a thing for models, and he'd known she had the face and the body to rise to the top. He wanted to be recognized for *making* her, as if he had some sort of Pygmalion complex. He paid for her to attend a modeling school and was her biggest cheerleader when she started getting booked for ads in national magazines.

After a year or so, he became frustrated. He believed she should have climbed further by that point in time. Her good years were short, and like a carton of milk, the expiration date wasn't far off. He didn't say that exactly, but his anxiety about the trajectory and speed of her career was a constant presence. He wanted to see her on covers, he wanted her face recognized everywhere. He wanted people to know her name. He took it upon himself to talk to photographers he'd been put in touch with through his publishing clients.

From these conversations, he came to the conclusion, whether the photographers actually said this in so many words, or he had his own issues that filtered what they'd told him, he decided she was too restrained. Her polite exterior and classy demeanor were assets, to a point. To a *point*. He repeated this so many times, she wanted to stab the point of a pen into his tongue. It became a mantra that made her feel there was something wrong with her very nature.

She couldn't let herself go, he said. She needed to project an image of dark desires in her expressions or with her body, he advised. She couldn't capture that certain something inside of herself that makes a model stand out from the rest — that sense of entitlement, that knowledge of her own beauty and desirability. She looked like any other attractive woman, and that wasn't good enough, not if you wanted to be a superstar.

She needed to be wild. She needed to be willing to get naked in front of a camera. Not just physically, but emotionally naked. The emotional nakedness was almost more important, he said. She needed to expose her soul. That's what drew people to images — a mixture of intense self-confidence and strength coupled with vulnerability so that those viewing your face, your body, felt as if they possessed you.

The solution to this was a photographer with whom she could strip herself down to the bones. A photographer who knew her inside and out, a photographer who could direct her to change her very nature because he wasn't focused on trying to create a certain feel and a set of images for a client.

A photographer who was focused on selling nothing but Eileen Cook to the world was the key to her success.

The photography studio already existed in Jim's unconventional third-floor room. He liked taking pictures, and he liked working with light. He'd photographed every woman he'd ever been with. He set the camera on a timer and took erotic pictures of himself with whatever woman he loved at a given point in time.

Over a period of three or four months, he spent every single evening in that tiny room with Eileen as his subject, wearing her down, breaking her down. As she sat in front of his camera, he demanded she tell him the story of her life in precise detail.

With each incident she related, he picked it apart and

pointed out what she'd done wrong. When she fell off the swing as a Kindergartner, she was *clumsy* and *lacking in a sense of her own bodily presence,* its shape and form in the world. At that age, a child should be bold and confident, and she had not been. She was *weak,* and she didn't grip the chains of the swing *properly.* She *let her fear overcome her. This was the cause of the fall,* not the natural inexperience of a child, the natural result of gravity and physics and accidents.

He walked her step-by-step through the hurts of her childhood and high school years.

She wasn't even sure why she'd told him all those things. They were the most painful stories of her life, and she told them to a man who clearly wanted to use them to wound her. But she couldn't help herself. He wanted to know everything. As if they were made for each other — vulture and prey — she told him. He stood behind that camera taking it all in as if he were sucking the marrow right out of her bones.

She told him because she had no other choice. She wanted to be successful, and she wanted to make him proud of her success. He seemed so sure of himself. He was so much older than her, more experienced. She was only twenty-six at the time, and she'd been raised by a single mother who had given her very few tools for facing the world.

The only knowledge she had for dealing with other people were the words of the Bible and the amorphous help that came through prayer. These were useless in standing up to a man like Jim Kohn, a man much older than Eileen. He possessed a lifetime of knowledge and skills that she knew nothing about.

He believed he was right, insisted he was right. His words seemed to make sense. He must be right. Look at all the success he'd experienced. He obviously had some insight into how the world worked. Most of all, he'd talked to the experts in her field.

And besides all of that, she loved him! He made her feel like an angel. He was charming and strong. He was so good-looking. She was obsessed with him. Her mother had been right about that. She wanted nothing but to be with him, to listen to his smooth tenor voice, to watch him do the simplest tasks, to lie in bed for hours while he made her body into something that felt like magic. He brought out desires in her that she hadn't known existed inside of any woman. Maybe he really was a modern-day Pygmalion.

By the time Jim was finished offering critical commentary on every choice she'd made, every effort she'd undertaken, every hurt and failure, and every lesson her mother and her church had taught her to believe, she felt as if the inside of her had been scraped clean. Eileen was gone, and all that existed was a blank canvas.

During the process of verbally eviscerating her life, he took photographs. When she cried, he moved in close and captured the contortions of her face, the sadness, and fear and shame in her eyes. When she felt guilty or uncomfortable, he snapped the camera so fast the sound made it seem as if she was in a room filled with crickets. When the photographs were printed out, he critiqued those as well.

Then he moved on to her body. He took close-ups of every imperfection in her form and every unwanted break in her skin — unsightly hair, the red bumps of ingrown hairs, pimples, moles, aberrations in her flesh and all the parts of her that didn't conform to his view of what physical perfection looked like in a woman. He took pictures of her splayed baby toe and the damp bit of dirt he found deep inside her navel.

She never questioned him. She never said no.

She adored him.

Surely this would help her shed all her insecurities, all her shame. If she was emptied out, if she no longer cared about keeping anything private, no longer cared about herself at all, if she was just a body to be photographed, then anything could happen.

When Eileen was finished with her story, we were both well-beyond tipsy. Two empty wine bottles stood between us, and a half-eaten slice of chocolate cake that we'd shared sat in the center of the table.

If I hadn't already killed him, I wanted to kill him all over again.

51

Drinking two bottles of red wine with Eileen, followed by martinis for both of us, then a dazed subway ride back to my apartment did nothing to help me get back into my running habit. I missed it terribly. I missed the clearing of my head, the breathing of outdoor air, even if it wasn't exactly fresh and pure in Mid-town New York. I missed feeling strong and fit. I missed knowing I could outrun almost anyone, should the situation ever arise.

One weight-lifting session and a stroll on the treadmill doesn't generate a sense of well-being and fitness that you can feel in every fiber as you walk down the street or climb the stairs, or even climb out of bed in the morning.

I gorged my way through an ill-advised breakfast of leftover pasta and two cups of coffee. I filled my water bottle and drank the entire contents before refilling it to take to work. During a longer than usual shower, I let the water run cold in an effort to drain the sludge out of my brain.

My body was aching from the previous day's weights and aching from too much alcohol and aching from leaning my elbows on the table, listening for two hours to Eileen's horror story, I decided to wear comfort clothes to work. I pulled on jeans, a silky camisole, and a long, soft sweater with a v-shaped neckline. I wore flat knee-high black boots and brushed my hair into a ponytail where it was staying more securely every day as it continued to grow.

The sky was clouding over, making the emerging day look like I felt. I packed my umbrella and wrapped up in a wool coat with all the extra knitted gear required for a New York December. As I turned down the heat, I thought for a moment about Tess sweltering in an Australian summer. For half a second, I wished I was there, wearing nothing but flip-flops and a sundress. I pushed the thought away and reminded myself of the way cold weather can energize you. I thought about the beauty of pouring rain or the drifting snow or a sky filled with sharp, white clouds. You can have the clouds in summer too, but for some reason, they're more breathtaking in winter.

I stepped onto the landing, and as if my foot had hit a lever in the floor, Victoria's apartment door swung open.

She grinned. "Just who I wanted to see."

"I'm on my way to work."

"I only need a quick chat. A question, and some great news."

"What's that?" I shifted my bag to the other shoulder and dropped my keys into my pocket.

"First, when are you going to give me that letter to forward to our former neighbor?"

"You mean, Nick?"

"Well you didn't know him, so I thought I should be clear who I was talking about. But yes, Nick."

"I gave it to the manager. He said he'd take care of it."

"Oh. I told you…"

"Why are you still talking about it? You're making me think a letter from the FBI has something to do with you. Or Rafe."

She stared at me, bug-eyed, then quickly recovered. She ran her fingers through her hair, readjusting the tufts. She giggled. "Where did you get that idea? I was just trying to be helpful."

"Well, no worries. I need to get going. I can't miss my train."

"Wait." She slid her hands into the pocket of the cargo pants she wore paired with a pale orange t-shirt.

"Shouldn't you be working?"

"Rafe has everything under control."

"I thought you were your own woman."

"I am, but I can take breaks."

I smiled.

"And speaking of being my own woman." She pulled a thin stack of bills out of her pocket. "This is for you. One-hundred-and-ninety-three dollars."

"What for?"

"We made some investments for you. We invested five hundred dollars. This is the return. Already! Amazing, isn't it? Can you believe how easy it is? When did we talk? Right before Thanksgiving, right? And already almost fifty percent in your pocket."

"What we talked about is that I don't want you making investments for me."

"You didn't want to put up cash yet. But this was no risk on your part. We did it because we like you. And we think you haven't given the potential of day trading enough thought."

"I don't need to give it any thought. You can put that

away." I tightened my scarf around my neck with a yank, feeling as if I were strangling myself. And maybe I was, to stop myself from talking any more about this tiresome subject. I stepped around her and started toward the stairs.

"Why would you not want money? Everyone wants more money. It's not like you owe us anything."

"I doubt that."

"You seem like someone who is incredibly open to life and its possibilities. I don't understand why you're so stubborn about this. I don't understand why you aren't even willing to keep an open mind."

"Because it's not what I want."

"Money?"

"Sitting in front of a computer looking at numbers and charts all day. It's not me. Please stop talking to me about it."

"Then let us do it for you. I know you'd be great at it, but if you really feel so strongly about it, let us invest for you."

"No."

She stomped her stockinged foot on the floor. "You aren't making any sense."

"I don't have to make sense to you. Only to me."

She shoved the money into her pocket. "Okay. I'm sorry. Let's start over. I really like you. I thought we could be friends and I don't want to *alienate* you."

It was far too late for that. She was a pest. Both of them were, when it came to their fanatical love of trading stocks. She thought I made no sense, but I felt the same way about her. About both of them.

"How about if we go ice skating. At Rockefeller Center. Just you and me."

"I haven't ice skated since I was twelve."

"You never forget how. You might be wobbly at first, but it'll be fun. And you're in shape. You're strong. I bet you'll be skating circles around half the people there after five minutes."

"Sure. That sounds fun."

She smiled and bounced slightly on her toes. For a minute, I thought she was going to rush at me and wrap me in a bear hug. "That's so great! When should we do it?"

"I don't know. I probably missed my train. I really need to go. I'll text you."

She nodded.

She stood by her door and watched me walk down the stairs. When I could no longer see her, she called after me — "Don't forget to text! Maybe next week. Don't forget."

I didn't shout back. I doubted the people on the floor below us wanted to hear a shouted conversation echoing in the stairwell at seven-thirty in the morning, at any time.

Outside, the clouds were thicker, and the wind was blowing, but it felt good after standing in a stuffy apartment building wrapped in wool. I tried to picture myself ice skating, but I failed.

52

As if nothing had ever happened to disrupt the connection between us, Joe suggested I spend the upcoming weekend at the house. I felt he wanted to keep an eye on me. I sensed his desire had shifted from my body and my company to a burning need to see what I was up to, to make sure I didn't step out of my place, whatever that was. I felt him watching every move.

Maybe he'd always been watching.

After all, he'd made a big point of telling me his job was to anticipate. He'd watched me when his boss grabbed and pawed me, and he'd done nothing. I still wasn't sure how I felt about that. I don't need rescuing, but don't people usually speak up, make themselves known when they see something wrong taking place? Well, of course they don't. Most do not. I suppose most are like the Good Samaritan that we were told about all through my childhood, but never worked very diligently to imitate.

We see someone dying on the side of the road, literally or figuratively, and we cross to the opposite side, walking away with our minds focused on our own problems and plans.

Minding our own business.

Maybe I felt him watching me because I was hyper-alert now, reading into every gesture and glance. Before, he'd watched me with the eyes of a lover, and now he had a different set of eyes, and they felt oppressive, while the others had been pleasant.

Maybe I felt him watching me because it was a house full of watchers. They'd taken a cue from their boss who watched a woman tear her life into barely-there pulp like a soggy, over-used tissue. Ed was tracking my movements, and Nell watched me.

I'd walked into the middle of something, but I couldn't figure out what it was.

Before the limo was due to pick me up at seven, I took the subway to Fifth Avenue. I went into Saks and walked directly to the men's department. I bought a pair of chocolate brown driving gloves made of leather so soft it felt like a baby's skin. I had them gift-wrapped and included a tiny card that said simply — *Thank you.*

There's nothing like expressing a little gratitude.

When Dirk opened the back door of the limo, I put one foot into the car, ready to climb in. I turned and handed the slim box to him. "I appreciate you driving me back and forth all the time. You don't work for me, you don't really work for Joe, and I just think it's really nice."

"This wasn't necessary," he said.

"Most things aren't necessary."

I climbed in, and he closed the door. He walked around to the driver's side. He placed the box gently on the seat beside him. When he pulled away from the curb, I knocked on the glass. He pressed the button, and the window in the partition slid open.

"What I really want to thank you for is that first night. Something bad happened to me after the dinner party. And riding back to my apartment, being comfortable and able to be alone with my thoughts and knowing I'd get home safely meant everything to me."

"It's my job."

"I realize it's your job. I realize you're paid to drive, but that doesn't make it less important. It's a job for which I imagine you don't get a lot of feedback, unless you screw up, of course."

He laughed. He had a nice laugh.

"I'm in a talking mood," I said. "I'd like to leave the window open."

"If that's what will make your ride enjoyable."

"It will."

He stopped for a red light. I felt him watching me in the rearview mirror. He did it without angling his head, a very subtle shifting of his eyes. "You're sure you're comfortable?"

"Absolutely." I opened the fridge and took out a split of champagne. I removed the cork with a slight pop and poured some into a glass before the light turned green.

"I can see that you're comfortable now," he said.

I lifted the glass toward the mirror. "Cheers." I took a sip. "I'm curious...what will you do when Jim's brother takes possession of the house?"

"I'll stay on, if that's what he wants."

"Is it hard to find a position as a limo driver?"

"No. New millionaires are minted every week. But...not as easy when your boss is dead and can't give a reference. Either way, I'm not worried."

"Good. You do a great job."

"You have a lot of experience with limo drivers?"

I laughed. "None. But you seem flawless to me."

He laughed with me. "Thanks."

"How come you don't live at the house like the others?"

"Not all of the staff does."

"True. But I thought since you seem like you might be needed on the spur of the moment..."

"I prefer not to."

"Do you mind me asking why?"

"I want my own life."

"I would feel the same way. I lived in a house with the people I worked with once. It was an awesome house, like this one, but..."

"No privacy," he said.

"Yes."

"I need my space. My own life," he said.

"Exactly." I took a few sips of champagne. "I guess Joe sort of has to live there."

"Does he?"

"Well if you're responsible for things running smoothly twenty-four-seven."

"Hmm."

I faced what I'd known from the start, — Dirk wasn't going to give me any gossip about his peers. Not easily. The risk of dissing someone to a stranger who is in a relationship with that person is too great. And the others...I wouldn't get information about them by asking direct questions. I'd have to make some wild guesses and take a chance.

I sighed. "Nell doesn't like it that I come over. It makes things difficult."

"Uh huh."

"She has a bit of a violent streak."

He nodded.

I looked down at the rising bubbles and smiled into my glass. "Was she always like that, or…it seems like something happened."

"There was some unhappiness over the distribution of Mr. Kohn's estate. Some people expect too much."

"Just because you work for someone who's wealthy doesn't mean they're going to give you money when they die."

"That's right," he said. "We're paid well. But some people don't have the character to be around money without it turning their heads, without awakening the greed monster."

"You do?"

"I'm happy with what I have. And I like to earn what I get. I don't need handouts."

"I guess Nell and Ed are the same in that — in wanting more." Another risk, but it was my opinion, after all. It wasn't as if I was pretending to have inside knowledge that Dirk could easily see for the lie it was.

"They all are."

I sipped my champagne very carefully. We drove for several blocks in silence. I spoke in a low voice, but with my face turned directly at the open window so there was no chance he wouldn't hear me. "Even Joe," I said. It wasn't a question.

"Even Joe."

We drove the rest of the way in silence, the window open between us. It was a comfortable silence, each of us enjoying our own space, not feeling the need to fill the car with talk and not feeling the need to close the window to ease the pressure of expectations.

As he pulled around the driveway of Jim's house, the window in the partition rose partially. "You be careful in there," he said. The window closed and the car stopped by the front steps.

53

Now, I was watching Joe. Very carefully. He seemed unchanged, but what can you tell from the outside? His smile was as genuine, seeping into his eyes as it always had. His kisses were as warm and deep, and he still talked easily. The subject of the photographs hadn't come up again, and there was no evidence that he still didn't trust me…or evidence that he did.

I'd arranged the contents of my bags carefully, and each time I opened one of them, nothing had shifted, suggesting he was either very careful, or not looking. Of course, there was no longer a need for the key to the armoire, so it sat in its elegant simplicity on the nightstand in my apartment.

Joe had pulled a backgammon board out of the storage room and was teaching me to play. We sat on the living room floor beside the coffee table, the fire providing all the light we needed. Beside the game board were two glasses of wine, the half-empty bottle, a small bowl of popcorn, and a small finger bowl with a soft towel to wipe our buttery fingers before we touched the game pieces.

The game was a sensual pleasure all in itself, with the hard plastic pieces and dice that felt like polished stones, the sound-absorbing playing surface with leather triangles that cast a satisfying significance over every move, and the shaker with the periodic clunk of that stone-like plastic against leather.

We played until the wine bottle was empty.

For the first time in many visits, I slept all the way through the night. Waking as the sun was coming up made me wonder if the movement of Nell and Ed throughout the house in those dark hours had woken me in the past. Despite the solid doors and thick interior insulation, it seemed as if I'd sensed their wandering as they kept an eye on their territory. This time, had they remained in their beds?

It was raining. Hard. The wind was blowing with enough force that I could hear the branches of the enormous oak tree at the side of the house scraping against the eaves. I turned onto my back and took a deep breath, letting the warmth and weight of the blankets settle over my limbs. I moved my arms to the side and felt a shock of cold beside me. I opened my eyes and raised myself onto my elbow.

Joe's space was empty.

I threw off the covers and got up. I pulled on yoga pants and a hoodie. I zipped it up and ran my fingers through my hair. On my way to the door, I grabbed a glass with a few inches of water remaining. I gulped the water, set the glass down, and opened the door.

It wasn't a panicked reaction at his absence, just surprise. And an intense need to find out right away why he'd slipped out of bed without waking me, curious about what he was up to, and hoping to catch him at it.

The house was silent. I wasn't sure sounds from the first

floor were audible up here, but I expected to have some sense of a person, or people, moving about. I walked to the landing. The air around me remained quiet while the storm continued to rage outside the large picture window at the side of the landing.

I went to the window and looked out at the sky. It was as black as if it were five in the morning, but it was now past seven. Trees swayed and bowed under the wind. The rain fell at an angle, pummeling the shrubs and the house.

Looking down, I saw Joe, Nell, and Ed standing near a large maple tree near the side of the lawn, as if they thought it might provide some shelter, which of course, it did not.

Why on earth were they standing outside? If they'd wanted a conversation away from my hearing, surely the house was large enough. The cigar room came to mind. The library with the door closed. The entertainment room. What could be so secret and desperate that they couldn't trust a solid wood door? What was so important that they woke at daybreak and stood in a storm getting soaked, talking with quite a lot of gesturing to punctuate whatever they were saying.

Nell held an umbrella that was doing nothing to keep her dry. I was surprised it hadn't flipped inside out. Her jeans were dark with water, as were Joe's and Ed's. They all seemed to be talking at once.

According to Dirk, they weren't pleased with their minor mention in their former employer's will, but this looked like outright fury. Only Ed was talking now, his arms clenched around his body. It was the first time I'd seen him without his Rubik's Cube. His head and shoulders moved and bobbed as he spoke. The others' body language suggested they wanted to shut him up, to have their say, but as Joe's and Nell's mouths opened and closed, Ed kept right on going.

I was mad with curiosity. I ticked through the things I knew about them. One of them had the humiliating photographs of Eileen. Joe and Nell had some sort of history that wasn't entirely clear. At least one of them had known previously about the existence of those photographs even though Eileen thought they were a secret between her and Jim. And someone wanted them so badly they broke the lock to get them. There was animosity between Ed and Joe although I wasn't sure if it went both ways. All of them were angry their former employer hadn't been more generous to them with his vast wealth.

Despite what I'd said to Dirk, I sort of got it. They'd not only served him with class and dignity and expertise, they'd given up their own freedom and a certain amount of privacy to make Jim's life better. Where was the compensation for that? Dirk didn't think there was enough money in the world to make that kind of arrangement worthwhile.

Yes, they lived in surroundings far nicer than anything they could acquire on their own. They consumed superb food and enjoyed the use of his home gym, his pool, and possibly some access to his limo driver. I was with Dirk — unsure whether those luxuries are worth your freedom and the ability to call your time your own. So I understood the additional expectation.

In the first half of the nineteenth century, so-called company towns were common. People lived in houses on property owned by the company they worked for, their housing subsidized by their employer. But what kept them from being considered indentured servants? Their lives were dangerously close to enslavement. If your home is under the watchful eye and ownership of your employer, and you can't afford to buy food and staples anywhere but the company store, are you really a free person?

The scene outside became more animated. They were all shouting at each other now, voices that were probably lost in the storm even if I'd been standing twenty feet away from them.

It was entirely possible they were arguing about the photographs. Joe had been extremely upset that I might have taken them, which suggested they were valuable to him. And still, the only use I could think of for those pictures was blackmailing Eileen. Or Stephanie, if any of them even knew she existed. But neither Eileen nor Stephanie had a significant amount of money as far as I knew.

Did Joe and the others believe there was some kind of leverage with Mark Kohn? Was he the kind of man who would be ashamed of his brother's sickening semi-voyeuristic tendency? Enough to be vulnerable to blackmail?

54

I stood transfixed by the drama taking place three stories below me. It was like a silent movie. In fact, the rain and their dark clothes beneath a charcoal sky gave the scene a black-and-white appearance. I squinted, and their animated gestures turned into the jerky movements seen in early films.

It was close to fifteen minutes before the scene ended.

Ed was the first to leave. He strode across the lawn, water splashing as his boots sank into the earth. His head was bent in an effort to keep the driving rain off his face. It didn't work — his hair was soaked, and water ran down the sides of his face in sheets.

A moment later, he disappeared from my view.

Joe and Nell remained under the tree. Neither one appeared to be speaking. The umbrella was collapsing around Nell, the fabric so saturated the metal spokes couldn't keep it taut. After a moment or two, Joe walked away from her, also headed toward the back patio. Within two minutes, he would have time to dry and come upstairs.

I reluctantly turned away from the window, finding it hard to put my attention toward where I was going. I thought of

Nell under the tree — water cascading off the branches onto her bedraggled umbrella, water and wind lashing at her legs.

She must be freezing. Why on earth was she still standing there? Why was I?

I hurried down the hall and into Joe's suite. I closed the door softly. I stood for a moment trying to decide whether it was believable that I'd still be sleeping, trying to decide whether my racing heart and cool skin would give me away if I climbed into bed and pretended sleep.

I filled the glass with water from the nearby pitcher, pulled my tablet out of my bag, and settled on the small couch in his sitting area. I scrolled through email and then the news. I read the weather report. I looked at Twitter and checked in on what Tess was posting on behalf of TruthTeller — the same old stuff.

Joe hadn't returned.

I desperately wanted to see whether Nell was still standing under that tree. I finished the water and closed the cover of my tablet. I did a few stretches and went out of the room, manufacturing a small yawn in case anyone was coming up the stairs. I went to the picture window on the landing and looked out. Nell hadn't moved. I moved close to the window and pressed my nose against the glass as if it would help me see her more clearly, which of course, it did not.

The umbrella lay on the ground, collapsed and useless. Rain poured down on her in such quantities she looked as if she were standing under a waterfall.

I could think of only one reason a woman would stand in the rain like that. She was crying and wanted the water to hide her tears. Either she was truly engulfed in torment or she was having a pity party. Knowing her, I guessed it was the latter.

I started down the stairs, expecting to meet Joe or Ed coming up. Instead, I reached the first floor without encountering either of them. The house still felt deserted. I walked through the living room. It was dark and comfortably cool. The dining room was the same, and the kitchen was also devoid of life. There was no aroma of coffee lingering from earlier in the morning, no signs that anyone had been in the room.

The breakfast room was empty and dark. Now I was confused. I'd seen both of them walking toward the patio. They were sopping wet. It wasn't as if they could just slip into the house without a trace. I began a methodical search of the first floor. It was empty, and there wasn't a drop of water anywhere on the floors.

I went into Jim's study and looked out at the front yard. The garage doors were closed. Was it possible they were continuing their conversation in there? Without Nell. Everyone looked angry when they'd split apart, so was there a new alliance forming now?

I walked slowly toward the back of the house again. I wanted coffee, and my stomach was growling. I stood in the hallway between the breakfast room and kitchen, trying to decide whether my body or my mind would win the battle.

It took a rather long time to decide, but I could always find coffee and food. Nell wouldn't be standing in the rain forever. I grabbed a yellow slicker, matching hat, and rubber boots from a closet near the library. I dressed and went outside. It didn't matter if Joe or Ed saw me talking to her. It was natural that I would go outside to help a woman standing in the middle of a rather vigorous storm, only partially dressed for the weather.

As I crossed the yard, my feet squished into the grass and slurped at the mud below. Every step threatened to send me skidding forward, my feet leaving the ground and my butt going down hard in the swampy yard.

She didn't look up as I drew closer, but it was clear, even with all that rain, that she'd been crying. Her face was swollen and red. She looked like the poster child for misery.

"Nell. You should come inside."

She stared at me.

I moved closer and took hold of her upper arm. "You're going to freeze."

"I won't."

"You're sopping wet."

She shrugged.

I picked up the umbrella. "Do you need help?"

She laughed. She looked at me and laughed harder. Her voice rose, the pitch tinged with hysteria.

"Are you laughing or crying?"

"Does it matter?"

"Maybe not." I tugged on her arm. "Come inside."

"I'd rather not."

"I was going to make coffee and breakfast."

"Go right ahead. You think you own the place. Why not rearrange the furniture while you're at it."

There was no reason to help her, except my addiction to finding out what was going on. That overwhelming need helped me to swallow the sharp words ready to slide off my tongue, and to push away the memory of her shoving me face first into the snow. "Isn't it better to sort things out in comfort rather than in the middle of a storm?"

"I'm in the middle of a storm all the time. I prefer this."

"What's wrong?"

"Nothing I'm going to talk to you about."

"Fair enough. Joe and Ed have disappeared."

She let go of the blank stare and looked directly at me. Her expression softened to one of self-protective analysis — should she trust me or the ones who seemed ready to leave her behind in whatever they were up to? "Coffee sounds good."

"I'll make bacon and hash browns."

She smiled. "You're one of those people who thinks food solves every problem."

"It does solve most of them."

"Not true, but I'm hungry. And freezing."

We walked together toward the patio. I dropped the shattered umbrella near the doormat, and we went inside. We slopped our way to the back bathroom, took off our jackets and left them in the large oval bathtub — a useless feature in a guest bathroom. I removed my boots, and she pulled off her running shoes. We dried ourselves and piled the towels on the jackets. I realized she would probably be the one responsible for cleaning it all up later.

I made coffee and fried bacon and potatoes. She didn't say a word. Neither did I, but somehow, I felt I'd made progress.

55

Portland

Carmen wanted to plot carefully how we would search the basement for the missing case of Barbie Dolls. Even though the boys had intruded into the girls' territory, giving us every right to investigate theirs, she didn't want to be caught. I'm not sure why she was so convinced this was an undesirable outcome, but it was strong and kept her focused on figuring out a way to ensure the boys did not get the upper hand.

At least that's what Carmen said, at first. Getting caught would be the *worst thing*.

But the look in her eyes at the thought of engaging in battle with my older brothers was nothing short of Wolverine. The pupils were tiny dots that refused to grow larger to adapt to the dim afternoon light coming from a sky filled with dark clouds. She stared at me with a look of hunger, more interested now in a chance to get the attention of the boys than she was in making sure the Barbies were returned. Even her teeth, exposed between her unconsciously parted lips, glistened with saliva. Her eye teeth seemed longer than average. Was it my imagination?

We sat on the floor, both of us with our legs crossed at the ankles, staring at each other.

"How do we know when they aren't down there?" Her voice was a whisper, and her eyes blinked rapidly. She jerked her head from side to side, looking around the room, afraid that she was being overheard or watched, or perhaps just demonstrating that she was a very jumpy kid.

There was a weird energy about her — the way she bulldozed her way through the front door and around my bedroom, the way she tried to use the same ramrod approach toward me, offering her opinions as if they were undeniable facts. She'd taken possession of our house and my life as if anyone would be glad to yield to her. As if she was used to everyone yielding to her.

I could see her desire to go into the basement and search through my brother's things. I wondered whether she cared if we found the suitcase or not, preferring that my brothers did catch her in the act of trespassing. She would be the center of attention as they chastised her for daring to intrude where she'd been told not to.

I wished I'd discovered earlier that the suitcase was missing. It would have been much easier to retrieve it myself. I'd been into the basement many times. I could have easily slipped down there after dinner or before my brothers were home from school. Now it was turning into a major expedition.

The boys were due within the next fifteen minutes or so. Because the day was gloomy and colder than usual, they would hang out in the basement instead of taking off on their bikes.

"We need to lure them," she said.

"It's kind of hard to lure three boys anywhere."

"Why?"

"If you had brothers, you'd know."

Her eyes filled with tears, but they weren't entirely from self-pity. Her voice was sharp. "Don't say that. It's not my fault I don't have brothers or sisters. It's God's will."

"It is?"

"God gave my parents the perfect child for them. He probably knew they couldn't handle more kids like me."

"Is that what they said?"

"Maybe. Why can't we lure them?"

"They aren't stupid. There's nothing we could do that would interest all three of them."

My brothers treated me with a decent amount of respect. They didn't like me in their things, and they didn't always want to hang out with me, but most of the time, they did. They liked watching me argue with my father. I was their untrained monkey, saying what they wouldn't, a monkey they felt very affectionate toward.

They were not so keen on Carmen. They'd said as much, and their contact with her had been minimal.

"She's weird," Tom said every time he encountered her, even for half a minute.

She's a brat. She's a pest. She doesn't know when to shut up. She's annoying. She's a know-it-all, and she really doesn't know anything.

"Maybe I should get the suitcase when you're not here," I said. "It would be a lot easier to get in there by myself, especially when they're doing homework."

"That's not fair. They're my Barbies. I want them back. Now."

Since she'd given the dolls over to me, the sudden desire to possess them seemed quite fake, but I'd already seen what she was up to so I suppose she had to pretend some kind of concern for her former toys.

"We could lure them with a snack," she said.

"My mother gives them all the snacks they want."

"Maybe we could lure them outside."

"With what?"

"Something in the woods? There are lots of tree frogs."

"They know that. It would have to be more interesting. Don't you know anything about boys?"

"Yes. I know a lot."

"Then you know they think a lot of things girls do are dumb. And they already think you're always trying to trick them."

"Why?"

I shrugged.

She bit her lower lip, her sharp teeth pulling it inside her mouth, the flesh turning pale at the edges and bright red where her teeth seemed ready to pierce the skin. "That's not very nice."

I laughed.

"You could pretend you fell and hurt your ankle. I could tell them you need help."

"That doesn't require all three. And they'd probably tell you to find my mother and stop bothering them."

She sighed. "This is too hard."

"It was your idea."

"You have to think of something. It's your turn," she said.

"I already told you. The best time is when they're doing their homework. They aren't allowed to leave their rooms until my father looks at their assignments to make sure everything is done."

"Don't you have homework?"

"Mine's easier. Homework is harder when you're older."

She nodded.

Finally, she decided I would ask my mother if we could bake cookies. The boys would want to lick the bowl, and while they were doing that, she'd sneak down to the basement.

We approached my mother. Of course, she was thrilled to bake cookies with us. When the time came for bowl licking, my mother said we'd earned it. Carmen assured her she didn't like raw dough and she really wanted to be nice to my brothers.

My mother thought this was so sweet and so kind and so generous, she called the boys. They trudged up the stairs, knowing it was hardly worth the effort. A single bowl with a thin layer of dough on the inside was hardly enough for one, much less three of them to really dig into, but they weren't going to pass up something sweet that wasn't on the usual after-school snack menu.

Carmen closed the kitchen door. She grabbed my mother's wrist. She whispered in a voice my brothers could surely hear that she had to use the bathroom. Immediately. She darted out of the kitchen to the foyer and circled around to the pantry that was between the kitchen and the door to the basement.

Within minutes, the bowl was wiped as clean as if it had been washed with a sponge. The batters were equally clean, and my brothers were pleading for a freshly-baked cookie. I was a little surprised Carmen's plan had worked so well. I didn't really think all three of them would be kept busy with such a simple diversion.

They were each handed a warm cookie and were now heading back toward the basement. Carmen hadn't returned.

56

One of the most perplexing things about Jim Kohn's house was that his study was kept unlocked, the doors often open, while a seemingly innocuous storage room and photograph studio remained locked. Of course, the exploitive pictures of Eileen explained some of that, but the rest of the room was mundane, and the armoire had had its own key, so the door locking seemed excessive. Maybe he'd done it to keep the photography sessions more private, to set a standard that the space was off limits.

Now, I was more intrigued by the unlocked study. Surely that would be a source of many things he might want kept private. So why was it so accessible? When I'd been in there, I hadn't seen locks on any of the drawers or cabinets.

It was a long shot, an extremely long shot, truly an impossible shot, but I wanted to see if I could locate any part of his trust or will or whatever documents he'd prepared for the end of his life. There was a ninety-nine-point-nine percent chance all important and interesting papers were in his lawyer's possession. But the staff had been notified of its contents, so maybe a document remained at the house. It was worth checking.

Besides, I might stumble upon something else.

There are so many possibilities in every situation, in every moment, in your life, in the world. You never know what might unfold in a truly unexpected way.

Given the habits of the occupants of the house, I wasn't sure how I would look through the study without attracting attention. But it might be fairly easy to look innocent, if I were caught. If I kept myself alert and didn't turn my back to the door, it would sound plausible to cover my actions under the guise of heading into the smoking room.

I was only staying at the house for one more night, so my only chance would be during the early hours of Sunday morning.

I woke at one-thirty and went downstairs, holding tightly to my cigarettes.

I closed one half of the double doors, leaving the one that had a line of sight to the staircase partially open. I placed my cigarettes on the corner of the desk and got to work.

It was tricky to figure out where I should stand because the desk faced toward the windows. Opening the drawers meant turning my back to the doorway. After moving about, shifting this way and that, I found I was able to stand with my back to the desk, pull open a drawer and look inside, while frequently glancing toward the foyer. I wished I had something to alert me to any sounds. They were all so damn sneaky. Like me, I suppose. Maybe we'd found each other through some common approach to the world that drew us irresistibly together.

I quieted my rambling thoughts and tried the center desk drawer. It was locked — not a promising start.

I pulled on the handle of the top side drawer, and it slid open. I sighed with satisfaction that it wasn't one of those desks where the center lock secures all the drawers.

The top drawer contained pens, a tape dispenser, boxes of paperclips, a fancy stapler, an elaborately carved wood letter opener, and a jar of foreign coins. It was tidy and minimalist, as I'd expected. It also suggested Jim was sentimental about the office accessories of the past.

The second drawer had a locked metal box that looked like it might hold cash. I lifted it out of the drawer, lowering and raising it in my hands, trying to feel by its heft whether there was anything inside. It seemed rather light, but I wasn't sure I'd notice the weight of bills, and large bills weigh the same as singles. I returned it to the drawer.

In the last drawer, I struck semi-pay dirt. It was full of file folders hanging from a metal rack. I stood and stretched my neck and shoulders, peering into the dark foyer. Given how much I'd been looking down into the drawers, I was no longer confident I'd be able to spot someone headed in my direction. Thinking this ratcheted up my adrenaline, making me want a smoke.

I stared blankly into the foyer, trying to decide whether I'd be able to carry the folders into the smoking room and relax with a cigarette while I flipped through papers. There were at least twenty file folders. None of them were over-stuffed, but it was still a lot of paper. I closed my eyes and pictured the cigar room. There was no place to hide the papers if someone came in — no throw pillows on the leather couch, no shelf or drawers under the coffee table.

My eyes flashed open. I couldn't be sure if I'd heard a sound. Nothing was visible through the partially opened door, but my heart beat faster as if my body sensed someone was there. I pushed on the drawer, closing it as carefully and as soundlessly as I could manage.

Those papers seemed critical and yet I couldn't think how I would read them. I could empty my messenger bag into my overnight bag and take the papers home with me. I considered this while I tiptoed to the doorway and looked out. The foyer was empty.

Finally, I opened the drawer again and flipped through the folders as quickly as I could manage. As best I could see moving quickly, they contained documents about the house and appliances and landscaping work, just as their labels indicated, not a secret stash of financial information. Quite a few of them seemed oddly unimportant to keep in such a readily accessible place.

I closed the drawer. I needed to focus on covering as much territory as possible. Taking the papers for a closer inspection meant a trek upstairs and a return trip.

I studied the built-in bookcases and cabinets along the left wall. The top of the cabinet section that extended out farther than the shelves was still lined with the photographs of Eileen. She seemed to be an entirely different person from the woman I'd observed in those other pictures. How could she have looked so confident and serene when posing for public view and so utterly broken in the photographs hidden on the third floor? I wondered which had been taken first, or whether they'd been shot during the same time period.

I took my eyes off the phony images. I walked slowly toward the window seat where Jim had shoved his tongue in my mouth and his hand down the front of my dress. I pushed the memory out of my mind. It should be as dead as he was.

I ran my fingers along the spines of his books, knowing his skin cells might be lingering there and that he would never touch his books again. If I really wanted, I could possess any one of his books. I could find the one that had been touched and marked the most, tuck it inside my bag and walk out the front door, never looking back at his house. But I didn't want his books — knowing I could have them was enough. Knowing the cells of his body were wiped off the face of the earth was enough. In fact, judging by the dust-free wood and picture frames, Nell kept this room as spotless as the rest of the house. Those cells were caught in the feathers of a duster and captured by soft cloths that had already been washed and dried.

I opened the door of the cabinet adjacent to the window seat. It was filled with photo albums, many of them with worn leather bindings. I assumed they were family photos and closed the door.

The next cabinet contained sturdy leather boxes of plaques and ribbons from college debate competitions and sports events. He'd been quite the debate star and a rather good tennis player. None of this was surprising. The fact that he kept it all boxed away, but couldn't part with his past glory enough to put those things up in the storage room wasn't surprising either.

The last double cabinet had two shelves. Both shelves were stacked with cigar boxes. I opened the lid on the first one. It contained the odds and ends that many people collect as they move through their lives, saving trinkets as if they'll use them to find their way back home, like Hansel and Gretel's breadcrumbs. There were small magnets, buttons, pens labeled with the names of companies, and key chains. This was surprising. He didn't seem like someone who would keep useless odds and ends. Maybe he'd forgotten.

I pulled out the box beneath it and lifted the lid. Inside was a disheveled stack of photographs. Most people don't have a lot of printed photographs, everything is on their phones or their laptops, stored in the cloud. Photographs are printed as needed.

I recognized the subject immediately. A fistful of images of Nell, with her long, ironed blonde hair. Her perfectly shaped face with its small nose and mouth.

All of them were seductive poses in which she was half-dressed. They weren't nearly as degrading as the photographs of Eileen, but some touched the edge of porn. Others were typical boudoir shots. Many would debate the difference between those types of photographs, but that didn't concern me.

I wondered if she knew they were here. I guessed she didn't, or I wouldn't have found them.

57

The email to Alexandra was almost complete. Stephanie had written most of it in the heat of the moment, sitting in her office on Thursday afternoon. Now, she was studying the final, carefully and repeatedly edited result on her phone, her finger poised to hit send.

It wasn't a good idea to send important email from your phone, but she'd wanted to let it settle in her mind before she did it. And now, on Sunday afternoon, it seemed the perfect time, so it had to be her phone.

With the email out of her draft folder and into cyberspace, she could spend the rest of the day thanking God for being with her and leading her to this solution. She could prepare a nice dinner for Eileen. They might even have a glass of wine again. She could watch a little TV. She would be free, and God would take care of driving the message home to Alexandra's heart. The Bible insisted His words were like swords, and this email proved it.

If she sent it today, Monday morning would be a fresh start.

She very much liked the idea of the email intruding on

Alexandra's weekend, spoiling whatever hedonistic activities that girl was up to. Everyone read their work email on the weekends. If something popped up from a colleague or your boss, you couldn't help yourself. You had to know what was going on, had to know what was so important that it warranted working on Sunday.

The message had turned out to be much longer than she'd hoped, but there was a lot to say. It was so good to feel God's hand upon her shoulder, to feel his warm presence inside of her while she'd been writing the message. Knowing she had a solution to her problem, and knowing that she'd healed the damaged areas of her heart by seeking forgiveness gave her a sense of power she'd only experienced a few times in her life.

It was intoxicating, maybe she'd didn't need a glass of wine after all. How had she forgotten that this was how good it felt to be doing God's work, to be aligned with His Purpose? There was no feeling on earth to compare.

Seeking Diana's forgiveness had gone a little more smoothly than her experience with Trystan. Diana was softer and less dismissive. She was a kinder person than most. And she was female. Women were always more open to healing their relationships, to making sure the undercurrents were smooth. They didn't want buried hurts that festered, prone to erupting in an unpredictable, dangerous, and uncontrollable fashion. Men tended to simply push those things out of their minds instead of addressing them.

Diana had held her gaze, hadn't interrupted, and managed to make Stephanie feel okay about the shameful things she'd done. She'd assured Stephanie that no one looked down on her, that she hadn't jeopardized her job. After all, dinner had taken place outside of work hours. They were all having fun.

Trystan knew she was a valuable employee. Diana had even opened up a little and made the enticing comment — *That's why I don't drink alcohol. Things happen.* Stephanie had wanted to probe, but as she'd opened her mouth to speak, Diana kept going.

She talked about how thoughtful Stephanie was, how diligent. She laid on the flattery so thick that Stephanie felt slightly greasy when she was finished. It was not the right moment for prying into Diana's life. Prying would have contradicted the fact that, according to Diana, Stephanie was *discreet* and *straightforward* and *genuine*. She wasn't a *gossip*, and she wasn't *catty or petty*.

It almost felt like a string of lies.

Stephanie read the email for the twentieth time. It struck exactly the right notes. The tone was respectful. The words were truthful.

As her finger tapped *send*, she felt her spirits lift even more. It was almost a state of ecstasy.

Knowing that she'd found a way to get the upper hand with Alex, to make sure Alex stayed away from Eileen filled her with relief. She lay back on her bed, suddenly tired. She let the phone drop out of her hand onto the comforter where it sank into the feathery softness. She wasn't just tired, she was exhausted.

In some ways, the incident, or incidents, at the Thanksgiving dinner had been worth it. Those missteps and her pleas for forgiveness had given her a new spiritual authority.

The lowly will be lifted up.

The meek will inherit the earth.

She closed her eyes and let her mind become soft and filled

with scenes from the Bible. She saw herself possessing a new aura. Normally she avoided the word *aura*. The word implied new-age beliefs that came from a humanistic belief system, the delusions fostered by Satan to lure the ungodly to their ultimate destruction, but she couldn't think of a better one. Because of her new power, she would look physically different to people. An inner beauty created by the Spirit of God would emanate from her face, her entire body. She would no longer look middle-aged and frumpy and dumpy. She would look vibrant and powerful, her persona transcending her actual physical appearance.

Alex and Diana would be in awe of her presence. Trystan would look at her with radically new eyes. He would touch her waist again, and this time she wouldn't scream at him. She would sigh gently and return his gaze, letting him know how much she respected and, yes, cared for him.

His hand would move farther around her waist, which was miraculously narrower than it was when she saw her reflection in her bedroom mirror. He would pull her close, put his face in her hair, and breathe in the beautiful scent of her.

Until that moment in his office, she'd never thought of him as a potential mate. Why hadn't she? Possibly the timing wasn't right. But... She thought of his precious little girl. Of his kindness and goodness. She thought about how intelligent he was, and how lonely. He never talked about his private life. Surely he was lonely.

58

The cigar box full of photographs was tucked at the bottom of the stack of boxes in Jim's study. I was lying flat on my back on Joe's bed, unable to sleep. I'd smoked two cigarettes trying to work out what the photographs meant, but of course, I knew nothing, so I hadn't figured out a single thing.

Now, I was trying to figure out how to crack through the crusted surface surrounding Nell. The series of photographs had to be related to the pictures of Eileen, and whatever Nell had been crying about must be connected in some way. The most obvious answer was that she'd been in a relationship with Jim. But when? And how did she continue working as a maid in his house while she was seeing him? That was messed up in so many ways I couldn't list them all.

Was it possible this was going on when I'd killed him? Maybe she was on the verge of resigning? Or maybe he...that might make her overly upset about him not leaving money. But of course, if something new had just spun up between them, he wouldn't have thought to change his last wishes. Most people in the middle of their lives are hard-pressed to think about their final instructions at all. And even someone with his wealth, who had all of that taken care of, wouldn't rush to change it the moment he started up with someone new.

It was even more clear that he hadn't been trying to *help* Eileen with her career at all. He just liked to take creepy pictures of the women he was with. *Helping* with her modeling career was the method he used to make the idea palatable to her.

The questions spun in my mind. Sleep was entirely impossible. My thoughts chased one another in circles. I'd never discovered where Joe and Ed had gone the day before. When he'd finally returned to his suite, I was waiting for him, but he didn't say a word to explain his nearly two-hour absence.

I turned on my side.

Despite the activity inside my head, I must have fallen asleep because I was surprised to find myself waking as Joe stroked my shoulder and then ran his index finger down my spine.

Sleeping beside someone you don't trust is a harrowing experience. I don't trust most people to varying degrees, but I don't usually wind up unconscious and exposed beside someone who's manipulating me.

Dirk had said I should be careful. What did that even mean? It wasn't as if anyone was out to assault me, or murder me. At least I didn't think they were. I wished I'd pressed him for more details. He wouldn't have given them, but I wished I'd pushed. Maybe in the not saying he would have revealed something. Anything.

It was probably time for me to extract myself from the entire situation, but I really wanted to get those photographs first. They belonged to Eileen, and whoever had them was going to try to hurt her in one way or another.

By late morning I hadn't made a single decision about what I should do. Joe and I seemed to have run out of things to talk about, and I wasn't interested in another game of backgammon or a movie. I just wanted those photographs and a ride back to the city. I was running out of time.

He and I sat in the breakfast room, lingering over champagne with crab salad that had been prepared for brunch. The delicious food and the fine champagne hadn't brought Nell or Ed out into the open. I stabbed the last piece of crab meat, firm and tender and sweet. I put it into my mouth without dragging it through a puddle of dressing. As delicate and well-seasoned as the dressing was, I wanted the naked taste of the crab. It was exquisite.

Joe topped off my champagne. "When are you thinking of heading out?"

It was a rather direct dismissal. I finished chewing. I took a sip of champagne. "Soon. If you have things to do, I can entertain myself."

"Actually, I do."

"No worries," I said.

He remained in his chair although I could feel his muscles tighten, eager to get moving with whatever was on his mind.

I took a long swallow of champagne. I refilled my glass almost to the lip. I stood and picked up the glass. "I'll go hang out in your room."

"Let me know what time I should call Dirk."

I smiled. "Of course." I turned before his feelings crossed his face. I didn't have to see the shift in his eyes and the press of his lips to know he wanted me gone. He was too polite to simply carry my bags to the front porch and hustle me into a waiting limo.

Upstairs, I lay on the couch in his sitting room. I skimmed the headlines. There were two new emails showing in my work account. I opened the account. One message was from Diana about two clients I'd be photographing in the coming weeks. It wasn't clear why she felt I needed to know this on Sunday afternoon, but I supposed it was nagging at her and she wanted it out of her head and into mine.

The other email was from Stephanie.

The message was dense with text. There were only four paragraph breaks in a letter that looked capable of filling three printed pages. I skimmed it.

Most of it consisted of Bible verses repurposed in an attempt to pretend they were her own words. She had no idea how familiar I was with all those words, most of them embedded into my memory like hot spears, still living in my subconscious. She seemed to think I wouldn't recognize her mimicry. The letter was repetitious, the same fractured verses and passages used two, sometimes three times in a single paragraph.

In the end, her message was this — Eileen was possessed by the devil, and I had no idea what I was walking into. If I continued to spend time with her, my life would take a turn for the worse. Much worse. The implication was this would be some kind of vengeance from god, some vague description of dark angels, but the instrument would be Eileen. She craved money, and she would find a way to extract it from me, stopping at nothing to get it. I should be afraid. *Very afraid.*

59

As if the *unseen angelic forces* that Stephanie threatened had been released upon me, my entire afternoon began to shift and take on a new shape. Not true at all, obviously. But with her fiery, flamboyant email fresh in my memory, it was hard to stop my mind from playing around with her dramatic ideas.

Joe returned to his suite and informed me he had to go out. He gave me Dirk's cell phone number and told me to call when I was ready to leave. As a *by-the-way*, he told me the chef was off that evening. The implication of that was clear, although he underestimated my willingness to forage in the well-stocked kitchen for my own patchwork meal. Leftover crab salad came to mind.

It was good to know that one less person would be watching me.

As soon as he was gone, I searched Joe's chest of drawers. I looked through his closet and under the bed and under the mattress. I found nothing. It was the dullest collection of male possessions I'd ever seen. Almost too dull.

Aside from a dish of coins in the top drawer, his dresser held nothing but clothing. Beneath the bed was a vast wilderness of spotlessly clean carpet, and the closet contained clothing on hangers and three pairs of shoes. A single box sat on the closet shelf. It was filled with plastic Star Wars figurines.

I ventured into the hallway, itching for something to do that would move me closer to figuring out where Eileen's photographs had been stashed. I also wanted a conversation with Nell. I paused outside of her door. I raised my hand to knock. I pictured her sour expression. I remembered our previous conversations. I turned away and continued to the landing.

Outside, the yard was recovering from the storm. The lawn had lost the look of the Everglades. The tree branches were no longer bowed, and the branches that had been torn off and lay scattered about had now been cleared, even though I hadn't seen any evidence of a gardening crew.

I returned to Joe's room, got the champagne glass, and took it downstairs. I washed it and dried it. I walked along the length of the kitchen, opening and closing doors, looking for its home. Finally, I found the matching glasses in the cabinet closest to the back window.

Through the trees on the far side of the lawn that had been stripped of their remaining dead leaves during the storm, was a glimpse of the swimming pool. Ed was working with another guy to pull the cover across the surface of the water. I laughed out loud. Surely this was an indication things were not going smoothly if he'd forgotten all about the pool until the storm was over.

I went to the cabinet across from the champagne glasses. Inside was a box of powdered chocolate and a bag of marshmallows. I detest marshmallows in hot chocolate, but seeing them made me long for a warm, soothing chocolate drink. I checked the fridge and found a carton of low-fat milk. It wasn't the best for a satisfying cup of hot chocolate, but it would do.

After heating the milk in a pan and stirring in cocoa powder, I poured the mixture into a large mug. I left it on the counter and dashed up the stairs, grabbed my cigarettes, and brought my chocolate and smokes into the cigar room.

It was such a pleasant place to smoke. Watching the smoke magically disappear without battling a stiff breeze was very relaxing. But if I had regular access to such a nicely appointed room, I would definitely smoke too much. Already I'd inhaled more than I should have during my visits to the house. The extra smoking wasn't at all helpful in getting me back into running, but there was plenty of time for that. Later.

I was on my second cigarette when Nell opened the door and stepped into the room. She held a bottle of glass cleaner in one hand and a bucket in the other. "I smelled chocolate," she said.

I pointed to my mug.

She looked at it with envy.

I saw my chance and pounced. "I saw some pictures of you."

The bottle of glass cleaner fell to the floor. There was a sudden intake of breath. She bent over. Her ponytail swung forward and hid her face.

At first, I thought she might be having a panic attack, but she simply placed the bucket on the floor. She picked up the cleaner and dropped it into the bucket with a thud. The bucket wobbled but stayed upright. "Where? With the others?"

"What others?"

"Where did you find them?"

"What others are you talking about?"

She nodded toward Jim's study. "Hers."

"Eileen's?"

"Yes."

"When did he take them? The ones of you?"

"Stop asking so many questions."

She no longer had the upper hand, but she probably hoped I didn't fully realize that. I waited.

"Tell me where you found them," she said. "Are you the one who broke the lock?"

"No."

She nodded, looking as if she was satisfied with my answer and that it provided information she'd been searching for.

"Where did you find them?"

"When were they taken?"

We stared at each other. I finished my cigarette and stabbed it out. I picked up the pack and held it toward her. She crossed the room and sat in the armchair. I lit two cigarettes and handed one to her.

"A while ago. Right before he was killed."

"Were you two in a relationship?"

She shrugged. "Define relationship."

I was not the best person to define that term.

She seemed to recognize that fact at the same moment I did. She gave me a knowing smile. "About like your relationship with Joe."

"But you wanted more?"

Her eyes filled with tears but they didn't spill out. She inhaled deeply and tipped her face toward the ceiling. She blew the smoke up, and it dissipated in seconds. "I was stupid. I knew what he was like. I saw what happened with her, and he was really into her. I should have realized."

I nodded. She should have.

"He tried to help Eileen with her career, but she didn't have the *IT factor*. I do, according to him." She laughed with a harsh sound that turned into a cough.

I tried for the millionth time to get my head around a guy who was hugely successful in the financial industry but obsessed with models. Not just models, but in making women into models. Maybe it was just his shtick. The method he used to draw good-looking women into his life. Although he had plenty to offer besides that, at least from an outsider's perspective, so I didn't see the point.

"Where did you find them?"

"In a cigar box in his study."

She nodded. "I tried to look for them, but Ed…and Joe… they didn't know about them and I didn't want them to see me searching. They're always in my face, which makes it difficult."

"So you didn't break into the armoire?"

She shook her head. "I thought they were in there, but I didn't know who had the key. I tried looking for that too… but nothing. And then when the lock was broken…" Her lower lip trembled.

I put my cigarette to my lips and looked at her hard, waiting for more. After several minutes of silence, she put out her cigarette. "Thanks for this."

"What's going on here?"

"What do you mean?"

"I saw you arguing with Joe and Ed. In the rain."

She shrugged. "We work together. We argue."

"I think there's more to it than that."

"There's not. As you've been warned, you need to stop being so curious."

Had I been warned?

She must have realized she implied there was very much something going on. People don't go around issuing warnings when what's on the surface is all there is. "I mean…I didn't mean to sound so dramatic. I'm just saying, you should mind your own business."

"If I did, I wouldn't have found your photographs."

She stood. "Well, thanks for that."

"You were worried…about what?"

"No one wants pictures like that lying around. They're private. That's all. Don't make a thing out of it."

"Why were you crying?"

"I loved him. Okay? And…"

"And…?"

She sighed. "And I hoped the pictures were in that armoire. I just don't like…I didn't really want people to know what was between us. And I…that's all. I just wanted them back. They belong to me."

"You're welcome."

She gave me a deliberately phony smile. "Thanks."

She went to the door. She picked up the bucket and opened the door. "Mark Kohn is coming on the fifteenth."

"Good to know." I finished my cigarette and my slightly cool chocolate.

After I washed the mug, I texted Dirk and packed my things. I was standing on the front steps when the limo pulled into the drive.

As he waited for me to get into the limo, Dirk thanked me for the gloves. He called me Ms. Mallory, and when I asked that he open the partition, he said it was better to keep it closed.

60

Victoria was waiting for me outside my apartment door. Usually, she would lurk around her own doorway. The doors were only five or six feet from each other, so it always felt like she was encroaching on my space. This time she'd taken over completely, leaning against my door with the toes of her right foot pressed up against the doorframe, her heel on the floor as if she was stretching her calf muscle.

She wore white leggings and gray Ugg boots. Her top was gray with long sleeves as a shout-out to the cold weather, but was cropped to expose her abdomen. She'd dyed her hair a shocking gray, causing me to stop a few steps from the top of the stairs. I'd seen a gray-haired woman with an unnaturally young face a moment before I registered that it was her.

If she hoped for a comment on her appearance, I didn't give her the satisfaction. The color was obviously chosen for attention. Although I wondered why I'd never considered gray hair as part of my repertoire for disguising my appearance. Of course, maybe a young woman with gray hair attracts more attention than I'm usually interested in drawing to myself. Usually. Sometimes, I do want to be noticed and remembered so that my alter ego can slip by unobserved.

"I just wanted to ask you a quick question." She gave me a coy smile.

"I have things to do," I said.

"I'm sure you do, after being gone all weekend." She pouted. "It really hurts my feelings that you're so secretive about where you're going."

"It shouldn't."

"It shouldn't, what?"

"It shouldn't hurt your feelings. It's not about you."

"What's the big deal? So you have a boyfriend, and you stay at his place. Why can't you just tell me?"

"Where I go is none of your business."

"I didn't ask *where*, I..."

"What was your quick question?"

"You seem irritated with me."

"I told you I have things to do."

"You seem irritated with me quite a lot. Rafe too. We've discussed it."

I shrugged. "And your question?"

"Are you irritated with me?"

"Is that your question?"

"You make me feel like I'm living in Alice In Wonderland. Talking to you always makes me feel that way."

I laughed.

"It's not funny."

"Victoria. You said you had a quick question. I told you I had things to do. Please ask your question and move away from my door."

"Are you irritated with me?"

"Right now, yes."

"I'm just trying to be friendly. I thought we were friends."

"We're neighbors. Don't try so hard."

"Is that how it seems? That I'm trying too hard?"

"Yes."

She nodded. She looked surprised as if she'd been completely unaware of how she presented herself. Maybe alone, or with your boyfriend, in front of a computer all day, doing nothing but watching numbers parade across the screen damages your awareness of how others perceive you.

"I'm sorry," she said.

"No worries." I nudged her arm out of the way and stuck my key into the lock.

"What's the rush?"

I turned the key, and the deadbolt snapped back. I unlocked the knob and opened the door.

"Did you really give Nick's mail to the manager?"

"Yes."

"I'm not sure I believe you. And if you didn't, I'd like to have it. I texted him there was mail and he wants me to open it in case it's urgent."

"It's already on its way."

"So you did give it to the manager?"

"I told you I did."

"He's not always trustworthy."

"The manager? Or Nick?"

"The manager. I don't know if we can trust that he actually forwarded it."

"It's his legal responsibility."

"That doesn't mean anything."

"Why wouldn't he?"

"Because he's lazy."

"Well, I did the best I could."

"Nick's worried."

I stepped inside my apartment and dropped my overnight bag onto the floor. "G'night, Victoria."

"Wait."

I waited.

"You wouldn't lie to me?"

"About giving the letter to the manager? Why? He said he had Nick's new address and he'd take care of it."

"What if he doesn't? Maybe you should double-check."

"If he lied that he sent it on, why would he tell the truth about not sending it? You're not making any sense."

"I really need to see that letter."

"I can't imagine why." I could imagine. I imagined Nick knew nothing about it and she wanted to open it anyway. The part I couldn't imagine was what might be inside.

Finally, she took a few steps away from my door. "I want to be your friend. I don't mean to be a pest. Please, can we start over?"

This was at least the second time she'd asked me to start over. Who does that? I wondered how many other people she wanted do-overs with.

"We need to plan our ice skating trip," she said.

"I have a lot going on right now. Can we put that off for a few weeks?"

Her eyes turned glassy and took on a blank quality. I wondered whether she had any girlfriends, any friends at all. The two of them seemed to be inside their apartment most of the time, always waiting for a chance to step out and start a conversation with me.

"We'll do it, just not right now. Not in the next two weeks."

She nodded. She said nothing and returned to her apartment.

I shut the door and dropped my messenger bag on top of my other bag. I went to the kitchen and began mixing a martini. I was wound up. I felt slightly off track.

After a few sips of my martini, I went into the bedroom and picked up the key. I brought it back to the living room and placed it on the coffee table. I pulled off my boots and settled back on the couch. I took another sip and looked at the key.

I'd eased Nell's mind, but the pictures of Eileen were still out there. I wished I'd never seen them. I wished I hadn't tried to figure out what was happening with the people who used to work for Jim. It had nothing to do with me, and yet, I couldn't seem to stop.

61

It was late when I knocked on Kent's door, but I had to get
him to tell me what was up with my neighbors. I didn't have
his cell number, and I wasn't going to turn myself into the
apartment-building freak by slipping a note under his door.
This was the only way.

He answered right away. He was dressed and didn't look
overly perturbed that someone was knocking on his door at
ten-thirty at night.

A crease ran across his scalp, right past the shadowy part
where his hairline began. It made it seem as if someone with
a shaved head is more transparent — their thoughts visible to
anyone who's looking. "Is something wrong?"

"No."

"What's up?"

"Mind if I come in?"

He stepped back and let the door ease open.

The apartment was extreme minimalist. He had a TV
mounted to one wall and a love seat across from it. Above the
love seat was a framed photograph of the moon. There were
no tables, no floor lamps, no other decor. I wasn't even sure

where he kept the remote.

The kitchen table and its two chairs were metallic. The counters were bare — not even a coffee maker or a toaster or kettle. There was no rack near the sink to hold a sponge or scrub brush.

He gestured toward the love seat. I sat, and he settled on the floor, crossing his legs and lifting one foot onto the opposite thigh in a half-lotus position. It was surprising to see such a muscular guy move so easily into a partial yoga pose.

"What's going on?"

"I need you to tell me what happened with the former occupant of my apartment. I don't know if I should be more cautious around Victoria and Rafe. They're very strange, and their strangeness is growing."

"They *are* different."

"I don't know if I should be watching my back more than I am."

"Why are you watching your back?"

"As you agreed, they're strange."

"It doesn't mean you need to watch your back. Why do you think that?"

I shifted my position, crossing my legs, then uncrossing them. I wished he would offer a glass of wine, or at least water, but he said nothing. He was content to sit there mimicking a yogi while I squirmed. His gaze was steady and his breathing so light there seemed to be hardly any breath at all. His back was perfectly straight, and his hips were flexible and loose, not straining to hold the pose that many people can't begin to twist themselves into.

"They're overly aware of when I'm home, when I'm out, and how long I'm gone."

"And this means...?"

"I didn't want a Q and A. I want you to tell me if I should be concerned. I think I have a right to know what happened to the previous tenant."

"Unless there's something wrong with the apartment, I don't see why you have any right at all."

That was sharp. He said it calmly, lowering his voice so the words sounded gentle. They were anything but. "So there was no interaction between Nick and my neighbors that forced him to move out?"

"I don't know exactly what made him leave. I don't think he was forced. That's a strong word."

"Come on, Kent. Don't play word games with me. I know you know why he left and I don't understand why you won't tell me. Do you owe Nick something? Or Victoria?"

He shook his head. He pulled his right foot onto his left thigh, completing the lotus pose.

"That's impressive."

"What?"

I gestured toward his legs.

"It calms me."

"I know. I do yoga." I tried to decide whether this was a lie. My body hadn't seen a yoga mat in weeks. Suddenly, I missed it desperately. I almost wanted to slide onto the floor beside him and join in his Zen-like presence. But I wanted a glass of wine more. I wished I'd brought a bottle with me. It never occurred to me that he might leave me parched and wanting on the love seat.

"You look uncomfortable," he said. "All keyed up. You're not usually like that."

"I have a lot on my mind."

He nodded.

"So are you going to tell me?"

"I don't like to gossip."

"How is it gossip?"

"Talking about something when I only know part of the story. Something that might make you view your neighbors differently. Everyone deserves to be judged impartially when they meet new people."

"You really believe that?"

"Yes, I do."

"What if they're troublemakers?"

"*Troublemaking* is dependent upon the observer."

"Is that right?"

He smiled.

"Nick got some mail. From the New York City FBI field office. Victoria's acting as if I should have given it to her. She insists she would get it forwarded to him, but she's fixated on it, and I think she wants to open his mail."

He sighed. He closed his eyes for a moment. "I don't know much...I don't know everything. That's why I don't feel comfortable talking about it." His eyes opened slowly. "I don't like giving partial stories that can turn out to not be the truth."

"If you know part of the story, it's the truth."

"Context is required for truth."

I stood. "Do you have any wine? I'd really like a glass."

He smiled, somewhat condescendingly, I thought.

After I was seated with a glass of wine in my hand, he returned to the lotus position, adding a glass of Chardonnay to his pose. Maybe I'd misread the condescension.

"Victoria and Rafe are harmless. As far as you're concerned."

"That's a guarantee?" It didn't matter whether he guaranteed it, I wouldn't take him at his word. I would still push for the actual facts, even if they were partial, knowing some of what happened is better than running blind.

"Of course not. I can't guarantee anything about another person. I can hardly do that for myself." He smiled and sipped his wine.

"I wonder if I should ask the manager."

"He doesn't know anything about it."

"Look, I've already judged them. They're funny in a ridiculous sort of way, and they can be interesting to talk to, but mostly they're overbearing. So anything you say isn't going to make me like them any more or less than I do now."

He took another sip of wine and placed his glass on the floor beside him. "Victoria came on to Nick."

As I'd guessed.

"They slept together a few times and then she told Rafe."

"That's bizarre."

"As you said..." He smiled. "Rafe didn't confront the guy or do anything. But he sort of...hovered. Similar to what you've experienced, but a lot more intense."

"Intense, how?"

"He followed Nick everywhere. To work, out with friends. To women's apartments. Once when Nick unlocked the door, Rafe pushed his way in behind him. He stayed for hours, asking detailed questions about what sex with Victoria had been like. It was nothing harmful or dangerous. At least I don't think it was. Just really uncomfortable. And tiresome."

"Okay."

"So that's why I said it has no impact on you."

I thought his assumption showed a rather narrow view of sex, but I simply smiled and sipped my wine. We finished the wine. We each drank another glass and talked about nothing before I got up to leave. I thanked him for easing my mind. He didn't respond. He gave me a limp smile and remained in his lotus position while I let myself out.

62

It was clear that Joe still wanted my body, but he no longer wanted me — my curiosity, my mouth, my restlessness. This time, I saw his text message as a summons rather than an invite, and I wondered if it had been that way before…if it had been that way from the very first time and I hadn't seen it for what it was. Maybe I'd been blinded by luxury.

The limo ferried me out of the city, the partition between passenger and driver closed. I sensed it was a permanent closure. It's a bit fanciful, but it seemed to symbolize that all of this was coming to an end. The gourmet food, the nice wine, the gorgeous house, the perfectly-designed smoking room, and the absolutely fantastic sex with a very good looking guy were nearly over.

That wasn't to say I'd never have any of those things again. I had no doubt I would have them all, and someday, I planned to have them all permanently. At least as permanently as anything can be on this planet.

Joe greeted me with the same seductive kiss and touch of his hands on my body as he always had. The look in his eyes was warm and welcoming, and I suddenly saw what else I'd missed on that very first rainy day — he'd never trusted me. He didn't start using his pleasant face and genuine smile to hide his lack of trust after he caught me with his keys. He'd had the same warmth when we first met as he did now. At that moment, what I saw was not reflecting what was inside of him at all. He and I were made of the same stuff, to some degree. Every word and gesture were calculated. I just didn't know to what end.

Now, things were easier between us because I felt that we were on an even footing. I wondered if he knew that I knew.

For dinner, we ate game hens stuffed with cranberry dressing and wild rice. The candles flickered around us, allowing both of us to relax our outward expressions, taking a few minutes in which we could simply enjoy the food without having to communicate affection and trust and mutual respect, although maybe the mutual respect was there without our masks.

After dinner, we went directly to bed.

Joe brought a bottle of Cabernet upstairs. We sat up in bed, the sheets over our naked legs, and sipped wine.

"I think I've walked into the middle of something here," I said.

"What's that?"

"I don't know. You tell me."

"I suppose there's some upheaval. Since none of us knows what our future will look like."

I folded over the edge of the sheet and smoothed it across my navel. "No one knows the future."

"What I meant was that our lack of knowledge is imminent. Generally, people are deluded into thinking they know the future, that they can predict most of what's coming into their lives. In this case, we're conscious of the fact that unpredictable changes are coming soon."

"I thought you weren't worried."

"I'm not."

"Then why do I sense this tension with you and the others?"

"The others?"

"Ed. Nell." I left Dirk out of it. There was no sense suggesting something that might make Joe go after him sniffing for a sign of betrayal.

"I can't speak for the others."

"I saw all of you arguing. It was pretty intense."

"When was this?"

"The day of that huge storm. You were standing out in the rain. It looked like you were shouting at each other."

He took a sip of wine. He leaned to the side and picked up the bottle. He poured some into my glass then refilled his own.

I rested the base of the glass on my belly. "So what's the problem?"

"It's not any of your business. What are you really here for anyway?"

"You." I smiled without looking at him.

"This is probably it with us."

"I know."

"That's flattering." He laughed. "I guess you're good at faking it."

"I wasn't faking."

"Not ever?"

"Nope." I closed my eyes and leaned my head back on the pillows. The bed was so comfortable, I couldn't imagine getting out of it every morning to go to work. Especially if there was a man like Joe beside me. "Are you still hoping to stay on here?"

"It might be time for something new. We'll see."

"I guess a job like yours has a lot to do with whether you click with your boss."

"Usually."

"Did you click with Jim?"

"I thought we understood each other."

"You *thought?*"

"Don't read into it. Just a turn of phrase."

I didn't think it was a simple turn of phrase. It was the first and only slip he'd made, letting me know that Dirk's comments had been truthful, and that his advice had been correct.

"It's dangerous to interfere in other people's lives when you're interest isn't wanted," he said.

"Thanks for the tip."

"No problem," he said.

"Is that a threat?"

"Of course not."

"Another turn of phrase that I'm reading into?"

I could tell the second bottle of wine was loosening his tongue. I had the sense he was regretting some of the things he was saying, even as he said them. Or maybe, he was so upset with the others his emotions were getting the best of him, making him angry and irritated, stirring up indiscretion because anger has a way of pushing thoughts onto the tongue and out into the world.

He laughed softly. "You didn't know there was a surveillance camera in Jim's study, did you?"

A chill ran down my arms. What I'd done was indeed dangerous. I'd thought I was taking control of Jim's house and doing as I pleased, dancing on his grave. Instead, Joe had invited me in, made me relax, enticed me to let down my guard, and allowed me enough of the proverbial rope to hang myself.

A small, cautious part of me whispered that I should leave the next morning. But another, much louder voice was shouting that whatever plans they had for the photographs of Eileen, they had no right. The chance of finding those pictures was slim, but there was still a chance. Until I was physically removed from the premises, there was still a chance.

63

Waking in the early hours of the morning was, for the most part, a habit in this house. The supremely comfortable bed didn't hold me. When I slipped into it at night, I thought I could never leave, but when my thoughts woke and started creeping around, my body followed. I dressed, grabbed my cigarettes, and went down to the smoking room. This time, it was only a bit after midnight. Joe's mention of the camera had disturbed me enough that ninety minutes of sleep was all I'd been able to manage.

I stood in the study and looked at the ceiling. Nothing was obvious, but with the slick design of the house, the high-tech light fixtures, and recessed speakers, it could be tucked anywhere.

Clearly, he'd wanted me to know he'd seen me going through the drawers and cabinets in the study, but he wasn't going to do anything about it...for now. This meant there was nothing of interest in this room. Something far worse plagued me. Was there also a surveillance camera in the storage room? If he'd seen me with the key...but wouldn't he have done something? Or was he waiting for me to step into a much bigger trap?

I went into the smoking room, more wary than ever. My past enjoyment seemed naïve now. How on earth would I find out if there was a camera in that third-floor room, and if there was, what could I do about it?

The obvious answer was to kill Joe, but if all of them knew...I couldn't kill all three. I wasn't even sure I could kill him. My presence in the house was well-known, and now I knew, well-documented. And this was my last visit. I hadn't come prepared for killing anyone.

Committing murder in a house filled with my fingerprints and fallen hairs and skin cells would be a worse mistake than taking the key from Jim's body. And luring Joe out to a hotel wasn't possible. He wasn't a man to be lured anywhere.

I was on my third cigarette, slowly destroying my lungs while my body atrophied.

I stubbed out the cigarette and turned my attention to the nude paintings on the wall to my right. The paintings were tasteful — true art — but now that I knew more about Jim, I wondered at the choice. I glanced into the corner above the door, looking for a camera. The walls were smooth, the crown molding seamlessly fitted. I saw nothing. I stood and walked around the room, looking for the slightest imperfection in the plaster, peering into the glass cases that held all those boxes of cigars.

It was a room where Jim had wanted complete privacy.

The door opened.

I turned quickly.

Ed stood in the doorway. One hand was on the door handle, the other in his pocket. I wondered if his fingers twitched, if his brain was searching for those squares of color, feeling lost without the cube.

"I need you to leave."

"In a few."

"Not the room, the house. The new owner is coming on Monday."

"I keep hearing about this new owner, but it seems he's been coming forever. I wonder if he really exists."

"You're no longer welcome here. And really, you never were."

"Does Joe agree with that?"

His fingers clenched on the door handle. "I can have you physically removed. By the police."

I laughed. "That's a little extreme."

"Is it?"

He opened the door wider as if he expected me to walk through it, obediently pack my things, and leave. I no longer felt the need or had any interest in drawing him out, trying to understand what was going on with him. I had no doubt that whatever they were up to with the photographs, the images were likely in his possession.

In fact, I was no longer sure that he'd ever taken direction from Joe. Their relationship was the opposite of what Joe had tried to suggest. When I'd seen Ed shouting at the other two during the rainstorm, he made his position as top dog very clear. Whatever was going on, Ed was directing it.

"I want you to leave in the morning. First thing."

"I'm Joe's guest. As long as he invites me, I'm not going anywhere."

His face turned red, then the blood drained completely, and that was almost more unsettling than the obvious temper that made him redden. His eyes were blank, his lips curled into something that said he would do whatever was necessary to make sure I didn't interfere with whatever he was up to.

I returned to the couch and sat down. I removed a cigarette from my pack and lit it with Jim's lighter. I leaned back and crossed my legs.

"If you think you look sexy doing that, you do not."

"I didn't think anything. I just wanted a smoke."

Alert to the proper functioning of the ventilation system, he stepped into the room and let the door fall closed.

My blood pumped hard. My muscles tightened slightly, seeing how he looked at me. Still, I continued smoking. I was pretty sure he would not call the police. Whatever he was planning, he wanted the police far away from this house.

"When you're finished, clean the ashtray and don't come back into this room."

"I like it here."

"Do I need to have Joe drag you out?"

"You could ask him." I inhaled smoke and blew it out slowly. "I love this entire house. And Joe...it's not just the house...he and I have a fantastic connection." I smiled. "I'm thinking of moving in."

"You can't."

"Why not? There's plenty of room. I could help Nell."

His hands twitched in front of him, no longer itching for the mindless machinations of the plastic cube. His fingers strained to wrap themselves around my neck. They tightened with the desire to both shut me up and remove my interference from his life in a single, swift action.

The ash fell off my cigarette onto the couch.

He made a sound like a wounded animal.

When I looked at him, his expression was stoic. I picked up

the ashtray and swept the ashes into it as best I could. I stubbed out the cigarette and stood.

When I walked through the door, I felt his breath on the side of my face. It was strangely and unsettlingly cool, inhuman. It smelled like some kind of spice I couldn't identify.

64

The entire next day I was alone in the house. They all wanted me out, but it appeared they'd decided it was easier to remove themselves, perhaps assuming I'd get bored and take myself elsewhere.

I immediately got busy looking for Eileen's photographs. I searched every room as best I could, although I didn't page through every single book in the enormous library.

By lunchtime, I began to consider whether they'd left me alone because they wanted me to look for the photographs. I considered this for a while, but I couldn't come up with a reason why they might want that. Combing through drawers and closets and bookcases was taking a lot of time and energy. I was frustrated that I had this fantastic opportunity but no luck.

The only lucky bit was my search of the master suite. In Jim's bathroom, I found a half-used bottle of Valium. Confident that any surveillance equipment would be in the bedroom itself, I flushed the toilet to cover the sound and dumped all but two of the tablets onto my palm. I slipped them into my pocket. It was a bit of insurance, I suppose.

Of course, the rooms on the third floor, all but Joe's, were locked. I played around with a slender screwdriver I found in the pantry, trying to see if I could manage to pop the lock on the storage room and on Ed's door. I'm not experienced at that sort of thing, so all I managed to do was apply thin scratch marks to the finish. The lines were small enough that no one would notice, unless they went looking.

Utterly out of luck, I shot a few games of pool in the billiards room. After that, I entertained myself with movies in the theater, eating buttered popcorn and treating myself to two martinis, spaced nicely throughout the afternoon.

As the sun went down, I was still wandering around alone, my footsteps seeming to echo more loudly without other ears to absorb the sound. I'd never been alone in such a large house. I could have enjoyed it so much more if I didn't expect one or all of them to appear at any moment.

The dinner hour came and went. I sampled a few expensive cheeses with crackers and then made a grilled-cheese sandwich from a block of imported white cheddar. I drank water and returned to the library nibbling the second half of my sandwich, studying the books and trying to decide if it was worth the effort to pull each one off the shelf to see whether Eileen's photos were stuck inside. The trouble was, there were easily seven- or eight-hundred books lining the walls up to the ceiling.

I put the last corner of the sandwich into my mouth and chewed it.

"What are you doing?" Nell's voice came from behind me. Her tone was neutral.

I spun around, chewing fast before I answered. "Looking at books."

She nodded. Her hair was combed smooth, gliding around her shoulders as her head moved. She wore a baggy sweater, skinny jeans, and thick, soft socks.

"Was it nice to get away from here?"

She looked over her shoulder then turned back. "Yes."

A few seconds passed.

She slid the tips of her fingers into the pockets of her skinny jeans. "Do you want a glass of wine?"

"Sure."

She gestured toward the leather armchairs arranged to face the window, a small table between them. The drapes were still open. Obviously whoever had pulled them that morning hadn't been back. She went to the window and tugged on the cord. They moved silently toward each other, swaying vigorously as they met at the center of the window.

She turned. "Petite Syrah okay?"

I nodded. I took a seat although I sort of wanted to follow her to see if she went down the treacherous stairs into the cellar wearing those comfy socks.

Several minutes later, long enough to descend quickly into the wine cellar, choose a bottle, and climb back up, she returned with the opened bottle and two goblets.

We drank the entire first glass in silence, staring at the motionless drapes, lost in our own thoughts, although my thoughts were mostly of her. I doubted hers were of me.

Finally, she began talking. It was nothing important, just chitchat about working as a housekeeper, how incredible the house was. She said she'd thought about trying to make a name for herself on YouTube by telling funny stories about keeping house for a member of the one percent.

After the second glass, she was silent once again.

I shifted in my chair. "Are you close to Ed?"

"What do you mean?"

"Good friends?"

"Not really."

"Sleeping together?"

"No."

"I saw him once, coming out of your room early in the morning. Around five."

"He probably came by to talk about things. He does that."

I nodded. "What things?"

"Just things."

"Do you like him?"

"What difference does that make?"

"Just curious. I was going to tell you something." I had to tell her something, had to chip into the wall between us, widening the very slight crack that remained stubbornly in place instead of splitting wide. She was my only hope for finding out whether there was a camera spying on the comings and goings in the storage room.

"He's okay."

"I wondered because I had fun winding him up."

"What do you mean?"

"He really wants me out of the house."

Her face revealed nothing.

"I made him think I'm planning to move in. That I could help you with housekeeping."

She laughed.

"I can't figure out why I bother him so much. He's wanted me out of here from the start."

She emptied the wine bottle, pouring half into my glass, half into hers. "Should I get another?"

"Sure. Why not."

When she returned, I expected her to change the subject. It seemed clumsily obvious she'd refilled the glasses and gone for another bottle to avoid commenting on what I'd said.

She picked up her glass and stared at the red liquid. She held it up and gazed through it at the striped curtains as if she were looking through a prism. "I guess I can tell you this." She lowered the glass and swallowed some wine. "When you first showed up, no one could figure out what you were after. Ed asked Joe to keep an eye on you, which he did in spades." She laughed as if this were so funny she couldn't control herself.

I waited for more.

"They still don't know why you showed up and invited yourself in, as if this is your holiday home."

"Joe invited me."

"Don't get defensive."

"I'm not defensive. That's what happened."

"Well, he only wanted to see what you were after. They couldn't figure out if you wanted money, or were planning some kind of lawsuit…"

"Against a dead guy?"

"They just…we just didn't know."

"I thought I was pretty straight-forward with Joe."

"It was strange. We knew you didn't think much of Jim… you're very aggressive."

"Where are they now?"

"I don't know."

"The three of you seem like you want to take over the house as your own." This wasn't truly my impression because it was impossible unless Jim had left it to them, which he had not, but it was the only thing I could think of to shift the conversation to the track I wanted.

"Not at all."

"It's an amazing house."

"It is."

"The camera in the study shocked me."

She didn't respond.

"I was glad you got your pictures out of the box before someone saw me looking at them."

"Yeah. I said, thanks."

"I wasn't looking for another thank you, just saying. Joe or Ed might have seen them and grabbed them."

"Maybe."

"Are there cameras all over the house?"

"Just a few."

"Is there one in here?" I turned, straining my neck as if I were looking for a small device near the ceiling.

"No."

I sighed, anxious for her to reveal the locations.

She said nothing.

"What rooms have them?"

"Jim was kind of...he had weird habits."

"So I noticed."

"He had a camera in his bedroom. There used to be one in the cigar room, but he took it out."

"To move it somewhere else?"

"I don't think so. He just liked to watch himself — working, having sex, sleeping."

I shivered. "Photographing women?"

"What?"

"In his photography studio inside the storage room."

"Oh. No, he doesn't have one in there."

I held my breath to keep myself from exhaling too loudly, exposing what was inside of me — how close I'd come to being discovered with the key, and thus tied more closely to Jim Kohn than I'd ever intended.

65

Portland

"**W**hat happened to your girlfriend?" Tom shoved the entire cookie into his mouth and yanked open the pantry door. "I thought she was hot to make cookies and now mom's doing all the work."

"She had to pee."

My mother glared at me. "Don't use that language."

Tom rolled his eyes and mouthed *sorry* at me. He left the room, and I heard his footsteps starting down the basement stairs, Jake and Eric behind him, Eric kissing my mother's cheek as he grabbed three more cookies off the cooling tray. "Eric!" She laughed. "You can only get away with that once."

"Sure, Mom."

"Hey!" Tom's voice echoed up the concrete sides of the stairwell.

Footsteps thudded as the others descended more quickly.

"You little twerp."

I grabbed a cookie of my own and followed my brothers. Downstairs, Carmen sat on one of their couches with her legs tucked up beside her. Two sparkly pink tennis shoes were on the floor, thin white socks lying beside them. A smile of absolute victory sat in the center of her face. "I think the girls should get to play here today."

"Nope." Tom grabbed her upper arm. She smiled at him. "Don't be rough with me. You're supposed to treat ladies with respect."

"You don't belong in here."

"Why not?"

"You know the rules."

"Tell me again."

"Girls in the attic, boys in the basement. It's not complicated."

"It's a dumb rule."

"Lots of rules are dumb, but that's the way it is."

"Why?"

"Because. Come on." He tugged her arm.

She wrenched away from him and let out a little shriek. "You're hurting me."

"You hurt yourself. Get up."

"Scram," Tom said.

"I'm a guest here. It's rude to kick me out."

"You aren't a guest in this room."

"I'm a guest in the house."

Tom turned to me. "Get your little friend out of here. Now."

"Come on, Carmen. Let's go," I said.

"What about the Barbies?"

Tom let go of her arm. "It was a joke."

"I don't think so."

"You can have your dollies," Tom said. "Little girlies with their dollies."

I kicked him.

"Watch it," he said. "No kicking."

"Is that a rule?" Carmen giggled.

"Actually, it is." Tom took her arm again and tried to pull her off the couch. Jake grabbed her socks, pinched his nose with the other hand, and stuffed them into the shoes. "Out."

"But the Barbies. Why would boys play with Barbies? That's weird," she said.

"We didn't play with your Barbies."

She opened her mouth and made her eyes wide. "What would you call it?"

"Get out, you little shit," Jake said.

"I bet you aren't supposed to say that," Carmen said.

Jake dropped her shoes in her lap. "Take these stinky shoes." He went to the corner and opened the cabinet at the bottom of one of the bookcases. He pulled out the pink suitcase. He turned and stared at the corner as if he were looking for something. He unzipped the suitcase a few inches and peered inside. He zipped it closed and glanced at Tom, who shrugged and let go of Carmen's upper arm.

Jake walked around the couch and handed the suitcase to me. "It was just a joke. Get your friend out of here."

"A nasty joke," Carmen said. She slid off the couch, clutching her shoes.

She followed me out of the room without saying anything more. We were two steps up the staircase when the door slammed closed behind us. I heard their voices, talking urgently, starting to argue with each other, but I kept climbing.

66

If you looked at things through a particular prism, everything she'd said in the email to Alexandra was the truth. It might not be literal truth, but it was a higher level of truth. It was the truth of knowing every person was far deeper than you gave them credit for. There were so many twists and turns, memories and beliefs inside a person's soul. The truth of their lives could be looked at in a thousand different ways.

And Truth, real Truth, spiritual Truth was not bound by facts that could only be seen in the material world.

In Eileen's case, that beloved baby girl, the beautiful young woman Stephanie had tried to shape, had sold her soul to the devil. Stephanie hated thinking in such drastic terms, but it was true. All Eileen cared about was her physical appearance, getting attention, making money, and sex. Because that's what the fashion industry was selling underneath all that glamor.

It wasn't too late to reclaim Eileen's soul, but the *Truth* was, for now, Satan was her master. There was no end to the kind of evil a person like that could inflict upon others. The influence of darkness was obvious in her appearance — all that dark, heavy makeup, the gaunt condition of her body, as if she were no longer even a woman but some sort of spectral beast...the vacant look in her eyes. No amount of makeup could hide that.

So telling Alexandra to be aware that Eileen had attached herself like a succubus was the Truth.

She'd laid it out in no uncertain terms. Eileen wanted money, and she would manipulate and lie and deceive to get it. Alex needed to stay out of Eileen's life, or she would find herself lending money, giving money, drained dry of all her resources. If there was one thing Alex seemed to care deeply for, it was money.

The two of them were the same in that — all Eileen talked about was money. She talked about her hourly rate, and how much other models were making. She talked incessantly about that man — being dead hadn't weakened his hold on her — going on about his influence, his knowledge of how her career should be managed, all because he had power and money. And the power came from his money.

The Bible was clear about how money should be viewed, about how selling out to worldly influences destroyed you.

She knew Alexandra didn't care about spiritual things, but she cared about money.

Stephanie had gently but directly laid out in writing that she was aware Alexandra didn't believe much in that aspects of life that weren't tangible, but despite her unbelief, dark forces would be released into Alexandra's life if she continued to spend time with Eileen. It didn't matter whether or not you believed such things, it was the Truth.

She hoped her warning was strong enough. She hoped

Alexandra didn't brush it off as something outside the material world she worshipped. It was strongly worded, written to generate fear in even the most unbelieving heart.

Time would tell.

For now, Eileen was in her room, ears plugged as music or motivational podcasts or God knew what else pumped directly into her brain. She'd skipped dinner, taking two apples and a mug of green tea to her room for sustenance.

She was so secretive lately. It started with that man, grew worse when he died, and now seemed to have intensified even further. She was hiding something. It was clear from her behavior, her refusal to make eye contact. A secret was nibbling away at her as relentlessly as she carved away at her body, scraping off fat with back-breaking exercise. Mothers could see that kind of deceit in the flick of a glance, in a daughter's posture, in the very hairs framing her face. What she could not see was any hint of what the secret might entail.

Stephanie's heart ached as she tried to think of a way to gain entrance to her daughter's life. She'd managed fairly well to shove Alexandra out of the way and close the door on that, but she'd found no way to do the opposite.

Why was it so much easier to be rid of people than it was to draw them closer?

67

After sipping my way through two bottles of wine with Nell, I slept from eleven-thirty until six-fifteen. Knowing a camera hadn't recorded my unlocking of the armoire had carried me into a deep, peaceful sleep — dreamless and satisfying.

The space beside me in bed was empty.

I showered and dressed and packed my things. I was annoyed that I didn't have the photographs, but the disappearance of Joe and Ed made me realize the likelihood of getting my hands on them was slimmer than ever. Pretty much nonexistent.

My finger was poised over the phone, ready to text Dirk for a ride, but I hesitated. I really needed coffee. A nice strong rejuvenating sip of dark roast. The limo was well-stocked with champagne and wine, hard liquor and soft drinks, but there wasn't a coffee pot built into all that luxurious space. Sitting in commute traffic would be more tolerable after a cup of coffee.

I stopped in front of Nell's door on my way to the stairs. There was still something standoffish about her, a strong sense that she wanted me out of the house as desperately as

Ed and Joe did, she was simply going about it with more subtlety. There was a sense that she'd risked more than she should have in telling me about Joe's calculated interest in me. Beyond that, I sensed there was a whole lot more to be said.

I knocked softly.

The thuds of someone moving inelegantly around the room came through the door. I waited for nearly a minute, but she didn't answer. I went downstairs and made coffee. As I pulled two slices of bread out of a bag, I thought about her again. She was obviously awake. Why hadn't she opened the door?

I ran back up the stairs, certain she'd want some freshly brewed coffee and toast.

This time I knocked with more force. I waited. Again I heard a few soft thuds, but no sound of her approaching.

"Nell? I made coffee."

I was answered with silence. After a moment I heard a faint whimper. This was followed half a second later by a sharp cry that was unmistakably pain.

"Are you okay?"

Again, silence.

I tried the door handle. It was locked, of course.

Her voice sounded weak. "Please go away."

"Is something wrong?"

"I'm fine. You need to go."

"I don't think you're fine. It sounds like you're in pain."

I heard a grunt and a few more whimpers.

I stood there for ten minutes, thinking of my coffee, continuing to knock every thirty seconds or so. Finally, she opened the door a crack.

The one-inch crack was too much. If she'd thought she

could hide herself, she was wrong. If she truly didn't want me to see her, she shouldn't have cracked the door open at all.

I pushed gently on the door, opening it another inch before she resisted.

Her face was battered and bloody. A gash filled with dried blood ran across her lower lip. One eye was swollen shut, the other was red and watery. A purple lump dominated the right side of her forehead. Blood and mucous bubbled in her nostrils.

"Let me in." I pushed on the door. She held firm.

"I'm fine. Just go away."

"Who did this?"

She sighed.

I couldn't begin to imagine it had been Joe. "Let me in. You need help. We should get you to the ER."

"It looks worse than it is."

"I doubt that."

"Nothing's broken."

"Well isn't that nice."

She started to cry.

"Let me come in. You need ice. I'll be back."

She sighed.

I hurried downstairs. I shoved four slices of bread into the toaster. I found a tray in the pantry and put two mugs of coffee on it. I filled a bowl with ice and draped a linen towel over it. I buttered the toast, plopped it on a plate, and walked upstairs as quickly as I could while taking care with the coffee.

Inside her room, I wrapped ice in the towel and held it first to the bruise on her forehead and then to each cheek while she tried to part her lips enough to sip coffee. I gulped down my own coffee, turning away from the purple and yellow and bloody mess of her face to steady myself. I spoke, still avoiding looking directly at her face. "Is he here? In the house?"

"Who?"

"You know who. Ed."

"I think so."

"You need to leave."

"I can't."

"What's to keep him from doing this again? Or worse?"

"He was pissed."

"So?"

She shrugged, followed quickly by a wince. "He wanted me to get you out of here. He was pissed you're still here."

"That guy sure has a lot of interest in someone that has nothing to do with him." The irony of what I'd said fluttered in my throat. I swallowed the laugh.

"He's concerned about Mark arriving and seeing we abused our privilege here. He's worried about his job."

"So he beat the shit out of you?"

"He wanted me to make you leave. I told him it was no problem, but I dropped the ball. You seemed so nice, I just felt like talking. And the wine..."

Now, I really wanted to laugh. I didn't recall anyone ever saying I was nice. They said a lot of things — they admired me, they envied me, they thought I was confident and strong and didn't take bullshit. They said a lot of less admirable things. But *nice* never entered the picture.

Maybe if you live with a guy who takes nude photos to exploit you for his own craving, and then you hang out with a guy who smashes up your face because you don't do what he says, common decency is interpreted as *nice*.

"Why are you staying?"

"I need the job."

"How are you going to convince Mark to keep you on when your face looks like this?"

She started to cry again. "I didn't think about that."

I took the towel into her bathroom and dumped the ice into the sink. I wrung out the towel and dropped it into her dirty clothes basket.

We ate the toast and drank coffee. Nell looked worried the entire time.

I wasn't sure what to do. I couldn't be responsible for her. There was no way I could help her. Not immediately.

68

It was clear to me that Ed was not a man who added any value to the world. The wreck he'd made of Nell's face stirred up a wave of nausea every time I recalled the pulpy mess of it. Whatever he was up to, whatever they were all up to, he was unnecessary. Joe and Nell could carry on without him and his Rubik's Cube.

The job would be more spur-of-the-moment than I like, but at the same time, it seemed as if the house had been designed for this very thing. And the added benefit was that once I was rid of him, I'd be able to access his suite and, hopefully, I'd finally get my hands on Eileen's photographs. She was going to owe me a huge debt of gratitude. I wouldn't call her on a debt, wouldn't demand it. I wouldn't even mention it, obviously. But I was sure it would be given all the same. Debt is not a good way to start a friendship, but I suppose there are worse ways. Luring someone into a relationship in order to take control of them is one that comes to mind.

In the end, Ed almost made it too easy.

Nell was in her room, her stomach rattling with four

Ibuprofen to ease the pain in her head and reduce the swelling. Instead of sleeping, she was worrying about how she might explain the condition of her face when Mark Kohn showed up the following day to decide whether or not he wanted to retain the household staff.

I gave her a Valium, insisting that rest would help her heal. She didn't argue, and after a few minutes, she drifted off, hopefully to a place without dreams. I took two tablets into her bathroom and dropped them into a glass. I used the stone obelisk sitting on her bedside table to crush the tablets into a fine powder. I shook the powder into a small plastic bag I found in the vanity drawer. I washed and dried the glass.

While Nell slept, I went for a run around the property. I set my app to track three miles. No matter how boring it would be crisscrossing the same garden paths four, five, six times, I couldn't put it off one more day. I also needed to burn adrenaline. I adore running, but I'd been behaving as if it were a chore. The weather and the weekends cozied up with Joe had spread a lethargy over me that I needed to scrape off ASAP. I'd been smoking like an addict and lying around eating rich food.

I like to be strong and fit and ready for anything. I like to run easily up a flight of stairs, or two. I like to feel my body move efficiently and work hard, pumping blood to every cell and nerve ending. My running shoes and clothes had waited hopefully in the overnight bag every time I visited Joe, but they'd remained stuffed to the bottom.

Starting was rough, but after half a mile, I hit my stride. Just before the two-mile mark, I had the crawly awareness of someone watching me. I was circling around the area past the back end of the pool, through a grove of birch trees. The ground was carpeted with natural covering instead of a paved walkway, but packed solid so I didn't have to keep my eyes continuously on the ground every time I planted a foot.

Another series of tingles ran across my skin. The birch trees were slender and graceful in the cool breeze, much too narrow for anyone to hide behind. Besides, the entire property was surrounded by a thick wall, and I expected there were cameras, so I couldn't imagine it was a stranger's curious gaze.

Still, I felt a pair of eyes tracking every step. A mind calculating where I would turn next, a gaze traveling over my body, watching.

Maybe I felt these things because I was already alert to Ed's constant presence. His attention to me was a good thing. Knowing he was watching me run, knowing he'd continue watching me until he figured out how to get me out of the house, gave me a slight upper hand. I needed that because luring him to the place I'd chosen was going to be tricky.

As my route took me around the front edge of the pool area, I saw him. He stood in the breakfast room, close to the windows. He was using a pair of binoculars. I circled around to the front of the house. My app said I'd completed one-point-eight miles, but I decided that was enough. I felt victorious for having overcome weeks of stagnation. Now, there were other things to do. My mind wasn't on my body, and that's a perfect way to land your foot incorrectly and wind up with a strained ankle.

I walked around to the back of the house again. As I crossed the patio, the spot where Ed had been standing was vacant. I went inside and upstairs to take a shower.

When I came out, Joe was sitting on the couch. "You're still here?"

"Something came up."

"I can't think what that would be."

I sat down and shoved my feet back into my running shoes. "Where have you been?"

"I don't think I'm required to update you on my plans," he said.

"I wasn't checking, just curious."

"I went to visit a friend."

"A friend?"

"A friend of mine has cancer, okay? It's probably the last time I'll see him."

"Oh. I'm sorry to hear that. It's just that the timing seems odd, since I'm here."

"The timing isn't about you. And I thought you were leaving."

I shrugged.

"You need to." He pulled out his phone. "I'm texting Dirk."

"Not yet. I will soon, but not yet."

"There's no point in hanging around."

"I still don't have closure."

He laughed, a genuine, hearty laugh. "Please."

"I'm going to get something to eat. Can I bring you anything, or do you want to join me?"

"Let's not prolong this."

"I'm hungry."

He turned his attention to his phone and didn't say anything more.

In the kitchen, I made a grilled cheese sandwich. I went

into the living room to eat it. One bite into the second half, Ed appeared in the doorway. "We have a breakfast room, and this isn't it."

"I'm eating lunch."

"Please take your crumbling sandwich into the kitchen or the breakfast room. And then, you need to leave. I think Joe was quite clear that you're no longer welcome." He turned and disappeared into the foyer, but I felt him standing out there, ready to follow me when I went upstairs, keeping himself just out of sight.

When I was finished with my sandwich, I got two glasses out of the cabinet and poured a shot of Jim's expensive scotch into each one. I turned on the faucet to cover the sound, and shook the powdered Valium into one of the glasses, stirring for several seconds until it was absorbed by the liquid. I returned to Joe's suite. The drink looked slightly cloudy, so I kept my hand around the glass as I handed it to him. I clicked my glass against his. "To your friend." I took a sip.

He swallowed some. "I needed this." He sighed. "Thanks. You're strangely cold, and interesting, at the same time. I like it and I hate it." He took another sip. "So...what are you buttering me up for?"

"Can I ask you a huge favor?"

"What's that?"

"Do you mind if I take a bottle of wine from the cellar?"

"Yes, I mind. That's...."

"It would give me the closure I'm looking for."

"Stop with the bullshit."

I walked to where he was half reclining on the couch, his lower legs dangling over one arm. I climbed onto him, straddling his hips.

"I don't think this is a good idea," he said.

"Wouldn't a gift from the wine cellar end things on a nice note?"

"There are wines in there that cost hundreds of dollars a bottle."

I leaned forward, brushing my lips across his. Beneath me, I felt him shudder, then try to resist the sensation. "I'll show you what I choose, and if it costs too much, I'll pick something else."

He groaned.

"Does that mean yes?"

"You're kind of a user."

"So are you." I climbed off.

He sat up, dug around in his pocket, and pulled out his keys. He slid one off the ring and handed it to me. "Bring it back...*with* the bottle of wine. And then you're out of here."

"Absolutely."

He picked up the remote and turned the TV to a football game. I left, holding the warm piece of metal in my left hand. He'd be asleep when I left for good.

69

When you think of luring someone, you think of pleasing words, enticement, curiosity. You think of seduction. But none of those things would work with Ed. He wanted one thing — me out of the house. Certainly, he wanted other things, but I wasn't sure what those were, and his primary focus was blatantly me and my air of entitlement and my interference in whatever he was up to.

I returned to the kitchen. First, I got out the high-tech blender. From the well-stocked liquor shelves and fridge, I retrieved bottles of vodka, banana liqueur, and pineapple juice. I dumped ice into the blender, filled it with the appropriate measurements of alcohol, and turned it to high. It was disappointingly quiet.

I poured the cocktail into a glass and took a sip. It was sweeter than what I normally like, but quite good, especially mid-afternoon when the craving for something sweet surfaces. I took another sip, added more ice to the blender and turned it on. This time I left the lid slightly askew — enough to keep the ice chips inside but allowing the sound to intensify, certain it would alert Ed to where I was.

I set the alarm on my phone for two minutes and turned the volume up to the highest setting. I selected the most annoying tone — the one that's a combination of electronic notes and honking sounds that drives you batty after three or four rounds.

I pulled a plastic bag out of a tub in the pantry and shoved it into my pocket. It bulged slightly. I pressed my fist against my hip bone, forcing out the air trapped inside the plastic. I turned off the blender and took another sip of my dessert cocktail. I dumped the rest down the drain, washed and dried the glass, and returned it to the cabinet. I went down the short hallway to the wine cellar.

A moment later, my alarm began ringing. I inserted the key into the cellar door and opened it. I stepped inside and started down the marble stairs, glad of the rubber soles on my running shoes that ensured my feet landed solidly on each step.

The alarm was still going. I walked back up and stood near the open door so the sound would carry out into the hallway. On the fifth repeat, Ed appeared, coming from the kitchen.

"Where did you get that key?"

I smiled and turned off my alarm.

He held out his hand. "Give it to me. You need to leave. Now. You're not welcome here."

"Joe said I could take a bottle of wine."

"Joe's wrong."

"Are you going to stop me?" I took a step down.

"Actually, I am." He moved into the space at the top of the stairs. I saw him waver for a moment as he made the mistake of glancing down to the floor below, throwing off his equilibrium. It was a strange, and almost deliberately unsettling design with the railing fixed to the wall and the opposite side completely unguarded.

"If you touch me, I'll say you tried to assault me."

He laughed. "And who are you going to *say* this to?"

"The police, when they come to take me out of the house."

"I don't need the police to get you out of here." He took a step down and grabbed the handrail. I don't think he realized that I saw the bone white of his knuckles on the iron railing. He took another step, leaving his hand slightly behind him, still gripping the railing. He was now one step above me but his long, skeletal frame towered over me.

I rested my shoulder against the wall. "Why do you hate me so much?"

"I'm not here to have a conversation." He grabbed my upper arm.

I tightened my grip on the handrail and took another step down, my back pressed against the wall. My movement pulled him awkwardly so that both of his arms were stretched out, one slightly behind him, unwilling to loosen its grip on the railing.

I moved again, and he was forced to make a choice. He let go of the railing.

I jammed the key into his stomach in the vicinity of his navel, just above his belt. He cried out and let go of my arm. He wobbled on the narrow, slippery step, his arms thrashing behind him to find the railing, to find anything to grab onto. I shoved him hard, not caring that the key rattled and pinged its way to the floor below.

He began to fall, grunting but not crying out. His bones and muscles hitting marble made more noise than the whimpers coming from his lips. The steep trajectory of the stairs added momentum, keeping him moving, tumbling, his limbs tangled, flailing as he tried to reach the railing that was now too far above him.

About halfway down, the momentum of his fall pitched him over the side. He landed on the cellar floor with a smack. I hurried down, sure-footed in my running shoes, pumped with adrenaline.

His eyes were closed and his breath shallow. His body was motionless. His head lay at an awkward angle to his shoulders. I yanked the plastic bag out of my pocket and pulled it over his head, holding my hands around his gaunt neck, feeling rigid tendons and soft flesh and surprisingly smooth skin.

Unconscious, but still driven by the unquenchable fight for life, he struggled, but not hard enough. I sat on his hips and was able to keep him in place. Despite my lethargy the past few weeks, I still had years of weight-lifting and age on my side.

I didn't like watching him die. It's not normally how I like to do things, but sometimes, you have to go with the flow. I turned my head away, but that didn't stop me from hearing and feeling his movements beneath me.

When he was still, the bag slack against his face, empty of oxygen, I stood.

Not worried, but compelled to check, I looked up at the stairs. No one was there. They were lost in their dreams.

70

Up in the attic, Carmen unzipped the suitcase with a dramatic sweep of her hand.

The Barbies and Kens lay naked on their enormous pile of clothing.

"They're naked," Carmen said.

"I can see that."

"They weren't naked the last time we played with them."

"My brothers must have taken off their clothes."

Carmen's eyes widened. Her pupils were large and inky. "I know. It's disgusting."

"Why? We take their clothes off."

She flipped the lid back in place to cover the naked dolls. She sat on the couch and pulled her still bare feet up onto the cushions, bending her knees and hugging them to her chest.

"Don't put your bare feet on the couch."

"I don't have cooties."

"But you have sweat and oil and dead skin."

"So do you."

"It's mine. And this is my room and my furniture."

"When we're blood sisters, we'll mix our blood so it's okay to mix other stuff."

"We aren't going to be blood sisters."

"You'll change your mind when you hear what your brothers did."

I walked to the window and looked out at the backyard. The wind whipped the trees into a dance that made me want to go out and run around, feeling it against my face. I wanted to listen to the sound of branches moving and the needles of the fir trees brushing against each other. Sitting in the attic listening to Carmen was tiresome. Her voice sounded dull and sometimes, the things she said reminded me of my father's opinions — irrational.

I liked having a playmate next door. I liked spending my afternoons with a girl my age. Some of the things Carmen said made me think, they made me smile inside. But some of her ideas were crazy. The blood sister idea was one of them.

"Don't you want to know what they did?"

I turned to face her. "What?"

"When I found them, the Barbies were doing sex."

At nine years old, I had only a sketchy idea of what that meant. I knew it involved being naked and I knew it involved letting another person see you naked. I knew there was a lot of touching and kissing. I also was quite clear on the point that you weren't supposed to talk about it or even think about it, although I wondered why this was since you were naked when you were born and naked for baths, and everyone talked about those things. I knew the Bible had things to say about when and how and with whom you should do it. I knew my church had classes for kids my brothers' ages where they were given a lot of details about these requirements.

Carmen clapped her hands. "Pay attention. Aren't you going to say anything?"

"No."

"It was nasty."

I remembered what she'd said to Jake — that taking the dolls had been a *nasty joke*. It had seemed a weird thing to say. Now, I understood.

"It's not really nasty. Even the Bible says it's okay. You just have to…"

"They shouldn't do that. Would your mother want them doing that?"

I had to admit she would not.

At the same time, the Barbies were lumps of plastic. Their bodies didn't even look like real bodies. None of them had nipples. The Ken dolls had lumps where their penises should be, and the Barbies had absolutely nothing, which should have told me a lot right then and there about how the world often views women.

"Would she?"

"No."

"Then it's nasty."

"Well, we have them back now. So we can put their clothes on."

She flapped her arms as if she might take flight. "You don't get it! Your brothers are *bad*. They shouldn't be doing stuff like that. If we were blood sisters, you wouldn't have to play with them so much. You'd have me."

"I like my brothers."

"But they do nasty things. And they don't tell you about it. I bet they do lots of things they aren't supposed to. They don't want you around when they do that stuff."

I shrugged. "Sometimes they do."

She glared at me. "Blood sisters are stronger than anything."

"I already told you I'm not doing that."

"Because you don't like me?"

"I like you. But I don't want to cut myself, and I don't want to mix up blood."

"It's like magic."

"I don't believe in magic."

She stared at me as if I'd been transformed into a unicorn right before her eyes.

The argument wound down after that. About twenty minutes later, she went home.

We still played together most days after school, but she never mentioned being blood sisters again. We played with the Barbies until my mother went up to clean the attic. She was upset to find the Barbies, but she didn't tell my father.

She sat me down on my bed and perched beside me. She slid her arm around my waist like she always did when she told me serious things that I needed to know in order to grow into a godly woman. "Those dolls make women think they're nothing but objects."

I nodded.

"Do you understand what that means?"

"Yes."

She sighed. "A woman is more than nice clothes and a thin body and large breasts."

"I know."

"That's not how God sees you."

"I know."

"What matters is what's inside your heart. I'm disappointed that you let Carmen bring those dolls into the house when you know that's not how we want you spending your time. God gives us precious time on earth, and you should use it for good things, for valuable things."

"Okay. I know."

"This is just a reminder because it seems you forgot, even though I know you realize these things deep inside. If you didn't, you wouldn't have hidden them from me."

I didn't tell her about my brothers. I also didn't tell her about blood sisters.

The Barbies went back to Carmen's house. She never brought over any more toys, and she never brought the makeup case again. A few weeks later, a For Sale sign appeared in the yard next door.

Carmen informed me that her father had a new job and they were moving to Houston. Her eyes looked blank, empty. A few days after she was gone, I saw that my cactus was also gone. I guess she'd slipped it into her backpack. My mother took me shopping and let me choose two new plants. These had even longer, thicker needles. I felt safe with the needles, knowing Carmen wasn't around to see them as tools for letting blood.

I always wondered what happened to Carmen. We exchanged addresses, and I wrote her a letter once, but she never wrote back.

After a while, I figured out that I'd disappointed her. But I didn't know how to do anything else. She wanted too much from me. That's happened again and again in my life. People want things from me that I don't have to give.

It happens with women as often as it does with men.

71

I did not take the Rubik's Cube. They're cheap enough to buy. And I realized I didn't want one after all. I don't need to prove myself to anyone, not even to myself. I already do things that most others don't, can't, and of course, would never.

The cube was sitting on the dresser when I entered Ed's suite with the key I'd dug out of his pocket. After retrieving his keys, I'd left him on the floor of the wine cellar. With sure feet, I'd climbed the marble stairs and closed the door to the cellar.

The Rubik puzzle was solved, the colors lined up with their counterparts on all six sides. There was nothing else on the chest of drawers. He obviously cherished it even when he wasn't holding it, endlessly turning the pieces this way and that. Not unlike the way my mind had twisted back and forth the past few weeks, looking for the matching pieces to click together.

It wasn't hard to find the photographs of Eileen.

They were lying in the otherwise empty top drawer. He hadn't even put them in an envelope.

Beside the photographs lay the memory stick from the camera. There was also a copy of a page from what appeared to be a will or a trust. I took it out and sat on his bed to read it.

I felt my lips part slowly as I read a line near the top of the page.

For a reason I couldn't begin to comprehend, Jim Kohn had left four million dollars to Eileen Cook.

As the paper fluttered in my hand, the questions rushed into my head — Why? He'd broken up with her. She disappointed him. How had Ed gotten ahold of the document? Did Eileen know about the inheritance?

One question did not arise. Clearly Ed, and to some extent, most likely as full collaborators, Joe and Nell planned to use the photographs to extort money from Eileen. She'd seemed somewhat unconcerned about the fate of the photographs, but was that put on for some reason? Or did she truly not care and was immune to their scheme? Maybe Jim had broken her in a way that left her no longer caring what anyone thought of her. She would pursue her career with a vengeance and perhaps didn't think the exposure of degrading and, in my mind, humiliating pictures would hurt her at all.

Perhaps she adhered to the belief that there is no bad PR — that not being talked about at all is far worse than being talked about negatively.

My mind relaxed, satisfied that I now understood the behavior of Ed and Nell. Joe would have told them of my connection to Eileen's mother. They wanted to be rid of me, but they also wanted to keep watch to see what I was after. Wanting two things at the same time rarely works out well.

Once Joe or Nell found Ed's body, would they carry on with their plan? Four million dollars would entice a lot of people. Especially when your face is smashed up, and you're pretty sure you're not employable for the near future.

I took the entire contents of the drawer and closed it.

I returned to Joe's room where he was collapsed on the couch, his arm dangling over the edge. The glass sat on the floor beside his hand. A thin pool of liquid remained in the bottom. His head was turned to the side, his mouth beautiful even though it was slack as his body languished in drugged sleep.

I took a step toward him then decided touching him was not a good idea.

I washed the glass and left it on the bathroom counter. I shoved the photographs and the page from Jim's will into my messenger bag and carried both bags into the hallway. I returned to the room and picked up his keys off the dresser. I scurried down the hall to the storage room.

Inside, I woke the computer and opened the file manager. Of course, none of the folders had Eileen's name on them. I opened the photo app and scrolled through it. There were hundreds of pictures of women. Most of the images were like Nell's — boudoir-slash-soft-porn shots. Eileen's were the only ones that tried to strip away the subject's emotional dignity.

I began deleting photos but soon realized it would take forever. I didn't see any evidence of cloud storage being enabled, but the computer wouldn't let me delete the app itself. I sat staring at the screen, trying to figure out how to get rid of everything.

Finally, I decided the only one who mattered was Eileen. I scooped through all of those images, deposited the digital files in the trash and emptied it.

I know there are ways to retrieve deleted files, but I doubted Joe or Nell possessed that expertise. And Mark Kohn wouldn't know there was anything to retrieve. If he knew of his brother's fetish, there were plenty of images. One missing woman wouldn't be apparent to him.

The printed and digital images belonged only to Eileen, as much as they ever could.

On my way to the stairs, I stopped outside of Nell's door. A small part of me wanted to offer a good-bye to her, and to Joe. But I couldn't. Once they woke, how long until they went looking for Ed? If I were gone, they'd assume he'd fallen.

Joe would wonder, but he wouldn't *know*. And without the photographs, as his share of four million dollars slipped between his fingers, he would need to put his attention on either impressing Mark Kohn or making his way to a new life...making his way toward the home he'd never given any thought to. Now it was poised to come rushing upon him faster than he'd expected.

Finally, I thought about the things people seem to want from me. It was likely Nell wanted my help now, even though she'd initially done everything in her power to be rid of me. But I couldn't give her any more. I'd found her photographs. I'd punished the man who brutalized her. That was all I had to offer.

In the end, she might have mixed feelings about me. Along with the death of her attacker, she'd have to face the death of her quest for easy money.

I texted Dirk, picked up my bags, and went to the foyer to wait for the limo.

72

In an alley, four blocks from the office, where there were no lights but the dim glow from windows covered with blinds, Eileen and I found a metal trash barrel.

I pulled Jim Kohn's fancy lighter out of my bag and fired it up.

Without speaking, Eileen reached for my hand. She touched the side of the lighter. I released the starter and handed it to her. She produced a flame and held it to the first photograph, dropping it into the metal barrel before the flames could lick toward her forearm. The flames spread quickly, and the ink began to bubble, melt, and then the paper curled and started its transformation into flakes of ash.

We stared, mesmerized by the hot, dancing flames. Each time the flames receded, Eileen flicked the lighter, touched the fire to another photograph, and dropped it into the trash.

As I watched the smoke billow into the air around us, stinging our eyes, scraping at our throats, I wondered whether Stephanie had any inkling that her threat had as much substance as smoke. Eileen and I clicked nicely, and I knew there would be more shared workouts and martinis and possibly shopping trips.

Once there was nothing left to consume, the flames grew calmer, and the heat no longer rose up into our nostrils and touched our skin with its intensity. When it was mostly a pile of ash except for a small fire still searching out pieces it had leapt over earlier, I dropped the sleek, expensive lighter on top.

When the flames were finished with every pixel, and had lashed at the casing of the lighter, scarring it thoroughly, we walked to the end of the alley and turned the corner.

"Thank you," she said.

"No need to thank me."

"I'm still in shock about the money Jim left me."

"I can imagine."

"It's confusing. I don't understand, and I'm not sure yet how..." She stopped abruptly.

She was quiet for several minutes as we walked toward the subway. "Don't mention it to my mother, please."

"Absolutely not."

"I'm not sure how it will change things for me, but it will definitely change...something."

She laughed, but there was a nervous and possibly grief-stricken undertone.

We parted on the subway platform, with plans to meet for dinner a few days before Christmas.

She gave me a hug which wasn't unexpected, but not something I'm very good at.

Still, I managed.

At home, I made a martini and sat by the window. I looked out at the starless sky. The rain was due to start in the next half hour or so, and I couldn't wait to watch it thundering against my window and slashing at the trees.

The city seems so strong and stable, invulnerable to the forces of nature, but it's not. Not at all.

73

For Christmas, I decided at the last minute I needed a break from icy cold weather, numb fingers, and the winter storms. I went online and found a great teaser deal on Qantas. I would have thought people in the Northern Hemisphere would be clamoring for the warm summer weather, but Qantas was trying to lure even more people to Australia's beautiful beaches and restaurants.

I flew to Sydney and spent eight days lying in the sun in Tess's back yard, drinking sweeter-than-normal cocktails with the banana liqueur I'd discovered a taste for. I closed my eyes and listened to cockatoos and magpies and kookaburras cackle and shout. It's a raucous sound that has a way of making you feel very content with the cacophony of the world's voices.

I told Tess as much as I could about Joe.

She told me what was new with the TruthTeller app, which was nothing. Still.

When Tess went off to work, I took the old-fashioned key out of my suitcase. I settled on the lounge chair and rested it on the bare skin of my belly. For a moment, I thought about letting the sun darken my skin around it. I decided that was foolish because Tess would surely see me in my bikini again. Then I fell asleep.

For the rest of the trip, I wore my one-piece swimsuit for sunbathing. Tess thought that made no sense, but I just smiled and ate a cracker smeared with caviar.

I put Victoria and Rafe's mind games and Stephanie's threat of the demonic, money-lusting danger lurking inside her daughter out of my head.

It did rain while I was in Australia, but the storm, filled with thunder and brilliant flashes of lightning, sent rain cascading down through warm air.

A Note To Readers

Thanks for reading. I hope you liked reading about Alexandra as much as I enjoy writing her stories. I'm passionate about fiction that explores the shadows of suburban life and the dark corners of the human mind. To me, the human psyche is, as they say in Star Trek — the final frontier — a place we'll never fully understand. I'm fascinated by characters who are damaged, neurotic, and obsessed.

I love to stay in touch with readers. Visit me at my website: CathrynGrant.com

To find out when the next Alexandra Mallory novel is available you can sign up for my new book mailing list here: CathrynGrant.com/contact.

As a thank you for signing up, you'll receive a free Alexandra short story — Death Valley.

CPSIA information can be obtained
at www.ICGtesting.com
Printed in the USA
BVHW040948120920
588372BV00005B/36